PIRATE PASSIONS

Robert Bringston was born in 1961 in a small town near Heidelberg. His forefathers came from England, which is how he became fascinated with English history, the basis of many of his erotic stories. Today, Bringston lives on an old farm in the Teutoburg Forest and devotes his time to writing.

Robert Bringston

Pirate Passions

An Erotic Novel

Translated from the German by
Nicholas Andrews

BRUNO GMÜNDER

1st edition
© 2013 Bruno Gmünder Verlag GmbH
Kleiststraße 23-26, D-10787 Berlin
info@brunogmuender.com

© Robert Bringston
Original title: Unter Freibeutern
Translation from the German: Nicholas Andrews
Cover art: Steffen Kawelke
Cover photo: © Guillem Medina, www.guillemmedina.com
Printed in Germany

ISBN 978-3-86787-522-6

More about our books and authors:
www.brunogmuender.com

For Josua

Prologue

The year is 1586. Plymouth, Devon County, in the southwest of England. Take a look at this city, one of the richest in the country. In recent years, Plymouth has developed into an important trade harbor—a fact many of its inhabitants have to thank for their comfortable lifestyles. Above all, merchants depend on secure shipping routes to France and Spain to maintain their businesses. This is the only way they can sell wares from other parts of Europe at cheap market prices and make a profit on their own products. For some time, however, more and more loaded ships have gone missing on the stormy seas. But weather isn't the biggest danger to valuable freight: pirates and buccaneers hijack these cumbersome trade schooners. With their light, nimble caravels, their prey is child's play; their barbaric propensity for violence makes any resistance futile. The few men who survive these struggles bring back reports of horrifying duels with these robbers of the sea. Prisoners, if there are any, are sold into slavery in new colonies overseas.

Two years later, in August 1588, vice admiral Sir Francis Drake, in the royal commission of her Majesty Elizabeth the First of England, will set forth with 34 ships from Plymouth harbor and lay siege to the Spanish armada. But that's another story. My adventure begins on an early summer evening in a secluded cabin on the outskirts of Dartmoor Forest ...

*E*verything was prepared. A bottle of wine was cooling in a pail of fresh spring water, the aroma of fresh bread permeated every corner of our humble abode. Today would be the last time we would see each other for a long time. I yearned in anticipation of my beloved. Yes, over time that word had become much easier for me to say. My heart beat faster every time I thought of him. From the timid shoots of honest friendship, a fragrant bloom of profound love had sprung, bringing us to a level of complete harmony neither of us had ever experienced before. I longed for his tender hands on my skin, for the whispered nothings he would murmur in my ear, making me shake every time; for his open laugh, so contagious that we would fall on top of each other snorting, teasing, and poking one another, eventually laying down exhausted next to one another, while his blue eyes examined my heated body.

My cock was already tingling imagining the next few hours, snaking down my right pants leg in expectation. I made myself comfortable in our favorite spot, where we'd enjoyed so much refuge in the past. A large blanket on fresh, fragrant hay would give us shelter for the night. Where single rays of sun fell through the missing tiles in the roof, casting shimmering patterns on the walls, soon the first stars would shine down on us, making our last night truly special. Full of anticipation, I closed my eyes. My thoughts wandered back a few months, to when it all started …

As I had often had to do in recent weeks, I was supposed to send an urgent message for my uncle, Walter Moore. Cheerful and proud that he had entrusted this crucial dispatch to me, I set out bright and early in the morning. I carried the letter in a double leather case inside a backpack slung on my shoulders. My uncle's faithful cook maid had equipped me with ample provisions for the journey.

"Here, take this skin, I've filled it with fresh spring water," she said, winking at me roguishly, "… and topped off with a bit of cold beer."

A few strands of fog still hung over the damp meadows, but the first rays of the sun were already streaming down over the crowns of the trees of the neighboring forest. It would be a warm, sunny day.

The merchant I was supposed to carry the letter to lived on an estate not far from the city limits of Plymouth.

"Thomas, you visit me almost as infrequently as your uncle," he greeted me warmly. "You think he could tear himself away from his work sometime? He'll come to a bad end. It's good at least that he has you to help him with all his work."

William Ambrose was a small, squat man with gradually graying hair that was already noticeably thinner on the back of his head.

"Those were the days, when your uncle and I travelled together to the sea. My boy, we had some real adventures. But come in, Thomas. You can lay the package on the cabinet there. You've come in perfect time for lunch. You are staying, aren't you? Of course you'll stay. Your uncle will be able to do without you for a couple hours. Sit down! Have I already told you about the horrible typhoon in Sumatra? No! It was the worst weather you could imagine. It's only thanks to your uncle's skill that we didn't sink without a trace. Well … of course I did my part as well. But that worthless captain very nearly had our blood on his hands. Ah, there comes the food. Beautifully braised quail in mushroom sauce. My mouth is watering already. But where was I? Oh yes, the storm …"

Thanks to William Ambrose's well-known hospitality, my stay extended late into the afternoon hours. Uncle Walter knew very well to send me rather than going to Ambrose himself. Both of us liked the old merchant a lot, but his stories had gotten more and more repetitive in recent years. When I was a little boy, I had hung on his every word and demanded more tales of adventures, but today I was getting impatient.

"Now I've really got to get going, Mr. Ambrose. My uncle will worry if I'm not back before sundown."

"That's a shame, my young friend. I was intent on showing you my newest trophies. Just arrived yesterday. More capital stag antlers and—my true pride—a black bear pelt for the large hearth room. Did I already tell you how the brute almost gnawed off my leg? I was just about to …"

"I'll be glad to hear this adventure the next time," I interrupted him. "But regretfully I really have to get going now." Impatiently, I stood at the door of the enormous room, the walls of which were already decorated with stuffed animal heads from all over the world to the extent that I could not imagine where he would ever find room for more trophies.

"Yes, yes, of course. The next time, the next time. And send my greetings to your uncle. It's always a pleasure doing business with him. Now get on your way, my boy!"

He ushered me officiously towards the door and let me go with a flood of best wishes, grinning as he slipped a change purse into my pocket.

On the way back, my fingers gladly examined the coins in my pants pocket. Even though I was well over 20, to Mr. Ambrose I was still the little rascal he used to slip sweets to. Shaking my head I set off on the narrow path that led through the forest. A few years ago, when I really was a kid, I only dared to take this path in the company of my uncle. I held his hand tight and pressed myself close to him as the crowns of the high trees closed above us like a dark roof, and the bushes to our left and right grew thicker and thicker. Creepy cracking sounds in the branches and rustling in the undergrowth—it was all really unsettling to me, and would always make me flinch.

"Think of the delicious roast Mrs. Hambrow has waiting for us in the oven," Uncle Walter would say, trying to distract me. "Can't you smell it already?"

Thinking of this, my mouth started to water. I thought of how the cook had skinned a rabbit early this morning.

"Don't come back too late, otherwise nothing will be left over for you," she called after me, waving.

It was already dark. I would have to hurry to get home in time for dinner. With quicker steps, I hastened along the narrow path, when suddenly out of nowhere a figure appeared in front of me. The prince of darkness himself, I couldn't help from thinking.

"In such a hurry and all alone, buddy boy?" the shadow snarled derisively. "You're Tom Moore, aren't you?"

"Yes, that's me," I responded defiantly. "What do you want from me?"

Even though my knees were shaking, I tried to keep my fear hidden. My companion's visage was disfigured by a scar that ran from his right hairline over his forehead down to his left cheek. He must have been waiting in the forest for unprotected travelers. No, it was not the devil who had emerged from the hazy twilight, but an impudent highway robber. But if he believed he'd found easy prey in me, he was fooling himself. I turned on my heels, took a powerful dash and … ran smack into his accomplice. He was more slender than his companion and the impact brought us both out of balance. He took me to the ground with him. My quick-witted attempt to flee had failed.

There were actually three of them. Another wretch was soon standing over us, laughing and ridiculing: "Have you ever seen a thing like that? What kind of moron have we snatched up here?" In an instant their leader was next to me, grabbing me and lifting me up.

"Now, my handsome fellow. We don't want anything from you. Must surprise you, right? You're pissing your pants already because you think we're going to attack you." He ran his tongue over his enormous lips. Saliva dripped from his unshaved chin onto his stained shirt. The man was nearly a head taller than me, with broad shoulders and arms thick as tree trunks. With his hands loosely at his hips, he stood before me smirking.

"But tell your uncle he still owes the one-armed man a few pieces of gold. Soon it's going to be payday."

His dark smile was not made any more inviting by the black gaps between the teeth in his grinning mouth.

"Otherwise, we'd be happy to take you. As a kind of deposit, so to speak!" For an instant, his brandished dagger flashed, reflecting the last rays of sun. Then he approached me with two quick strides and ripped my shirt apart.

"Clothes off. All of them." His companion had positioned himself behind me. "Well, get going, boy. What are you waiting for?" Haltingly, I followed his instructions. "Is this going to happen today, or should I help you out?" His eyes gleamed with lust as I stood before him completely naked. Behind me, a hand slapped my naked buttocks. Both the henchmen laughed darkly.

"Shut it back there!" the leader hissed grumpily. "If anyone makes jokes around here it will be me."

He grabbed my balls roughly and pulled down on them, taking my breath away, then blew his bad breath into my face.

"Not bad at all. Who would have expected such a jewel in this wasteland? Beautiful men like you fetch a pretty price, did you know that? There are lots of nice men who would love to amuse themselves with you."

He placed his blade against my throat, then slowly led the tip down to my right nipple. A shudder ran through me. A pure sweat of terror ran from my armpits down my arms.

"Ah, that's the smell I like," the leader grunted contentedly, sticking his nose underneath my arm.

"You'll probably piss your pants again in a minute. Or wait … you can't, since you're not wearing any." He laughed a dirty laugh. "It's been ages since I laid hands on a creature as pitiful as you."

Disdainfully, he stuck his knife back in his belt. With his free hand, he suddenly tweaked my nipple. In my pain, I yelled out loud, "Nasty scoundrel!"

"Want to have a little courage, young lad? No one can hear you out here. It's a shame." His throaty laugh repulsed me.

He nodded encouragingly to his accomplices behind me. Out of the corner of my eye, I only saw a fast movement, then felt a dull thud at the back of my head. As I fell I heard the leader say, "Pack up his things and let's get out of here. That should be enough as a warning." Then everything around me went black.

While I was blacked out, I had a strange dream: Out of the deepest darkness a ray of light fell upon me. The fire of a brightly blazing torch burned on my face. Behind it a being appeared with the face of an angel. Blond, curly locks framed perfectly even facial features. Sensual lips formed into a beautiful smile, blue eyes looked at me with understanding. Then the warm light was extinguished and the face disappeared in darkness once more. I felt my body floating. Then I came to sitting on a horse. The angel was nestled up tight behind me. His strong arm held my upper body tightly against his chest. Powerful legs pressed against my ass from behind. With his free hand, the angel held the reins loosely. He clucked his tongue and we fell into a slow trot. Shortly afterwards,

I felt his hand on my naked chest. His glove's soft leather stroked fleetingly over my hard nipples. A warm prickling spread over my skin. The horse's rhythmic movements sent pulsing waves through my swelling cock. With the animal's every step, it grew larger and harder, smacking between the knob of the saddle and my stomach.

I could feel a quickly growing serpent rising up my back as well. At first it seemed to stop at the height of my navel, then reached a little bit higher. My companion's pleasure pole beat firmly against my skin. His deep breaths sent showers over my back. His hot lips, so near to my ear, whispered secretive words. He had let go of the reins. Instead, he held his hand tightly around my cock. Slowly, he pulled my foreskin back from the bulging head, then slid it carefully up again. Gradually he sped up his rhythm. The horse seemed to fly as the man pumped the tip of my cock till it seemed it was about to burst. It was harder and harder for him to pull my foreskin over my swollen cock head. At the same time, my balls were wedged pleasurably and painfully between the saddle and his hand. I let out a moan and he started to stroke my nipples as well.

I wanted more, I stretched out my arms searchingly and pulled his head towards me. The moment our lips touched a radiant heat fell over my body and spread through me like wildfire. Animal groans emerged from my throat. Hot lava rose in powerful waves from my cock and streamed over his hand.

Wild shudders shook my entire body. Cold night wind flowed over my body. Deep darkness surrounded me again. But soon again the face of my protector appeared above me, framed by an aura of light.

"Are you an angel?" I asked.

"Good that you're awake again. You slept all day. I'm Brian and … no, I'm not an angel," the stranger answered me with a friendly smile.

"I found you yesterday unconscious by the edge of the forest and brought you to the estate of my father, Lord Hamilton. They must have done a number on you. You had a big bump on your head. But everything is looking better this morning."

I carefully lifted my head and looked around me. I was lying on an enormous, soft bed with a canopy of heavy fabric hanging down on either side to the ground. The few pieces of furniture in the large room were made of dark, precious wood. A crackling hearth fire warmed the room. Through the artful stained glass in the high windows, the dark red evening sun shone in.

A sudden pain in the back of my head made me groan out load. My savior hurried over to me and helped me up.

"Take it slow," he said. "Otherwise you'll pass out on me again."

His strong arms were holding me tight, but his soft gaze left me somewhat dizzy. The thin, white blanket couldn't hide my painfully stiff cock.

"I'm glad everything is in working order again," he said, laying his hand carefully on the tensed fabric.

"I had a dream," I admitted with embarrassment. "You brought me here on a horse, and …"

I faltered.

"That wasn't a dream," whispered Brian. He kissed me briefly on the mouth. Our eyes met and absolute silence reigned for a moment. For the first time in my life I was certain that another human being was peering deep into my soul.

Powerless, I opened my innermost being to this strange man, looking deep into his blue eyes. I knew he understood me. My heartbeat raced through my entire body. A pleasant feeling I had never known before began to spread through me. Dazed, I shut my eyes. When I opened them again, my angel was still sitting next to me.

"So, it really wasn't a dream," I murmured.

"I ran a bath for you in the next room. Right over there!"

As he stood up, Brian pointed to a side door at the back left of the room.

"Take your time, no rush. I'll go grab us something to eat, then I'll be back with you soon." In the doorframe he lingered and looked back once more.

"What's your name, actually? Maybe your parents are concerned. We should let them know where you are!"

"My name is Tom, Tom Moore. I don't have any parents. I live with my uncle, the merchant Walter Moore, on Penrose Street in Plymouth."

"Then I'll have a message sent to him that you're all right."

And on that, he disappeared. Carefully I tried roll out of the bed without jerking my head at all. A bath would do me good right about now. All my limbs were horribly cramped. My back felt as if I had been heaving sacks of grain around all day. Hesitantly, I opened the door to the next room and encountered another surprise. A wood tub stood steaming in the center of the room; this kind of luxury was something only truly wealthy nobles could afford. At the back of the room, a fire crackled in a small hearth. Some soft thick towels had been hung over the armrest of a lounge chair. The water smelt of fresh pine trees. I got in carefully. Instantly I was surrounded by a pleasant warmth that let me forget all my pain. Again, I closed my eyes and thought about the last night, then I took care of my dirty skin, rubbing myself with a soft cloth. In the process I paid some much-needed attention to my cock. Just a few powerful strokes of my hand and it reached its full size. Its bulging head had already risen eagerly above the surface of the water when I was startled by the sound of someone clearing his throat next to me.

"Pardon me, Sir. My name is James. I'm the young lord's servant."

I bent forward hastily to hide my erection, but the man continued speaking in a deadpan voice: "I was asked to help you with your bath. May I soap up your back? It seems you have not quite managed yet to remove all traces of yesterday's accident."

"Umm ... yes ... my name is Tom," I stuttered, bewildered. "Wash my back ... of course ... that would be wonderful. I can't reach it very well."

Embarrassed, I looked up at him. James seemed to be just a little bit older than I, but his exaggeratedly genteel behavior made him seem much older. He dipped a small washcloth in the warm water and spread soap evenly upon it. Then he began to rub my shoulders firmly. He had to bend far down to reach me, propping himself up on the edge of the tub with one hand while he worked his way slowly right and left down my back. He seemed to take his assigned task very seriously.

"My lord has quite strong muscles," he observed with appreciation. By now he had laid aside the cloth and was rubbing his flat hands in wide circles over my back. I was unused to such careful treatment, and I liked it.

Once James was finished with my back, he focused his attention on my arms. Then his hands drifted gradually from my shoulders down to my chest.

"My lord has quite strong muscles," he observed again, but he seemed to be primarily fascinated with my nipples. Clamping them between his thumb and index finger, he rubbed and pulled them until they stood out straight and hard. A shudder ran through me.

"Mmm ... that feels really good."

"Then may I continue?" James asked hesitantly. Without answering, I leaned back in the tub and gave him full access. His hands wandered further down, deeper into the soapy water, exploring the small mountains of muscle on my stomach. Just before he reached my navel, he ran into my stiff sentinel.

"Oh ... so big!" That was all he said before pulling his hands back without any further explanation. I looked at him with disappointment, but his mischievous expression calmed me.

"It looks as though I'll have to offer more in-depth services," said James, beginning to take off his clothes bit by bit as I looked on in astonishment. He lay each article of clothing neatly over the back of a chair. His tailored servant's uniform had already highlighted his well-built body, but seeing his square chest and strong arms without their covering exceeded my expectations. Unconsciously, he flexed his graceful muscles. A fine line of dark brown hair led down over his flat stomach to his navel. The sight of his thick package made me swallow involuntarily. Slowly, the servant peeled off his pants and underwear. His cock sprang expectantly out of its cramped hideaway, while my best part was trying desperately to reach the surface of the water, as if to get a glimpse of him.

"All right, now there's no more danger of my clothes getting wet. Slide a bit forward, Tom!" This time, James abandoned all pretense of formality. His face seemed much more relaxed as well. He gave a friendly, excited smile as he knelt behind me in the water, ready for his next task. He started massaging my neck with his powerful hands.

"Bend a bit further forward and lean your arms on the edge. It will be much more comfortable for you and I can soap up further down your back. I couldn't get that far beforehand."

Delicately, James' deft hands kneaded their way down my back. It was a long way from my neck to the start of my crack, but the expert servant worked thoroughly and untiringly.

"You're so tense here. I'll really have to give this area a beating," a determined James said, letting his hard cock slap against my ass. A contented sigh escaped my mouth.

"Well, that sounds very nice. But wait a minute, it gets better," he whispered, bending over my back. His thick cock rubbed firmly against my ass crack. His hands embraced my chest while his fingers circled around my nipples. His right hand wandered further downwards. With great skill, he massaged my firm abs. At each stroke, my firm cock slapped against his hand.

"You want more, don't you?" he breathed in my ear. He grabbed my rock-hard shaft and continued massaging. A pleasant tingling spread through my crotch. My ass rubbed eagerly against his hard-on.

"I'd be happy to loosen you up on the inside as well and slip my cock into your warm ass, but it's not slippery enough."

"What do I need to do?" I breathed impatiently.

"A little fluid from your mouth should do it," he grinned. In a flash I turned around; his thick cock throbbed towards me at eye level. James had stood up, holding his meat expectantly in front of my face. His retracted foreskin was tightly pulled behind the bulging head. Gleaming veins snaked down his powerful shaft. Thick hairs covered his sack, weighed down by huge balls. Searchingly, I took them in my hands, kneaded them lightly and flicked my tongue against the bare skin of his sack. Immediately, his balls pulled upward and the skin tightened together. James looked down at me with a grunt.

"You were going to get my cock wet, I believe." Teasingly, he wagged his thick soldier back and forth in front of my mouth. I tried to catch it but he slapped it lightly against my cheeks.

"You've got to try a bit harder than that."

Determined, I grabbed onto it with both hands. I squeezed his shaft quite tight, making the head grow dark, then rolled my lips over the tip of his cock. My tongue played in the little slit at the end, where I unexpectedly tasted sweet, fragrant juice. Delighted, I spread the fluid and began to lick his cock from all sides. My tongue felt his pulsing veins as it ran up and down his shaft. Both my hands were eager for new ground, so they grasped his firm ass tightly. My curious fingers examined his twitching back door.

I would have loved to give his thick hard-on more attention, but his heated motions made it clear that he was racing towards climax already. It took me some effort to free my mouth from his demanding cock.

"I think that's enough," I said, gasping for air. "Now you can get back to your assignment."

Standing, I bent forward and leaned my hands against the rim of the tub. I turned my head back, looking expectantly into his lustful eyes. James' left hand stroked my back, while his right hand wiped some fluid off his cock and began to smear it on my asshole. I pushed firmly back against him as he pressed his wet finger deep into me, then pulled it back a bit. Circling, the tip of his finger explored my narrow canal. Then he added a second and a third finger to his examination, gently widening my tight muscle ring. With each movement, my cock twitched gleefully back and forth. Bright flashes shot before my eyes. When James pulled his fingers out entirely, I wanted to protest. But then his stiff cock head was pushing against my narrow hole. Carefully, he increased the pressure and I felt the head of his cock slip inside me. A light pain ran through me, making me wince. James stopped right away and waited.

"Is that all right?" he asked with concern. "Maybe it is a bit too big for you."

But I managed to relax and courageously sank down further on his hard pole. Inch by inch, James slipped into me. The tension in my sphincter felt as if it was going to tear me apart. Shaking, I faltered, gave in a bit more, and then it was over; his huge hammer was inside my ass, down to the last inch. I could feel it pulsing within me. Timidly, but with a pleasant feeling of fullness, I leaned back against him.

"I can feel my cock throbbing inside you," he said.

"Yes, me too," I answered. "It's enormous. But it fits beautifully."

Cautiously, I pulled myself forward a bit. What had started as pain was gradually being replaced with a pleasant, warm feeling streaming through my ass. James was still standing behind me without moving while I rocked cautiously back and forth, sliding his cock faster and deeper within me. Soon his strong hands were feeling along my stomach, surrounding my cock and grasping it tenderly. My soft moans left no doubt how aroused I was by this touch. And my erection pulsed in his hand, filling his narrow fist as if to confirm it. I could feel two or three thick calluses on his palm as they rubbed along my shaft. So I could work this servant hard, he wasn't afraid to get down and work. As if James had guessed my thoughts, he pulled me roughly into him.

"You seem to be enjoying my piece," he guessed. "Your stiff pole shows me you're ready for more."

Without waiting for an answer, he let go of my cock, grabbed my thighs with both hands and shoved his shaft firmly into my hole. I could barely hold onto the edge of the tub. Water sprayed everywhere, sloshing over the edge. My cock slapped wildly against my stomach as his hot thrusts became more and more passionate.

"I brought something tasty to eat ..." Brian's voice broke off. He had returned unnoticed, and now he advanced furiously on us with his fists balled up at his thighs.

"James! What are you doing?" he screamed, out of control. "Tom had a bad head injury!"

James stopped thrusting so heavily, but didn't stop entirely.

"The young man needed a strong treatment," he said, trying to justify himself.

"But not without a soft place to put his head," Brian countered with concern. He rushed over to me, pulled his pants down in one go and held his stiff cock in front of my face. "Here, Tom, take this to support you better."

Dazed, I looked at him.

"Yes, take it into your mouth. It will take some of the impact off that big lug's thrusts."

Turning to James, he said devilishly, "You should have waited for me. I came just in time."

James returned quickly to his old rhythm. His massive shaft slid forcefully in my ass. His balls beat rhythmically against my thighs. Grasping me firmly with his strong hands, he maneuvered me back and forth. Brian's pulsing cock was in my mouth. His throbbing cock head rubbed against my tongue and tickled the back of my throat—especially when James pushed me forward, shoving Brian's cock deeper in my mouth. Brian had placed his hands on my shoulders, massaging my muscles tenderly.

"See, it's much better this way, isn't it Tom?" he asked. "You need to be taken care of from all sides. Yeah, suck my cock harder. Uhh … yeah … keep going. Oh yeah … that's really a heavenly way to thank your guardian angel."

Brian's hammer had grown thicker with my treatment. His imposing piece thrust more and more wildly into my throat. Excitedly, I felt the bulging veins running down his hard pole. James' vehement thrusts were growing more and more ferocious. He pushed forward at the same time as Brian, leaving me wedged helplessly between the two of them. My hard shaft beat unrestrained against my stomach. I would have loved to hold it in my hands. And as if James had read my thoughts, he was soon reaching for my cock. Impatiently, his fingers gripped the tense shaft. My moans were muffled instantly by Brian's enormous piece as he went at it more forcefully. James used his fist, clamped in an iron grip around my cock, to press me back deeper against his shaft. He peeled my foreskin far back and squeezed my balls lustfully. Pulling my hard-on forward, he pushed me firmly against Brian's cock, while only his cock head was left inside me. Slowly, I lost all control. Animal lust shook through me, unrestrained desire to be controlled by these two idols of manhood. Letting go of all inhibition, I sucked at Brian's cock as he suddenly roared and sprayed his semen in my mouth, shuddering wildly. His hot juice flooded down my throat. A strong, tantalizing odor spread from between his legs. My nostrils sucked it up greedily. Together with the sharp taste of his cream, I was bathed in a sensuous rush of lust.

At the same time James howled loudly, shoving his glowing sword hilt deep in my ass, hitting my sweet spot perfectly. It was too much for me. With the next strong stroke of his hand on my cock, my white load splashed into the warm bathwater. James held his breath. He stood there as if petrified, his thick cock still pulsing within me. Breathing heavily he fell onto my back, holding himself up on my shoulders, then bucked sharply, pumping his steaming fluid deep inside me. Exhausted, he leaned against me with all his weight, turning his head to the side; I felt his cheek lying against my shoulder. Pearls of sweat ran down my back.

"I needed that," he murmured. "It's really nice to soap you up, Tom."

His short chest hairs scratched against my sweaty back. His broad chest lifted and sank. It was a long time before his racing breath slowed down. Brian squatted down in front of me, kissing me tenderly on the lips. Then he licked the rest of his sperm from my face.

"Are you all right?" he asked with concern.

"Yes, fantastic," I grinned. "You filled me up nicely. But weren't you just saying something about food? The appetizers were quite substantial. But I could manage to take a little bite of something more."

"Yes, of course. I had no idea James was in such a hurry. Otherwise we would have taken care of that earlier."

With a laugh, Brian stood up and grabbed a few large towels from a chair.

"Here, James, you got Tom all wet, now rub him dry." He held the towel out to his servant.

James stood upright obediently. His beautiful cock slipped out of my ass, to my disappointment. Sighing, I stood up as well. James and Brian made sure to dry me off quite thoroughly. To my own astonishment, their firm rubbing revived my spirits. Brian was the first to notice my throbbing friend rise again.

"It seems we'll have a lot more work to do on you," he observed.

"As my lord knows, I'm ready to help any time you desire," James added.

"Or if I deem it necessary. This man needs as many hands as we can give him," Brian countered in an exaggeratedly serious tone.

"I hope more than just hands will be involved," I protested, laughing. James, now the perfect servant once more, gave a chuckle and helped Brian and me into soft bathrobes.

"As you wish, Master Tom."

He bowed politely, naked as he was, took his clothes over one arm and went to the door, where he turned around again. His cock bobbed loosely back and forth between his legs. This man had a truly imposing piece. And he knew how to use it.

"I will prepare a small table for dinner. If I am not needed afterwards, I will retire."

"Yes, that's all right, James," said Brian. "We'll manage all right on our own."

"And thank you for the thorough bath, James," I called after him, bowing gallantly. Smiling, he returned the gesture, then shut the door quietly behind him.

All wrapped up warm and cozy in my bathrobe, Brian led me back to the neighboring room. The hearth crackled, spreading comfortable warmth throughout the room, the last rays of sun glowed on the wall like pale red fire. As promised, James had set up the meal. A silver candelabra with five long candles stood on a small table by the window. The bread was still warm, giving off a wonderful seductive odor. Beneath a large silver platter, juicy pork roasts were steaming, and some crispy chicken drumsticks. My mouth began to water. The wine glasses had already been filled. Brian held his glass up to me. Lovingly, he looked into my eyes.

"To our friendship, Tom. May it last long and grant us many more happy hours."

"To my rescuer, and to our friendship," I responded. We drank the glasses empty in one swallow. Brian came over to me and pressed his moist lips to my mouth. I pulled him tightly close to me, dizzy at our profound connection. For this brief moment, the world around me seemed to sink into peace and calm.

"Let's eat something quick," I managed to say. "I'm getting dizzy. I think I've got a hole in here." I pressed my fist against my stomach, and it actually did give way a bit.

"I'd love a little dessert later." My gaze wandered to the freshly made bed across the room.

"One thing after the other," Brian grinned. "First sit down and get started. I don't want to be responsible for you falling to the floor again in a dead faint. Tell me a bit about yourself. Where do you come from? Where do you live? With your uncle, you said?"

"Yes, I've been living with Uncle Walter for more than ten years now. He took me in back then after my parents were killed in the huge city fire in Plymouth. You must remember, a whole district of the city was turned to ash. The flames went straight up to the heavens. I was with a friend when I saw smoke and heard the pandemonium in the streets. When I reached our house it was already ablaze. It was one of the first to collapse ... I was only twelve at the time, suddenly alone, without a family. Uncle Walter had only been back in the city for a year then. My mother had only mentioned a little about him beforehand. He was always the black sheep of the family, a good-for-nothing, as my father put it. For years, he had disappeared. No one knew where he had gone. But then when he came back he bought himself a large property on Penrose Street and had the best relations with many rich merchants. Wealthy nobles visited him at all hours. My uncle told me later that he had been dealt a lucky hand in all his travels. After he had seen enough of the world he returned to his old home town to settle down for good. "And as soon as a man has money, he suddenly has lots of new friends," he always would say.

In any case, I found a new home with him. It was not an easy time for me, but he always took good care of me. And there were always glimmers of light. My home tutor Mr. Dickens, who my uncle selected for me, was a strict but fair teacher and friend to me for many years. "Parlez-vous français? Hablas español?" were his first words to me. Later, he would have me recite French and Spanish poetry for hours on end. I read thick books and even spoke Spanish in my dreams by the end. "You need to be able to understand your enemies, Tom," Uncle Walter always said. By enemies, he meant his business partners from Spain. "If someone makes you a tempting offer you have to be able to tell if he's trying to pawn off a lead duck on you. So you've got to understand his own language better than he does. So, work hard and follow Mr. Dickens' instructions."

Yes, my uncle really meant well with me. Tomorrow morning I absolutely have to go back to him. He must be very worried and will want to know what happened."

"Sí señor. Nadie nace enseñado."

"How right you are. Masters don't just fall from the sky fully formed. And my master doubted my mental ability more than once."

"Oui monsieur. As tu remercié ton oncle de ses bons services?" Brian twanged in accent-free French.

"Oui, je l'en ai remercie. Yes, I thanked my uncle for all the hard years of studying."

During my report Brian had been chewing on a piece of bread, listening intently.

"I'm sorry about your parents," he said, reflecting. "My mother died giving birth to me. She was from a French family. In order to honor her memory I struggled through the French poets and philosophers as well. Also to do my father a favor. He never fully recovered from her early death. Later, he went on many trips. Or he would go for weeks to his estates in the north. After just a few days at home, his suitcases would be packed again and my father would be on his way to Paris, Madrid, Florence, or elsewhere in Europe. Fortunately, I have James. With him, it's not so lonely for me here." A fleeting smile passed over his face. "But please, dig in. You were so hungry before."

For a while, we were silent, lost in our childhood memories, good and bad. During this time, we dug into the delicious meal. The table was slowly emptied. The wine too dwindled. In just a short time, I felt as though I had known this young lord for a small eternity.

Gradually, pleasant tiredness fell over us. Brian sank deeper into his chair. Casually, he slipped his leg underneath the table onto the front of my chair, rubbing the sole of his foot against my cock while lost in thought. My cock was glad for the attention, and began to rise jerkily. With a relieved sigh, I slipped deeper, pressing my love shaft against Brian's foot. With my eyes closed, I let my head sink against the high armrest of my chair.

"Are you tired?" asked Brian softly. "Let's go to bed. Then we can make ourselves comfortable."

Smooth as a cat, he got and slinked over to the bed.

"Come on, follow me," he said demandingly, turning around. "Move it, otherwise you'll nod off at the table."

On his way through the room, his gown had slipped off his broad shoulders. The flickering shine of the fire in the hearth cast a dancing shadow play on his light skin and flawless body. Looking at his tight ass, those round white globes, his slim waist and broad back, I had to gasp for breath.

Brian turned around and laid his hands seductively on his arched chest. As if accidentally, he stroked his thumb against his nipples, which grew hard immediately. Then he leaned against the bedpost and waved me towards him. His cock lifted lightly up as he started rubbing his ass against the thick past.

"Come, grab your nightcap," he whispered secretively, letting one hand fall beneath his legs to massage his pulsing shaft.

In two swift strides I was next to him, falling to my knees to catch the first drops of pre-cum dripping from the throbbing tip of his cock. Brian moaned as my tongue touched his stiff manhood. Shortly afterwards, his piece sunk deep into my mouth.

"You don't want to let anything go to waste, do you my friend?" he said, overjoyed at my swift approach. Then he fell on his back, legs spread, onto the soft bedsheets. I threw myself on him with a laugh. My hard cock pressed firmly against his as I shoved my tongue deep in his mouth. We kissed long and passionately, rolling love-mad around the rumpled bed like two young whelps until we were completely out of breath.

"I surrender, I surrender …" I called out at some point, totally exhausted. I lay flat on my stomach, Brian with his full weight on my back. His teeth bit into my shoulder, my wrists were firmly in the grasp of his strong hands. The hottest part was his rock-hard hammer begging for entrance at my sweaty crack.

"You're not conquered until my battering ram has pushed through your locked gate," Brian whispered into the back of my neck. His hot tongue tickled my ear. Before I could turn my head away, he bit down and held me fast. My cock reacted immediately. Beneath me, trapped between my stomach and the bed, it twitched uncontrollably. Playfully, I attempted to throw Brian off. I bucked, shook and twisted beneath his weight. Fortunately in vain. Effortlessly, his strong legs pushed between mine, spreading my knees wide apart. With determination, he pointed his spearhead at the adversary and got ready for assault.

Brian let out a bewildered sigh when he found the supposedly barricaded entrance unlocked. Without much trouble, his shaft slipped into me.

"I did say I surrendered," I whispered once Brian was laying on top of me, his cock fully disappeared in my gate of pleasure. Then nothing happened for a long time. He lay on top of me without moving while his cock pulsed inside me, seeming to swell and swell. I answered this unexpected ceasefire by suddenly tensing my sphincter on my conqueror, who was sure of his victory. With all my strength and pleasure, I grabbed hold of my invader.

"Who's the real victor now?" I laughed triumphantly, pushing my ass mercilessly against Brian's trapped shaft.

"You rascal … just wait," he purred.

After the ensuing test of strength, we emerged as equally fero-cious opponents. Whenever Brian's hammer threatened to lose the ground it had gained, he slammed his pole deep within me again. At the same time, I hindered him as well as I could from pulling his hard spearhead out of my ass. The battle might have lasted longer if Brian hadn't suddenly developed a new tactic. Unexpectedly, he wrapped an arm around my chest, pulled me close to him, and rolled both of us on our sides. With his other hand, he grabbed my uncovered hard-on as it sprang free, rubbing it quickly and firmly. My ass muscles tightened together in jerks, but it didn't stop Brian from continuing his assault on my rear entrance. Then when he started grabbing my nipples and tweaking them, I lost control of myself. With a loud howl I shot my load in a warm stream, flowing through his hand onto my quivering stomach. In the same mo-ment my opponent gave in as well.

"The last shot wins," he said triumphantly, in heat. "Yeah, now you're going to get a full load. You're beaten. Here comes your con-queror.

I felt his twitching ram within me like a tree trunk tensed to the point of bursting; then rearing up once more, he sprayed a flood of hot juice inside me. Exhausted, the triumphant victor sank down on his overwhelmed opponent. His warm body cov-ered me, I felt his quick breath at my neck, his cock still twitching within me.

Later, Brian lay behind me, cuddling up close and stroking my belly tenderly.

"I love you, Tom," he said softly. "I've never felt so happy with another man. So peaceful and content, yet at the same time so aroused and worked up. When I'm near you, I can finally enjoy life again. I feel so peaceful when you're near me, so trusting."

"I love you too, Brian," I whispered. "We've only known each other for a short period of time, but I feel like I've been looking for you for ages and have finally found you."

I grabbed his hand, pulled it up to my mouth and kissed his palm tenderly. Then I pressed it back against my chest so Brian could feel the glad beating of my heart. He pulled the covers over us and kissed me softly on the shoulders. The last thing I heard was the soft crackling of the fire in the hearth.

"Tom! Wake up, Sleeping Beauty. It's a beautiful day."

Then he was shaking me hard by the shoulders. I lay stretched out flat on the bed. My hard cock stretched roughly against the bedsheets while Brian tried impatiently to wake me up. His shaking kept getting harder. By grumbling softly I tried to pretend I was still sleeping. But once a pair of warm lips touched my mouth and I felt the familiar taste of a warm tongue, I opened my eyes with difficulty. Brian was already dressed, standing in the room flooded with sunlight.

"What's wrong?" I asked, still half out of it, holding a hand in front of my face to protect it.

"Your uncle sent a messenger to pick you up. I sent the young man to the horse stalls with James, since he seems to be interested in our famous stallions. Although I have the feeling he had his eye on James more than anything when the two of them headed over to the stalls. Well, at least his pants got visibly tighter in the crotch." Brian winked at me. "But you should really get dressed. I don't know how long James will need for the inspection. The messenger has orders to bring you back home as quickly as possible. He even brought a second horse. Your uncle seems to be really worried about you."

On the word "inspection," Brian grabbed his crotch playfully. Then he pulled back my bedsheets and gave me a friendly slap on the ass.

"There's breakfast down in the kitchen," he laughed and disappeared down the stairs, whistling gleefully as a rogue after a successful prank. Still a bit groggy, I stood up and rubbed the last remnants of sleep from my eyes, then looked around the room for my clothes. Clean, neatly folded pants and a shirt lay on a chair. Brown leather boots gleamed in the sunlight.

Lost in thought, I pressed my upright hammer. Sitting naked on the bed I thought about the previous night. We had made stormy love more than once. Brian was a soft yet hot-blooded lover. Again and again I had solicited him to pull out his little lord and fill me up again. As reciprocation, Brian's tongue repeatedly made certain, through extensive searches, that the attack in the forest hadn't made any permanent damages to my best piece. Reluctantly, I tore myself from these arousing thoughts.

When I finally entered the kitchen, Brian, James, and a young man were sitting together at the table and chatting.

"There you are, Tom, we've been waiting for you," said Brian. "Your new clothes suit you perfectly."

"I have an eye for these things," James chipped in. He looked at the bulge between my legs, which the narrow pants highlighted perfectly.

"This is George." Brian pointed to the young man. "He was just telling us that you two don't know each other, that he's only been working for Walter Moore for a short while."

"But this morning he was the only one your uncle could do without. One of his ships came back unexpectedly early into Plymouth harbor. Now everyone is busy unloading the freight. But George well bring you back to your uncle safe and sound."

"You can trust him, Tom," James added when he saw me looking at the stranger somewhat mistrustfully. "I showed him our stalls. He understood right away what it takes to make a good stallion. He gave me a helping hand. In return I gave him some secrets for dealing with difficult horses."

Now the man came up to me and held out his strong hand.

"I'm George, the new blacksmith in your uncle's service. Your uncle sends his greetings. He expects us back before noon. While we were waiting for you, James was friendly enough to show me the stalls. As a blacksmith I'm always curious to see how hot iron is forged and fit to other goods."

George kept shaking my hand after he had finished. He seemed to be very excited to be standing in front of his employer's nephew on the one side and a real lord on the other side. He was nearly a head shorter than me. His short, strawberry blond hair curled up on all sides, giving him a youthful, eager expression, even though he was surely several years older than me. His friendly smile and sky-blue eyes added to my immediate first impression that he was a real likeable guy. When he noticed he was still shaking my hand, he let it fall abruptly, laughed embarrassedly, and sat down again. His ears flushed a strong shade of red.

I didn't doubt for an instant that James was the cause of George's confusion. The servant's contented grin had not escaped me when I entered the kitchen. Clearly he had cooled his glowing iron in the blacksmith's tight ass as soon as the man had given him a hand. Now George was sliding back and forth impatiently on his butt, casting James hidden glances while I tucked into the ample breakfast. Even Brian had realized what was going on.

"Go on, get the horses ready," he said after a while. "We'll come get you in a minute."

James and George disappeared, beaming.

"The two of them really seem to have taken a liking to one another," Brian observed with a grin.

"Just like us," I added.

I took his hand, pressed it tightly, and looked deeply into his beautiful eyes. For a long time we sat there wordlessly, until I said softly: "I have to go now."

"When will you come again, Tom?" Brian asked in a muted voice, visibly struggling to retain composure.

"As soon as I can. In three days at the latest you will have news from me."

Then my voice failed me as well. I pulled Brian into my arms and kissed him passionately.

"I promise. I will come back as soon as it's possible."

Together, we went outside. James and George pulled apart from an intimate embrace once we reached the courtyard. James ran his hand congenially through the blacksmith's wiry hair.

"See you soon, George," I heard him whisper as he helped him into his saddle.

As farewell, my companion and I both turned back to look a final time. Brian and James stood next to one another, watching us with glum expressions. Then our horses trotted off.

Along the way, George was sunk deep in thought, hardly speaking a word. And I wasn't in the mood for entertainment either. Too many confusing thoughts were swirling around my head. An hour later, when we reached the city and then my uncle's house, Walter was already standing on the front stairs, and he approached us gladly.

"Tom!" he called when we were still far off. "Are you all right? Have you been injured?"

When we were standing in front of him, he was completely out of breath. I had barely dismounted the horse when he took me into his arms.

"My little boy. I would never have forgiven myself if anything had happened to you."

"I'm not little anymore, Uncle Walter," I protested, returning his hug firmly. "Aside from a little bruise on my head nothing happened to me. Fortunately, the son of Lord Hamilton found me and took me in. He took good care of me."

"I think I know who sent out that band of robbers," Uncle Walter thundered. "These times are getting more and more insecure. But I promise you one thing, my boy: I won't put you in harm's way again." He embraced me carefully again, then led me back into the house.

Over lunch, I told Uncle Walter all the details of the attack. He was particularly interested in a description of the three bandits. I only mentioned Brian first in passing, but then I expressed a desire to visit him as soon as possible in order to thank him for rescuing me. My uncle didn't mention anything at first, but then merely two days later, as I was looking for a particular horse in the stalls, George was standing beside me saying, "Your uncle asked me to remind you that you still owe Lord Hamilton's son your gratitude. Since he doesn't want you traveling alone, he ordered me to accompany you. So, it looks like we've got to head out together soon."

A broad grin spread over his face. He said that Uncle Walter had ridden off at first daylight, ordering him first to remind me of my duty. It was my turn to grin.

"I was just about to come find you anyway to ask if you wanted to ride off with me. Now that we have an official order, it's even more important not to waste any time."

"Your uncle is traveling for business until tomorrow. In case we don't manage to get back before dark, he says we'd be better off staying overnight. He sent a letter for Lord Hamilton in case."

George waved an envelope at me.

"No, better not. Then Brian will be surprised," I teased, taking the letter and adding with a laugh, "And James too, of course."

Soon afterwards, we were sitting on our horses. We could hardly wait to see our friends again. It was a beautiful summer day. The sun shone down on us out of a cloudless sky, and it was already oppressively warm despite how early in the day it was. George drove his chestnut mare as if he wanted to reach his goal in half the time. An uncontrolled throbbing between my thighs drove me to hurry as well. The wide alley flew past us. Not even a farmer threatening us with his pitchfork as we galloped across his tilled field could make us stop.

Wrapped in a thick cloud of dust, we reached the Hamilton Estate. James was crossing over the yard. Astonished, he looked up to see who was riding towards him in such a hurry. As soon as he recognized us, he beamed at us with his white, spotless teeth.

"George! Tom! What a surprise," he called. "Come in. You look like the devil's been chasing you. I could see your dust cloud from a long way off. You must be thirsty."

With exaggerated care, James beat the dust off George's jacket and pants, looking at him mischievously with smiling eyes. Meanwhile I had to dust myself off all by myself.

"So, now I can lead you in. Perhaps a refreshing bath later?" As he asked this question James looked at me with a wink. He had taken us inside to the cool ground floor of the house. Brian ran down the large stairs beaming.

"I heard you guys coming. What a thrill to see you again."

His strong arms welcomed me eagerly, and he pressed his hot lips on my mouth. Somewhat surprised that Brian was greeting me so openly in front of James and George, I hesitated briefly before slinging my arms around him and pressing him just as warmly to me. This time James took the hint. "I wanted to show George our new foals," he said, saving the situation. "We'll see each other later for dinner."

Brian nodded without letting go of my lips. James and George had long disappeared across the yard laughing by the time we released one another from our intimate embrace.

"I missed you so much, Tom," Brian admitted breathlessly. "The last two days have seemed like an eternity to me. Every hour was torture for my heart."

"It was just the same for me. But I couldn't come any quicker. Uncle Walter had lots of work for me. To make up for it though, I can stay with you tonight." I pulled the envelope out of my bag, beaming. "I have a letter for your father. Uncle Walter expresses his gratitude once more for your heroic act and asks your father for safe accommodations for us tonight."

"Your uncle is really a very thorough man. But we can't ask my father. He's on his way to his estates again. As his substitute, I will have to protect you in my humble rooms. The safest place would be to have you right nearby, in my own room."

"I thank your lordship for the generous offer," I responded with a formal bow.

"You'll see, I will prove myself worthy of your hospitality and repay you amply."

"I hope so, Tom. I can hardly wait."

Brian pressed me close again. This time I could feel his hard cock pressing against my upper thigh.

"But there's still time for that," he whispered in my ear. "Beforehand, I want to show you something. Out in the forest, not far from here, there's a small cabin. I found a little hidden place for us where we can meet in the future without being bothered. I'll just pack the saddlebags quickly. Now that George is here, I don't think there's any sense in asking James. Why don't you get the horses ready? Then we can spend the whole afternoon in the forest."

Brian disappeared into the kitchen to take care of our provisions, so I made my way to the stalls to saddle up the horses. I would have loved to show my gratitude to Brian right away by freeing his cock from his pants. With my impatient tongue, I would have teased him until he begged me to take his shaft into my hot mouth. On this thought, my balls pulled together and my pleasure pole thrust upward in its much-too-narrow encasement. On the way to the stall, I tried to calm my thoughts again but the idea of feeling Brian's skin on my own very soon, breathing in his scent like a heavy drug, would not leave me, making it nearly impossible to walk with a stiff, throbbing cock in my tight pants. Involuntarily, I had to grin. An observer who had seen me cross the yard from behind would have found my hobbling walk very strange.

The large gates in the middle of the long stall building stood wide open. When I entered, the horses stamped their hooves nervously, snorting through flayed nostrils. I hoped to run into a stall boy who could help me saddle the horses. I looked left and right down the corridor; there were ten horse stalls on each side, nearly all of them occupied by large, splendid stallions—but no help was in sight. Then I heard soft cursing. Loose straw flew through the open grate of a stall into the corridor, then strange panting followed. Determined, I walked down the corridor. Just as I reached the stall, I heard a deep man's voice: "Now it's better. Stay there. Ohh ... yeah ... finally!"

Loud moaning followed. I could hardly believe what met my eyes. James, the lordly servant, was kneeling on all fours, naked, his face turned towards the outer wall of the stall. Behind him was George, my uncle's blacksmith. Legs spread wide, half-squatting, his upper body bolt upright, he was shoving his hard tool in James' asshole. His strong back, with a tight ass, moved carefully towards James until his low-hanging balls were touching his ass. Then George pulled back a bit carefully, and pushed forward again. At a leisurely pace, his loins continued their work. His powerful legs and tense thighs rooted on the ground firmly as tree trunks, barely moving, while his pelvis swung back and forth light as a feather pushing his hard shaft forward. My glance wandered upwards from his slim hips to the most impressive back I had ever seen. Right and left of the spine, wide mounds of muscle built up to the strong shoulders. His massive neck and steely arms lent this blacksmith the air of an antique statue. His sweat-covered skin gleamed in the dusty twilight, his white orbs separated by a clear line from his suntanned back muscles.

"That's the way you like it, right?" George grunted contentedly.

The answer was an incomprehensible moan.

"So we can change our pace to a trot?"

James responded with another moan of agreement, which turned to a suffocated gasp as George sunk his hammer faster into the narrow hole. Then I saw that a thick, plaited leather strap was clamped between James' teeth, its end wrapped around George's left wrist. He held the strange bit like a seasoned rider, pulling the bridle tight each time he shoved his crotch forward, pulling James harder onto his cock. The servant seemed to enjoy this treatment. His panting and moaning became rawer and more demanding. As George pulled a riding crop into his right hand and stroked it over his mount's sweaty back, James' entire body shook. Softly, the blacksmith traced his muscles with the rod, skillfully turning the broad end then wandering back, rubbing over his nipples. Suddenly James bent up.

"Not so fast, young stallion," the cavalry master silenced him. "Or are you not enjoying the ride? Time to trot off again!"

With that, he stroked his heaving belly with the stock. Alternately, he pulled the tip of the crop left and right past the twitching cock, pulling carefully on his tight balls and hitting his own hammer as well as it drilled into James' ass.

I had already freed my cock from my narrow pants and was rubbing my throbbing shaft. Leaning my back against the opposite stall, I enjoyed secretly watching these powerful men in front of me. Now George changed from a light trot into a gallop. Shaking, he shoved his loins against James' hot pleasure point. His legs were shaking lightly, he had dropped the bit and the crop, and his powerful hands were grasping James' shoulders. The servant reared up like a fierce stallion. I wouldn't have been shocked if his pleasurable panting had turned into a loud neigh. The rider was just speeding up his tempo when I heard Brian. He called my name. Shortly after that he appeared in the stall corridor. Conspiratorially, I lay a finger to my lips to keep him from talking. Confused, he looked at me. He probably hadn't expected to find me with one hand on my mouth and the other on my hard cock. I waved him over and pointed to the open gate in front of me. Carefully, Brian pushed next to me. His reaction to the two pleasure riders was similar to mine—he made a confused face. But he quickly recovered from the surprise. His glance wandered down to my hard cock. He grinned, slowly loosened my hand from my stiff club, and gripped his fingers around my throbbing shaft.

An animalistic drone distracted our attention to the two men in the horse stall. James reared up, tilted his neck back, screamed, and clasped his hands to George's ass. George had slung his arms around James, tweaking his nipples and pumping his cock unrestrained into the willing hole.

"Yes … harder … deeper," James demanded. "Shove your hot iron in my ass and show me how a blacksmith beats his horse."

The hard mounds in front of us began to shake. The hulk briefly stopped his movement, then shot his cream into James' ass with a long deep thrust. His ass muscles shook clearly, a throaty moan burst from his mouth. The servant's hands clawed into the black-smith's white flesh. Then James hurtled his full strength into an imposing climax. White semen flew on the wall in front of him, smacking against the dark ground and running in broad streams. James' whole body twitched and shook again and again from lust that did not want to end. He fell back against his rider, and his panting began to ebb.

At the same time, Brian bent over my cock—at just the right time, too: he pushed my cock deep in his mouth and soundlessly swallowed the juice from my exploding balls. I muffled my rising moan by pressing my fist into my mouth. After I had calmed down a little, Brian came up and whispered in my ear: "Let's go. These two need a bit of peace and quiet."

George was lying next to James, softly stroking his friend's back, the two of them making themselves comfortable on the ground, visibly exhausted but content. Noiselessly, Brian and I snuck back to the yard.

*T*hose two boys have quite an unusual riding session behind them," I said with a muffled voice.

"But James seemed to enjoy it. And you had your fun with it as well," Brian replied, somewhat accusingly. He pushed me up against the next wall. His tongue snaked into my mouth, still smelling of my semen. But more than anything I felt Brian's twitching cock as it beat against my crotch.

"Shouldn't we ride to your hideout now?" I interrupted him. My heart was in my throat out of sheer arousal.

"If we saddle up the horses now, we'll just bother the two of them. Besides, I can't wait so long." Saying this, Brian squeezed his hard cock through his pants, pulling a pained face.

"And you can't wait any longer either, can you?"

He was right, my shaft was rearing up again. Impatiently, it throbbed against my pants.

"Come with me," he whispered. He ran along the length of the building. Some of the horses stretched their long necks curiously out of their stalls. A black stallion watched Brian go, pricked up its ears, then looked at me as if to say, "Well, what are you waiting for?"

Brian disappeared behind the next wall. Hurriedly I followed him, but as I bent around the corner it was as if he had disappeared off the face of the earth. Irritated, I stood and looked around. Further off lay the horses' paddock, on the other side there was nothing but broad meadows. It was impossible that he had already reached the distant forest's edge. I felt somehow as if I was being watched. Then I suddenly discovered a ladder leaning on the back of the stalls. My glance followed the rungs up to where Brian was standing. Completely naked and uninhibited, he was leaning against one of the open gable hatches that ran along the long roof timbers.

"Where have you been?" He grinned down at me, turned around, and showed me his tight ass, then disappeared from view. Springing up two rungs at a time, I rushed up the ladder. In the darkness of the giant roof I had a hard time recognizing anything at first. Disoriented, I stumbled about in the twilight, then from further down I heard Brian's call: "Here I am, my lover!"

It was the first time he had used that word. It sounded strange and yet familiar. In my thoughts I had called him that many times as he lay in my arms looking up at me with his blue eyes. But now he had said it out loud. And it sounded right. I was his lover. Hearing it from his mouth meant that a part of me belonged to him from now on. Just the same, a part of Brian belonged to me from now on. This single call caused a warm tingling feeling to flood from my heart and fill my whole body. I breathed deeply and peacefully. Again, my eyes searched the hayloft in half-darkness for my beloved. Finally I saw him. Brian was sitting in a large old rocking chair, one leg lazily swung over the armrest, the other propped against the ground, rocking him from time to time. He had one hand behind his head, while the other stroked his stomach seductively—almost as if it couldn't decide whether to wander upwards to his chest and protruding nipples, or downwards toward his cock. The beauty hung down between his legs, foreskin already half pulled back. In gleeful anticipation of the coming hours I looked at the thick cock head with hunger, lightly trembling.

"Isn't it a great view from here? Come here, I love to sit and enjoy the view."

"Everything I want to see is right in front of me," I responded with lust. "Why roam in the distance when the best thing is so close?"

Slowly, I approached Brian. On the way, I slipped off my shoes, and my pants slipped down nearly on their own. I managed to get out of them without tripping. My shirt buttons flew open and soon I was standing naked in front of him. His eyes grew narrow as if he were appraising an unknown object for the first time. Unconsciously, he licked his sensual lips. A timid sigh escaped his slightly open mouth. Without another word, I stood behind the rocking chair, leaned my arms on the high armrests and whispered, "What view were you talking about just now?"

"I ... ummm ... I just wanted to ..." Confused, Brian scrambled for words. Then he pulled himself together and, stretching out his arm, pointing at the open side of the gables. "Take a look at that."

I looked up. What I saw was every bit the equal of those landscape paintings that were in fashion at the time, indispensable in any well-off citizen's living room. Framed by the massive black oak beams of the roof truss, Plymouth's typical soft hilly landscape spread before us in the afternoon sunlight.

"Whenever I need a bit of a break from the hubbub on the estate, I come up here," Brian admitted. "Look at these soft green hills."

My hands slid cautiously down his shoulders, slowly stroking his powerful upper arms.

"Yeah, I can feel them," I answered softly.

"Down there to the right, you can make out the last of the Venton Mountains with their bare rock peaks."

My hands wandered further down to the protruding domes on his vaulted chest. Carefully I pressed and twisted the sensitive nipples between my fingers. Brian's breath grew quicker. He slid up and pushed his upper body against my hands, moaning at my treatment.

"The cabin I wanted to show you is actually in the little forest below those peaks. We can always meet there undisturbed. If you look closely, you can even see the red roof tiles among the leaves."

I looked up briefly. Focused, my eyes found the spot he was referring to.

"The forest here isn't too thick though," I murmured, referring to Brian's body, my hands crawling tenderly through his short chest hair and following the fine line down to his navel.

"The little lake between those hills there leads out to the sea," Brian continued, describing the panorama while my fingers explored the landscape left and right of his navel. Tenderly, I stroked every nook and cranny until the small mountains of muscle began to twitch beneath my fingers.

"Just before the bluffs, there is a lighthouse standing on a height of land. As soon as it gets dark they light a fire to make sure the ships get safely into port."

My own big lighthouse had already come into view. Proudly raging up below Brian's navel, it cast a long shadow on his stomach. The low sun bathed it in golden light, making the tip glow even though it was not yet dark. And on the highest point of the rearing cock, a fluid diamond gleamed like fresh dew.

Surprised, Brian drew in his breath as I touched the gem with my tongue. I had knelt down between his legs and was now licking from the tip of his pulsing cock head down the long shaft.

"Oh, Tom," Brian sighed. "That's the best view of all."

I looked up at him. His beaming smile warmed my heart. He was visibly enjoying the view as I took care of his stiff rod with my tongue. Greedily, I kept tonguing down this imposing lighthouse until I reached the foundation. On my attack, his sack pulled tighter together. Eagerly I tried to put both balls in my mouth, though I was unsuccessful. A rich manly odor reached my nose and I sniffed it in deep. My nostrils opened and a wild groan emerged from my throat.

Brian's legs shook. I had placed my hands on his narrow hips and he let me pull him forward without resistance. I spread his legs wide apart and laid them on the armrests. Readily, Brian showed me his seductive pleasure gate.

"You're right," I gave a muffled gasp. "There are really beautiful views to discover here."

My breath made him shudder. When I lay the tip of my tongue on the sensitive skin, the entrance twitched approvingly. As if enchanted, I pushed forward. A hot eternity seemed to pass until I suddenly heard my name repeated as if through a fog, pulling me away from the moist gate.

"Tom ... Tom ... I can't take it much longer."

Panting, covered in sweat, Brian lay in the rocking chair. His hands twitched, his pulsing cock danced wildly up and down.

"Please take me," he begged. "I want to feel your thick cock inside me, my beloved."

Obediently I stood up, licking up his sack and the back of his cock as I did so. My tongue left a moist trail behind, running down on all sides into Brian's hot crack. I pushed my hard cock against his lighthouse, grabbing both shafts with one hand and spreading the overflowing nectar onto my shaft. With my other hand I leaned against the armrest. Eagerly, my tongue circled his stiff nipples. Brian nibbled at my ear.

"You make me so happy. I want to be with you forever. This moment is just for us."

A sharp pain ran through me. In his eagerness Brian had bitten my earlobe. Immediately, he took my head firmly in his hands and led it softly to his mouth. As our lips met I tasted a drop of blood. Worked up and overcome by emotion, we kissed passionately. Uninhibited, I enjoyed the sweet odor of the love we had for one another. Losing control, I sucked on his sensual lips until the kiss suddenly tasted like blood again—this time Brian's. In this strange way, we sealed our blood-brotherhood. It was clear to me that this moment had changed both of our lives forever.

Only when my legs began to shake did I release myself in a daze from our intimate embrace.

"Are you getting weak in the knees?" Brian asked, watching with amusement as I straightened up and tried to stand straight again.

"More like I have the feeling my back is about to break. And it's not exactly good for my knees to squat in front of you for so long," I admitted. "Although I found the view very exciting, and it gave me a taste for more."

My tongue ran unconsciously across my lips, leaving a wet trail. My cock was still raging up straight, bobbing back and forth excitedly.

"Then I have just the right thing for you," Brian said energetically. In one gesture he jumped from the chair, probably to make it clear to me that he expected more effort on my part and didn't want to hear any complaining about a little boo-boo. He grinned at me cheekily. His rod, sticking out from his body, whipped recklessly back and forth. Outside, the sun had already half-disappeared behind the hills. In the fading light, the colors of the forest and meadows began to gradually grow pale. Anyway, I only had eyes for Brian. He turned the rocking chair around so its back was facing the opening of the gables. Then he knelt down on the seat and propped his torso up on the armrests.

"Now you have to decide. Which view do you prefer? This beautiful idyllic land by sunset?" With a sweeping gesture he pointed to the landscape in front of him. "Or you do prefer this work of nature in front of you?"

At that, he pushed his ass towards me, pulling his two gleaming ass cheeks apart with his hands. When he looked around at me his eyes were glowing like a wildcat's at night. I played along with his game. With one hand I scratched my chin as if in thought, then with the other I rubbed my hard cock casually.

"Not an easy decision," I hesitated, walking towards him at an exaggeratedly slow pace. Brian tried to influence me by wagging his ass seductively.

"But maybe I don't have to choose at all!"

The firm tip of my moist rod aimed for Brian's twitching entrance. Full of anticipation, my hands grasped his loins.

"I knew you would do the right thing," my blood brother moaned as my cock head pushed against his most sensitive spot.

"Feeling is much better than seeing, isn't it?" I asked Brian.

A long, drawn-out "Yeees" followed by contented moaning was the answer. So I grabbed his hips tighter and pulled them close to me. The tip of my cock assaulted his welcoming gate. Effortlessly, my firm cock head slipped into the warm oasis.

"That's good," I grunted with relief. "I've been wanting to be inside you this whole time, my lover."

This time I was the one speaking the magic words. Just like that. Suddenly, unexpectedly, I realized that I actually loved this man. My heart seemed to burst in my chest. A sweet pain unlike any I had experienced before began to flood through my body. Warm waves of indescribable happiness spread through me. Yes, I was in love. A contented sigh escaped me. Arising in my burning crotch, lifted through my heaving stomach, encouraged by my beating heart and brought out by the triumph of lust, it made its way out of my throat.

"I love you, Brian." It was just a whispered declaration of love, but he understood. His blue eyes looked around, reflecting boundless love. His enchanting smile hit me like Cupid's arrow, along with a whispered, "I love you too, Tom."

Softly I pushed Brian's ass away from me. My hard cock appeared again, its dark skin set off clearly from his two white half-moons. The thick veins more than anything were clearly visible from above. Whether by chance or intentionally, Brian shifted his weight on the rocking chair so that his ass approached me again without my doing anything. When I pushed him away again, he simply sank back onto my tight shaft. I repeated this game for a while. Every now and then I slapped a bit of spit on my cock, increasing the tempo each time. The rocking chair was squeaking dangerously, but Brian's loud howling drowned it out. Like a little boy who had just discovered something new, he whipped back and forth wildly. I didn't need to hold onto him anymore. It was enough to hold him with my hard torpedo. He swung back and forth, rubbing eagerly on my pole. His back gleamed. Drops of sweat ran down his spine like a little river, falling between his ass cheeks directly on my rod, lubing it up.

"I could keep going like this for hours," Brian howled, overjoyed. "Your fat cock feels amazing inside me."

Swaying again, he fall back on me, pushing me deeper inside of him.

"I don't know if I can hold out much longer," I let him know, panting. "I think my piece is glowing already—soon it's going to catch fire."

Since my hands were free, I grabbed my nipples and kneaded them forcefully. I pulled the thick nodes harder and firmer. My cock answered by twitching strongly, arousing Brian even more.

"Look at the landscape, that will distract you," Brian snorted in a begging tone of voice. "I want to feel more of you."

Cool evening air flooded down on me as I lifted my head and looked out into the twilight. I could barely make out the silhouettes of the far-off chain of hills. The sun had long disappeared beneath the horizon, but the sky still glowed a weak dark red. But the sensation of Brian's tight ass on my throbbing cock was simply too strong. My entire body began to tremble. My legs shook and threatened to give way beneath me. Cramping up, I grabbed onto Brian's thighs and shoved my hammer so deeply inside him that my balls slapped painfully against him.

"Look," Brian called breathlessly. "The Plymouth lighthouse is lighting up."

Just as I saw the flames rise up in the distance, my hot cream made its way through my balls and my twitching hammer. I was burning within as if on fire. For an instant I thought my skin would glow like the evening sun. Uncontrollable heat collected at the tip of my cock, then with an animalistic roar I pumped my blazing fluid into Brian's ass. One wave followed the next, one cry after another. Breathing heavily, I sank down on Brian's back.

When I opened my eyes again, an eternity seemed to have passed. We had sunk down to the ground. My legs were unable to carry me any longer. My heart was still beating loudly in my chest, but it began to calm down gradually. Brian's breath was getting slower too. Deep darkness surrounded us, the only light came from the distant lighthouse guiding ships safely over the sea.

"That was amazing," I said softly to Brian.

"Yes, it was. I've never experienced anything so hot, so animalistic and at the same time so exhilarating," Brian responded seriously. And as if he had seen my eyebrows raised in the darkness, he added, "Yes, you make me truly happy!"

Lovingly, I took him into my arms and kissed his lips. *Yes*, I thought, *he makes me happy as well*. We gave free rein to our emotions and lay a long while, tightly entwined. Only the threat of a cool oncoming night led us to collect our scattered clothing. We climbed down the ladder and tried to cross the yard as quietly as possible to avoid waking the horses from their well-earned sleep. A crescent moon hung over the house, keeping solitary watch behind slowly passing cloudbanks.

We made our way to the side entrance of the house unnoticed. When we reached the dark hall, Brian gave me his hand. With a sleepwalker's certainty he led me up the stairs past the old suits of armor keeping watch in the corners and wall niches. I could only recognize their outlines, which made them appear even more threatening. We had almost reached our destination when I accidently tripped against an old chest holding a copper jug. In an instant, the door across from us flew open. In the light flooding out I recognized James, standing on the threshold looking at us with frightened eyes. Like two burglars caught red-handed, Brian and I stood there. James' facial expression changed from serious concern to mild annoyance to an amused, self-satisfied grin that seemed to spread all the way to his big ears.

"Look at that, a night-time visit! His lordship and his recovering new friend do us the honor of showing up after all. We were waiting for you at dinnertime." James' voice had a biting undertone. "But as I can see, your lordship preferred to inspect a hayloft with his new friend."

Just then, I noticed the remnants of straw on Brian's head. And he began to pull individual straws from my hair with a smile.

"I just had to show Tom the view from the hayloft in the horse stall. And we both fell down," Brian apologized without turning red from his lie. He knew that James must have put a lot of effort into dinner. His scolding was not entirely unjustified.

"And that's why you took off your dusty clothes right away to avoid dirtying up the whole house. Very praiseworthy. But it doesn't seem to have been much use." James shook his head and looked down at us appraisingly. It's true, we had slipped in naked with our clothes clamped under our arms. Then I realized that James himself was standing in the doorway completely naked. His imposing frame filled the door almost completely, while the quivering light of a crackling fire highlighted his compact silhouette. He turned to the side and looked back into the room. This brought his stiffly-standing cock into view, which had been hidden by the darkness until now. His jerky movement caused his enormous erection to wobble back and forth, the wiry hairs on his ballsac shimmering in the firelight. The lively shadow play of the flickering flames raced over his broad chest and square stomach muscles.

"Our two missing friends have showed up again," James called back into the room. "They were trying to slink past us like two thieves. What are we going to do with them now?"

"Maybe ask them in first," George's voice echoed from the room. "They must be frozen through. They need to warm up ... then we'll see."

A strange undertone was mixed in with the last sentence. I approached James and looked past him through the open door, where George lay stretched out and buck naked on the spacious bed. His back was to us, his head propped up on his large hands. His broad shoulders and muscular back lay in the dark, his well-formed, tight ass gleaming in the bright candlelight.

"Well, come in, you drifters."

James took a step back and waved us into the room.

"But you do need to be punished a bit," he said grimly, slapping his flat hand intently on my ass as I slipped past him. More out of shock than pain, I stumbled and found myself on the floor in front of the bedposts, on my knees looking straight between George's spread legs. He had sat up, his legs hanging loosely from the high mattress, looking at us in amusement. His fat cock rested slackly on his right upper thigh, already impressively large in this state.

"Don't be so harsh, James. Even though the lordships missed your excellent dinner, we can still offer them a nibble now," George said. "And if they make a bit of an effort they might even get to enjoy a special drink."

Playfully, the blacksmith grabbed his cock, pulled the foreskin back with relish, then slid it back over the head. In the glow of the hearth fire I thought I could see a drop of clear liquid gleaming on the tip of his cock. Now I understood what delicious drink George was talking about. I didn't hesitate any longer and dove right in to catch the drops with my tongue. Tenderly, I surrounded the sensitive zone, and soon was tasting the sweet juice.

"Can I get more of it?" I begged George.

"Serve yourself," he encouraged me. "I have enough of it. Also enough for the noble lord over there, who seems to be overlooking us at the moment."

George had lost all semblance of shyness in front of Brian. Curious and tranquil, he scrutinized the young man who was standing naked and freezing in front of the hearth trying to warm up. In this position, he didn't make a particularly noble impression, and his cock had shrunk up a bit from our nighttime flight through the cold. Looking at him, you wouldn't imagine what size his now unassuming appendage was capable of reaching. James was not deterred. Once more the helpful servant, he stood behind his master, first rubbing his back firmly, then roaming with his hands slowly over his shoulders to the front. He grabbed Brian's chest, stroking passionately across his stomach, and landed at the gem between his thighs. With a deep sigh, Brian relaxed and leaned back against James.

"Now I'm finally warming up," he said, acknowledging his servant's soothing efforts.

"Warm is all right. But I want more," James murmured softly, working on Brian's shaft more encouragingly by heating up his strokes. This procedure did not fail to have its desired effect. Beneath James' eager grasp, the swollen pole grew to a size I was quite familiar with from earlier that day. George liked what he saw. Leaning back relaxed on his elbows, he had been observing the whole show in front of him from the bed, and his cock had been revived. His seductive hard-on danced in front of my nose. I couldn't resist. Greedily, I dove on it. As his thick cock disappeared in my warm mouth, I smelled the familiar intoxicating odor of pine trees wafting from the blacksmith's crotch. George must have taken a bath after the adventure in the stalls. I could imagine very clearly how James had thoroughly scrubbed his riding instructor's back—and not just his back.

George grunted contentedly as I engulfed his thick weapon. Suddenly Brian was kneeling next to me, looking at me wide-eyed.

"You don't want to keep that all for yourself, do you? The offer was for me as well."

"Of course. We'll see how long it takes to get this fountain of youth flowing. If you help me it will go twice as fast."

Now Brian and I began indulging the growing mast with united forces. George sank back on the bed sighing. My beloved was bent deep over the stiff erection, his hands leaning on the spread upper thighs, his head bobbing rapidly up and down. With each downward motion he managed to engulf a bit more of the enormous shaft.

At the same time, my tongue explored the lusty blacksmith's balls. Each time I sucked the magnificent parts into my mouth, their anguished owner snarled out of pleasure. Brian, too, was howling loudly next to me. James had come up behind him and shoved his massive shaft in his ass without warning.

"I told you there needs to be some punishment. And this is a punishment that pleases me quite a bit. Your lordship will hopefully understand now that it's better not to keep me waiting by a finished dinner."

Mercilessly, James rammed his pole into his master's ass, growing harder with each thrust. At the same time, he beat his master's ass cheeks with regular, loud slaps of his flat palm. Brian took it all with composure. After he had pulled himself together, he continued his work on George's manhood with relish. His own twitching cock bobbing right in front of my face signaled to me that my friend was also greatly enjoying his punishment. I turned around and leaned my back against the bed. Brian's manhood thrust toward me in jerks. James' hard thrusts shoved his magnificent, throbbing cock head in my direction. All I had to do was open my mouth and my lips were already touching the sensitive head. Brian noticed immediately that his best friend had found a warm home. He made sure that the pulsing red head shoved deeper within me upon each thrust. Visibly contented, his ass alternated between James' thick shaft and my greedy mouth. My right hand had found its way to my own erection, stroking it pleasurably. My left hand grasped James' ballsac, making his balls dance by pulling together and then relaxing apart. Playfully, my fingers wandered further down his tight crack to his moist rosebud. James shoved his ass expectantly against my groping fingers. His joy at this unexpected visit caused him to let out a moan. My teasing at his greedy hole seemed to transfer directly to his cock and into Brian's. Suddenly, Brian's hammer filled my mouth completely. His sweet nectar was no longer merely dripping—it flowed in streams like honey down my throat. I could hardly move my head, Brian's ram was pressed so firmly against my face. My flaring nostrils dug into his short pubic hair. The manly heat rising from them drove deep into my lungs, spreading through my whole body.

James' ass bucked heavily under my finger's bold exploration as it dove more and more mercilessly into his warm ass. His narrow sphincter pulsed feverishly. But suddenly James seemed petrified for an instant. He held his breath and his legs began to shake. Then he draw in a deep breath like a drowning man rising from the water at the last minute, burying his seed deep in Brian's ass with a roaring "Yeah … I'm coming!"

Almost at the same time I heard George's uninhibited yell coming from the bed: "Here, your lordship, here's your delicious drink. Take it all." The whole bed shook as George's fountain overflowed and Brian lapped at the fertile spring.

My own hammer jumped in my hand. A pleasant burning spread through the shaft down to the tip. My heart was in my throat. As soon as I tasted Brian's bitter cream on my tongue, there was no holding back. My lover sprayed his full load down my throat. There was no way I could swallow it all. The warm flood overflowed out of the corners of my mouth down onto my chest, mixing with my own spurting fountain exploding from my cock.

Exhausted, I sank back against the bed. Brian lay next to George on the soft bedsheets. The blacksmith's powerful arm embraced his shoulder lovingly while his large hands fondled his sweaty back. Softly and with a tenderness unexpected from such a rough man, he sank fully into this sensual pleasure. James was resting contentedly on the ground. All his limbs were stretched out, and he grinned at me happily. His whole body gleamed in the warm light of the slowly dying fire.

"I wasn't expecting this tonight, my friend," he said.

"Me neither," I responded. "In any case, I'm not really sure if Brian regrets what he's done. This kind of punishment might soon make him succumb to the temptation of not showing up on time for dinner."

"Believe me, Tom," James responded, smiling. "I've known Brian long enough. When he's really hungry, he comes. My culinary skills aren't actually so amazing, but Brian generally doesn't like to miss out on my truly excellent dessert."

Mischievously he closed one eye and pulled lazily at his pubic hair. His thick cock was dangling loosely between his legs. Only the protruding veins winding along his shaft were still pulsing a bit.

All four of us spent the night in James' large bed. Brian kissed me lovingly for a long time, then turned away with a smile and pressed his back firmly against my stomach. Soon I felt his breath grow peaceful and more even. Behind me, James and George cuddled up close under the blanket. Their softly whispered declarations of love acted like a lullaby to me, drifting me off into dreamless, restful sleep.

The next morning, we were woken up by the bright sunlight of a cloudless sky. I stretched myself out fully. Brian lay to my right, sunk deep in sleep, his face angelic. On the other side of me lay George on his stomach, the blanket pulled back. His broad shoulders and powerful back muscles seemed to be working even in sleep. His narrow hips and full white mounds—I just couldn't get enough of the sight of this image of manhood.

I didn't notice James until he was standing right in front of me. He was already dressed, looking unexpectedly sexy in his tight work uniform.

"Doesn't he look good enough to eat?" he asked softly.

I nodded mutely and slid carefully out of bed. Softly, I collected my scattered clothes.

"We can go downstairs. I already prepared breakfast," James said quietly.

I took a bit longer getting dressed than I actually needed. It didn't escape me that James was secretly watching me, reaching down more than once between his legs to make more room for his pride and joy.

"Finished," I whispered, waving James after me. "Let's leave the two of them resting here a while. I can give you a hand in the kitchen until they come down."

Pleased, I went to the door. In the stairwell, the aroma of fresh bread wafted up to me.

"I didn't know you were also a baker," I stated with surprise. James answered with eloquent silence. Once we entered the kitchen I let out an impressed whistle at the sight of the amply laid-out table.

"Does Brian really appreciate what you do for him?" I asked James openly. "You really have all sorts of talents."

I was only a step away from him, looking openly at the thick package in his pants. Uncontrollably, my hand grabbed the tense material and pressed his winding cock. James bit his lower lip and grunted softly. All of a sudden we heard voices outside.

"Is there anything to eat here?" echoed across the hall. A second later, Brian and George stormed through the kitchen door.

"You were going to start without us," the blacksmith protested, casting a hungry glance on the tasty treats laid out in front of him. With relish, he traced his tongue across his broad lips.

"The question is … what were you going to start?" Brian grinned and looked at James and me with amusement. When he saw the heat rising to my head and my face growing red, he laughed out loud. James chuckled gleefully.

"Other talents are in order at the moment," he said, clasping my shoulder congenially. "May I invite you all to the table, my lords?"

He bowed nobly and let the three of us precede him. As I passed him he whispered in my ear with a conspiratorial grin: "But you can help me later with washing up."

It was an eventful morning. James actually did have need of my helping hands, while George showed Brian in the forge how skilled he was with glowing iron. The precious time passed much too quickly; as the sun reached its highest point at midday, George called for us to depart. The young lord and his servant didn't want to let us leave, but once we promised to come back soon they let us set off on our way.

*I*t was to be a full two weeks before I saw my beloved again. I almost suspected Uncle Walter of intentionally assigning me so much work that I fell into bed every night fully worn out, falling asleep in an instant with a last yearning thought of Brian. Early the next morning, my next assignments awaited me. Sometimes he would send me throughout the city with a long list of errands, then I was supposed to accompany another three-day transport of fine materials to Exeter.

"You will accompany our coachman Nathan and use this opportunity to seek out some of my business partners and deliver these papers to them," Uncle Walter had decided. "And don't lose them, my boy, our future depends on them."

A little while ago I would have been proud to have such an important mission entrusted to me. I would have given anything to see the stained glass windows of St. Peter's Cathedral in Exeter from within, or to gaze at the famous astronomical clock, or to wander around the famous harbor with its enormous trade ships. But right now, I missed Brian so much that I made the whole trip miserable for the coachman by being irritated and moody. Nathan had been in my uncle's service for many years. He was a large, rough man, but "his heart was in the right place," as Walter always said. To put it briefly: there wasn't a better or, particularly, more honest servant in all of England.

The trips to Exeter were not without dangers. Although the main streets were secured by mounted patrols, there were often attacks by vagabond bands of robbers. More than once, Nathan had defended our wares, and he had managed to save them every time. With his hard fists, he showed cheeky rascals what he thought of them. He had left more than a few highwaymen hovering between life and death in ditches on the side of the road, teaching these vermin to fear. But none of that concerned me at the moment. All that mattered was that I had no time for Brian, yet again. As I was packing, I took out my anger on my clothes and my pack; cursing loudly I stuffed my pants, shirts, and jacket into the much-too-small bag, then threw it angrily in the corner. Just a few days before, Walter had insisted he wouldn't let me travel so far anymore. "The times are getting more and more uncertain. I won't put you in harm's way again, Tom," he had said. His words still echoed clearly in my ears. Why couldn't he send someone else? Did it have something to do with the inconspicuous documents he had to deliver? I tried to get a look at the letters, but as expected they were sealed. With two wax seals each. Attentively, I examined the prints on the seals. One of them was the crest of the Plymouth trade union. The other showed an eagle on a tree branch. It was completely unfamiliar to me. After I got back, I would have to ask Brian what it was. If only it wouldn't be so long …

The trip to Exeter passed without incident. I could just as well have stayed at home. At our destination, we took a small room at an inn and set about fulfilling our duties. First, Nathan set off. After he had taken care of all necessary purchases, it was my turn. My assigned message deliveries went off without a hitch. On the second day, I passed the last letter on to its recipient.

"Let's go back home, Nathan," I begged afterwards. "If we hurry we can get back to Plymouth before dark. Mrs. Hambrow will have saved a hearty piece of roast for you, and you can get comfortable in front of the fire."

"No question, Tom. Today is the start of the county fair in Exeter. I'm not going to miss that. What's wrong with you, my boy? Once a year you have a free day in a new city and all you can think about is food? There will be acrobats jumping through the air. Muscle-bound fire eaters spewing giant spouts of flame over the spectators' heads. Giant colorful men on long stilts walking around between the people. And ..." On the following words he bent towards me conspiratorially: "... Then of course there are the pretty ladies on every street corner. Each one more open-hearted than the next, if you know what I mean. So, don't worry about me. I'll get something hearty to munch on here as well, and I'm sure it will be comfortably warm. Maybe in a different way than you're imagining, my boy."

Saying this, Nathan shoved his paw between his legs and licked his lips gleefully.

"We're leaving tomorrow morning, basta. So, what'll it be? Are you coming with me? Come on, be a man!"

I just shook my head, while Nathan, cursing, left our room at the inn. I lay down on the bed and fell soon into a deep sleep.

Late at night, Nathan stumbled drunkenly into the room. A cloud of beer stench billowed out from him that would have done a whole regiment justice. As he undressed awkwardly, I saw his giant cock in the moonlight for an instant, dangling between legs. Visibly contented, he stroked his fat snake, murmuring: "We made them all happy, didn't we, my big boy? None of the ladies complained, did they? Ha-ha, they could all learn something from old Nathan."

He fondled his sac sensually for a minute, then fell on his bed and was asleep in an instant, snoring loudly. He lay on his back, his hands placed protectively over his manhood. I had to grin at this man, who knew how to make the best of his life regardless of what fate had in store for him. Nathan was one of those people who didn't struggle with what he was given, instead seeing the best in everything. What was I so upset about? True, Brian was far away at the moment, but I knew he was waiting for me. And I knew that nothing could separate us. What did a few days matter when we had the rest of our lives together?

Contentedly, I fell back asleep until Nathan woke me up the next morning.

"Let's go, Tom. Time to head out. Yesterday you were in such a hurry." He held both hands to his head and strolled towards the door.

"If it's all right with you, I'm going to catch a bit more shut-eye later in the back of the wagon. Yesterday was a pretty rough night, you understand? If you had come with, you would have something to brag about to your friends." He grinned at me gleefully. Then he became businesslike again: "You can get the horses ready. I'll pay the innkeeper and follow you." And he was out the door.

Nathan was already sleeping off his hangover by the time we left the city of Exeter. I tried to get my thoughts in order and prepared the proper words to say to my uncle. I couldn't keep working like this. It had become clear to me on this trip: I was not Walter's messenger. I wasn't even his son. I wanted to lead my own life.

Later, Nathan sat next to me in the coach trying not to fall off his seat. Neither of us really felt like talking, so we stayed silent. When we finally saw Plymouth in front of us, Nathan coughed nervously and grumbled: "Your mood is unbearable, Tom. I'll be glad when we're back. You didn't even come to the big county fair with me. You should have seen the show. When you were a little boy we could barely hold you back when you saw the first church towers of the city, but now ... I'll think twice before taking you with me again."

"I'm sorry, Nathan," I defended myself quietly. "I've just got so many thoughts racing about in my head."

When we turned into our yard on Penrose Street, Nathan clapped me congenially on the shoulder.

"Keep your chin up. We're back. I just hope you're not lovesick. Because it certainly seems like it, my friend. But I can tell you one thing: women only cause trouble. If you try to make things right with them, everything will get twisted up for sure."

"Thanks for the advice, Nathan, but that's not it."

Shaking his head he jumped from the wagon and trotted off in the direction of the stalls.

A little later, Uncle Walter took me aside.

"I heard you didn't enjoy yourself in Exeter. Nathan said you were so quiet and dismissive the whole time. I hope the two of you didn't fight."

"No, we didn't. I just wasn't in the mood. It seems to me ..." I began uncertainly. "It seems to me that you've really been giving me a lot of work lately. Don't misunderstand me, Uncle, I like to work, but ..."

"But what? Is it too much for you? I just wanted to prepare you for the future."

I looked at him with wide, questioning eyes.

"Don't look so scared," he laughed, putting his arm around me. "At some point, you've got to learn to take over my business. And what I've seen in the last few days has made me very proud, Tom. You're a hard worker. I'm more than pleased with you. You've actually earned a day off. Tomorrow is Sunday. You could go visit your friend Brian again in the afternoon.

"Not until the afternoon?" I protested. "Then we'll only have a couple hours."

My mood had abruptly dropped to a new low.

"After church tomorrow morning I'm expecting a few merchants for lunch. You should really meet them. That's a part of business as well. What would you say if I didn't expect you back for … let's say three or four days? Would that be enough for the two of you?"

Uncle Walter winked conspiratorially at me. And I embraced him joyfully, tighter than I had in ages.

"Yes," I said to him in full conviction. "You can depend on me. After that, I'll enjoy my work more. I promise."

Our visitors had scarcely left the house the next day when I was racing on horseback through the narrow streets of Plymouth. Outside the city, I drove my chestnut mare to hurry up. We rocketed like a whirlwind over the dusty field paths. In my haste, I nearly ignored a low-hanging branch. Just in time, I pulled my head in and clamped tightly to my trusty horse's mane. Involuntarily, I thought of my first ride with Brian. Immediately, warm blood flooded my cock. I could hardly wait to lie in his arms again.

From a distance, I saw the Hamilton family crest waving on a flag on their majestic house. I hadn't noticed it on my previous visits. But now every detail increased my yearning for my lover. Where would we make love tonight? In his room again? Perhaps in front of the fire? Under the trees by the little lake behind the stalls? Or on the roof beneath the waving flag, with only the stars as spectators?

As I reached the courtyard at a gallop, it became clear to me that something was not right. Several coaches and wagons stood chaotically in front of the large gate. Mountains of boxes and suitcases were scattered everywhere. Chefs with white caps and aprons made an uproar grabbing their unwieldy pots and pans from overstuffed kitchen wagons. Servants in colorful uniforms ran excitedly from one wagon to the next, unloading bags and boxes until half of the wide atrium looked like a battlefield. Further off, a pack of hunting dogs were straining, while their caretaker was struggling to keep the animals in check. Two of them had broken away and were running around the coaches, sending the servants completely into desperation. My horse jittered back and forth.

"Tom! Tom, come here!" It was Rupert, one of the stall boys, running up to me, waving. Rupert was a lively boy, large and broad-shouldered. Last time, he had taken care of my beautiful Dario. And he knew how to handle horses. During my last visit, I had seen him proudly and triumphantly break in a two-year-old horse. He had managed to accustom to the young horse to its rider softly, without violence. Now as well he lay his hand calmingly on my nervous horse's forehead, rubbing it softly. His other hand grabbed the reins and led me hastily in the direction of the stalls.

"What's wrong, Rupert? I've never seen such masses of people here. Are they putting on a play or something?" I asked jokingly. But when Rupert turned towards me angrily, my laughter stuck in my throat.

"Lord Hamilton came back unexpectedly this morning. He was furious as a madman," he explained heatedly. "He even whipped two of the boys after inspecting the stalls. He complained about the apparently miserable condition of his horses. I really don't know what the problem was. The stalls were all fitted with fresh straw and the troughs were so clean we could have eaten out of them. All of the horses were clean and well-groomed. But Lord Hamilton grabbed Mr. Comstock, our stall master, and disappeared into the main house with him, fuming with rage. Brian is with them. Little William from the kitchen reported that they've been sitting in the large living room for hours already. There's been lots of loud screaming and nasty curses. None of the servants dares to go in to them. So you can see what chaos reigns here."

"And I wanted to surprise Brian," I sighed. "I would have loved to take a ride with him today."

"Nothing will come of that, I'm afraid. I'm really sorry, Tom. First, I'll get you away from here a bit. And Dario needs to be properly rubbed off. You must have ridden like the devil himself."

Rupert led Dario and me away from the hectic hubbub in the courtyard. He led us to a storehouse out of the way.

"It's quieter here. This part of the horse farm is not used very often. There are plenty of empty stalls here where we can keep Dario. Would you rather wait for Brian, or are you going to head out? I really can't say when my masters will be finished."

"I would like to stay, particularly because my uncle doesn't expect me back for two or three days. But now that Lord Hamilton is back. I really don't know ..."

"Let me think." Rupert scratched his wiry hair in contemplation. "You could wait for Brian here. Or there's a room under the roof over there that we don't use anymore. The stall master used to live there but for a few years now he's had his own house on the other side of the forest. When we have difficulties with stubborn horses, we bring them here and then Comstock sleeps up there in the chamber. Come with me. I'll show you where it is.. As soon as I see Brian, I'll send him over here right away."

Without waiting for my answer, Rupert marched off. A staircase at the back of the stall led up into a spacious room.

"Watch out that you don't trip," Rupert warned me as we entered. "There are old saddles and reins lying around that no one uses anymore. Good thing Lord Hamilton hasn't seen it yet. We have to clean it up. In the next few days he's sure to take a look at all of this."

Carefully, we paved a path through the dusty clutter. I followed the stall boy to a steep ladder at the other end of the room. He climbed it eagerly, and I followed. After a few steps, Rupert stopped suddenly. I nearly rammed my nose into his ass.

"Careful, the next rung is broken." He took a large step, his pants stretching over his firm ass. I would have loved to run my hands over Rupert's tight mounds, but the stall boy was already a step removed. His muscular arms pulled him effortlessly through an open hatch in the ceiling. When he got up there he looked down at me: "You must be dreaming, Tom. Not very safe in the middle of a ladder. Come up! You can daydream as much as you like up here, and wait for Brian however you like." He stretched out his hand to me. With a strength I had not expected, he pulled me up to him. Suddenly we stood directly in front of one another, looking at each other silently. I felt Rupert's fast breathing on my face. The strong aroma of aroused manhood wafted from his body. The air between us seemed to blaze. But then Rupert looked away and turned aside. In an instant, the magic of the moment was gone. He turned his back to me and rummaged a lantern out of a drawer.

"Here's a lamp with enough oil." Without looking at me he placed it on a small table. "And there is an almost comfortable place to lie down. In case it takes longer for your friend to get here."

"Thank you, Rupert. It's really very helpful of you to bring me here."

I grinned at him and embraced him tightly. For a moment I thought I could feel his hard cock pressing against mine. Then he broke the embrace, as if embarrassed.

"I have to go now."

Shortly before his head disappeared down the hatch, his dejected look met mine. Poor Rupert! I wished from the bottom of my heart that he could find someone who loved him as much as Brian and I loved one another. I breathed deeply and fell back on the bed. It was more comfortable than it had looked at first. The straw was dry and smelled good, and the large blanket was only a bit dusty. I closed my eyes and waited for my lover.

"All week long we slaved away, and now this outright injustice!"

"What are we working so hard for anyway? So his high-born lordship can lash into us whenever he feels like it? I'd like to teach him how it feels to have a back covered in welts."

"Yeah … it's always us who get the brunt of it."

"Dan and Peter probably won't be able to work for the next few days. The poor guys. We should do something for them."

"Be careful what you say. If anyone hears you you'll be wasting away in the sheriff's cells—if you even get that far."

The last sentence was spoken by Rupert. His normally soft voice now had a conspiratorial undertone. Shocked, I sat up. I was still in the former chamber of the stall master, where I was supposed to wait for Brian. It was almost dark outside. I must have slept for at least two hours. All the work of the past weeks had made me more tired than I had admitted to myself. But where were these voices coming from? From the room below me? Cautiously, I crawled to the open hatch.

"We should make use of what's left of the day, there's still a lot to get done," echoed a man's voice I didn't recognize. The statement was answered by strange laughter from the others. I had determined that the conversation wasn't taking place directly below me. A glance through the hatch confirmed my suspicion. Out of the corner of my eye I saw a weak light cast from a cracked-open door a few steps away from me. Since it was hidden by a clunky chest, I hadn't even noticed it as I came in. Softly, I crawled towards the light. Looking through the crack, I saw a narrow hall. In the hopes that the old door hinges wouldn't wake the whole stud farm, I opened the door. My heart was racing. Was some kind of plot against Lord Hamilton taking shape on the other side? Who were the men there? And what did Rupert have to do with them? The door opened without a sound. On tiptoes, I snuck down the narrow corridor. It ended in a head-high archway with low wood railing. Behind it was a drop of at least ten feet. I looked down on the huge loft above the empty horse stalls. All sorts of old devices were piled up there as well. I recognized some old furniture and worn-out tools, but the farthest end of the loft was hidden in darkness. What the glow of light did manage to illuminate in the center of the room took my breath away. Five men were standing in a circle, brightly lit by the halos of multiple lanterns. All of them were completely naked and stroking their cocks.

"We stall boys have to stick together," Rupert said in the stillness. He was standing with his face in my direction with both hands on his large shaft. "We even had to toil like animals on our day off. I didn't even manage to get into the city to let off some pressure with Rosalind."

His four colleagues nodded in agreement and understanding. A large man with thick legs started to squeeze his cock as tightly as if he were trying to tie a knot in a thick rope. His pleasure pole seemed long enough to me, but it was also as hard as steel. His assaulted plank stuck up straight as the man gave up his efforts and began tweaking his nipples firmly.

"Don't rush, Bradley. I'll help you. You can count on it, we'll manage to empty your sac tonight," said a boy with long blond hair bound together in a ponytail. I had noticed him on my first visit and James had told me he had only been working with the horses for a little while. His flawless facial features and slim body set him apart from the other stall boys, although his slim hips carried a respectably muscular torso. Now he sank down on his knees in front of Bradley and took his cock between his lips as far as it would go. Bradley shoved his pole forward impatiently and howled, "Man, Robin, swallow it to the hilt. Yeah ... more ... deeper."

Now Rupert kneeled to the ground. He alternated offering his lips to the twitching shafts of the two other men, who were sticking their tongues down each other's throats. I watched, enchanted. Motionless, I stood there and watched the stall boys continue with their unusual pleasure. All right, I'll admit it: not entirely motionless. As if it had a mind of its own, my pride and joy had freed itself from my narrow pants and found its way into my hands, which gladly took charge of my growing desire. Slowly that familiar pleasant feeling spread over me. I had to bite my lips to keep from moaning out loud. At the same time, I couldn't keep from leaning over the railing to better observe the spirited activity below me.

Robin was working on Bradley's hard tool with dedication. At the same time, his right hand was firmly grasped onto the man's balls. Mercilessly he kept pulling the hairy sac downward. Bradley seemed to like this rough treatment. He grunted contentedly and stroked his body with relish. His arms were stretched behind his head while he thrust his crotch hard against Robin's greedy mouth.

"Come, stall boy, show me you've learned to use your little mouth for more than just loud talk," Bradley grunted. "If you want to work here you've got to be able to handle big tools."

Robin's answer was an unclear murmur. True, I didn't know what the novice had accomplished so far in his work duties, but right now his full-body commitment seemed quite convincing. His hands had just found Bradley's ass cheeks, gripping the tight muscles firmly. His blond ponytail danced wildly back and forth on his back. His own shaft was sticking straight up between his thighs, jumping in time with his unbridled passion.

"Yeah, you're good at that, boy," Bradley moaned. "A bit harder … harder. Take all you can. Yeah, that's good. Finally …"

With a long sigh, Bradley sprayed his semen down Robin's throat. His hands pressed the stall boy's head hard onto his exploding tool. His ass cheeks twitched and twitched until he finally leaned over, relaxed and exhausted, onto Robin's shoulders, gasping wordlessly for air. His hot cream dripped out of the corners of Robin's mouth. He gave Bradley an expectant look.

"Well? Is that good for a start? Your sac already feels lighter."

Bradley rolled his eyes wildly as the younger man kneaded his balls jovially. His cock was twitching up again already.

"If you thought that was all, you were fooling yourself!" he snorted. "Stand up so I can shove my hammer in your hot ass."

The two other rascals, who had just been trying to shove both their cocks into Rupert's mouth at the same time, brought out a long table. Rupert grinned and shoved one of them on top of the table.

"Now you can give your back a break, Scott. Lie down! Randy and I will take care of the rest."

With that, he jumped up with a lightness known only to practiced riders, and in the next instant was straddling Scott's stomach like a horse's back. Then he bent over and the two of them kissed intimately. Meanwhile, Andy eagerly spit in his hand and spread his saliva between Rupert's ass cheeks with his fingers. Then he grabbed Scott's cock and tried to direct the thick spear into the oiled hole.

At the other end, Robin leaned with both hands against the edge of the table, offering ass to Bradley with a laugh.

"I didn't dare hope for it, man! I've been waiting all night for this. There's nothing better than a thick cock in your ass after a long day of work."

"You can have it, my friend," Bradley roared, pressing his moist hard-on against Robin's back entrance. "Your hole is twitching very nervously. You just can't wait, can you? But no worries … I'm here."

With that, the hulk grabbed Robin's shoulders and shoved his shaft into the hungry boy's ass in one motion. The boy answered with a delighted "Shove your stick in deep. Yeah, deeper, please!"

On the other side, Randy pushed Rupert's ass down onto Scott's hard erection. Rupert spread his legs and slid effortlessly down onto the waiting cock. A deep sigh came from his mouth. Then he sat up and leaned his hands on Scott's chest.

"Yeah, that's real good," he moaned. "I've been waiting for this ride for hours. We'll just have to see if I can teach this stallion a thing or two."

"Don't think for a second I'm going to make this easy for you," Scott grunted beneath him, jerking his pelvis up quickly and making his rider stagger on top of him.

"Just wait, you ungrateful nag," Rupert panted back. He pinched Scott's nipples and clamped his legs around his hips on either side. His back lifted and sank in a strong gallop while the stubborn stallion beneath him tried to throw him off. He lifted his ass up until only the head of Scott's cock was still clamped by his tight sphincter. For a second, there was peace. Then Rupert fell full force on the thick hammer. He repeated the process several times. Each time,

Scott moaned loudly, but didn't stop bucking wildly beneath his rider.

"You need to help me, Randy," Rupert called out to the other stall boy. "I won't manage to tame this beast alone."

Randy had been watching this rough lesson excitedly, massaging his thick tool. In the glow of the lanterns his shaft gleamed with moisture and his gaze radiated greedily on the energetic duel before him.

"This devil needs particular dressage. We need ..." Rupert bent over in pleasure as his opponent's cock pushed upward again full-force. His hard shaft slapped on Scott's stomach at each thrust. "... To work together to tame him. Grab his hind legs and make yourself useful!"

Randy understood immediately what the rider wanted. He positioned himself next to the table behind the two of them, grabbed Scott's narrow calves, and laid his legs on his shoulders.

"That's good," called Rupert. "I'll try to keep him calm. Until then, shove your riding crop between his cheeks. Maybe then he'll learn to obey."

"You can't do that!" Scott huffed as he realized what the boys were planning.

"You should have been more friendly, my dear. Now we have no other choice. But I'm sure that Randy knows how to use his punishing tool."

Rupert nodded encouragingly at his helper. With determination, he directed his "punishing tool" at Scott's twitching hole. Randy's strong hands spread the tight ass cheeks apart. He waited briefly with the tip of his cock at the entrance, then pressed against it with his full body weight. Scott lay on the tabletop without moving. Only his eyes were rolling wildly back and forth, and his sweat-soaked chest heaved lightly. His cock was still shoved to the hilt in Rupert's ass, while his own ass was being filled by Randy's hammer. Randy and Rupert used the opportunity to continue their riding session. In coordinated rhythm, they showed the disobedient stallion how real horse experts can make even the most steadfast thoroughbreds subservient. Scott howled with pleasure. He seemed to have realized that it was useless to defend himself against these two superior men. Instead, he gladly gave into the teaching session.

"I think we'll turn this wild beast into a cart horse yet. Let's end our schooling with a little show," Rupert suggested to his helper. "Whoever of the two of you jumps over the big hurdle first will get my scepter and can empty my trophy cup."

Both Randy and Scott licked their lips. I had to grin in spite of myself at Rupert's clever strategy. As soon as there is something to win, men drive themselves to perform at their best, regardless how worthless the prize is. But in this case I could understand why the boys were eager. Rupert's thick cock was a real treat for the eyes. The way it sprang from the boy's quaking loins made it actually seem like a monarch's rod. And its glowing red tip was dripping clear fluid onto Scott's stomach. That was a prize worth any kind of effort. I was getting a bit annoyed with myself for letting that magnificent trophy slip through my grasp so carelessly when Rupert suddenly looked up in my direction. His eyes seemed to focus right on me, and although I was certain he couldn't see me, I pulled back into the shadows instinctively. Did this man have some idea that I was watching his uninhibited lust from a safe distance? Or was his penetrating glance merely a result of ecstasy, and I was just imagining it? He grinned, then nodded gleefully and turned back to Scott. I was captivated by this show. Carefully I moved forward again.

The heated men were now galloping unbridled towards their destination. While Scott drove his hot cock wildly into Rupert's ass, Randy clamped his muscular torso tightly from behind, pushing his hips rhythmically against Scott's ass in loud slaps. Robin and Bradley were now looking eagerly over at the three of them. Bradley's hands grasped his friend's loins tightly. Legs spread, he stood behind him, pushing his cock forward in a fast tempo.

"You like that? You probably didn't think my plank would be back in action so quickly. I feel that sinister tingling in my balls again. Just wait! Soon I'll be flooding your hot ass." For a second, he stopped thrusting. He shifted, then focused his glance straight at Robin's neck and rammed his hammer forcefully in the tight hole, his whole body shaking. You could almost see the sperm flowing from Bradley's body into Robin's ass as the boy's moaning rose to a loud, demanding cry: "Damn it, Bradley … deeper … deeper … ram your cock balls deep into me!" His voice cracked. With his last strength, Bradley dug into him harder. Then Robin straightened up, pressed his ass so firmly against his friend that he nearly lost his balance, and spewed a load from his fire-red cock head. With an animalistic cry from the depths of his ribcage he un-loaded on the dark tabletop. His eager sperm spewed out without him even touching his cock.

All the while, my hands were sliding uncontrollably up and down my moist shaft. My thick cock head gleamed wetly in the dusky light of my hideaway and my legs shook. Fortunately, a bare wall offered support. I thanked the cold stones for helping at least to outwardly cool the blaze within me. Shaking, I shut my eyes and waited until my rapid breath calmed a bit.

"Let's go, Randy. Show us what you're made of. It would be ridiculous if you don't win this duel."

When I opened my eyes again, Robin and Bradley were standing to the left and right of the dangerously teetering table. It was Bradley who had just been encouraging his friend. "Or should I help you?" he offered. Without waiting for an answer, he kneeled behind Randy and buried his face in the boy's ass cheeks. This seemed to have its desired effect. Scott's loud moaning left no doubt about it that Randy's cock had grown in circumference and hit his most sensitive spot.

"Don't worry, Scott," Robin spoke up. "For the sake of fairness, I'll help you too."

He heaved himself up onto the table and dangled his thick rod encouragingly in front of Scott's face. The gem disappeared half-way in the stall boy's mouth.

My rock-hard tower of joy pulsed energetically in my right hand. Sweat ran over my chest while my left hand wandered indecisively between my hard nipples and my panting mouth. Desperately I pressed my fist between my teeth in order to suppress the incontrollable urge to cry out in lust.

Down below, Rupert reared up, shaking. As if possessed, he grabbed at his hair and gave a blood-curdling scream as semen burst from his cock. Everything went very fast after that. Randy grabbed Scott's ass and moaned, "Almost there, almost there!" Then he fired his load. Bradley fell back in the straw, tearing at his cock again like a madman. Meanwhile Scott sat up, wrapped his arm around Rupert, who was still shaking with cramps, and tried to calm him. His mouth pressed firmly to Rupert's throat, he reached his climax with a muffled howl. Randy grunted contentedly and shot hot cream on his hairy chest. Shortly afterwards, Bradley began panting and shot a white fountain over his stomach, emptying his sac for the third time this evening.

Laughing, the other four surrounded Bradley.

"I wasn't expecting that, my boys," he uttered with a gleeful smile. "No, I really wasn't. I think that might even be enough for today!"

He stroked his cock seductively as it sank gradually back down between his legs.

"Tom? Where are you? Tom?" When I heard Brian's voice, I shot up and turned around. My lover was standing with a lantern at the entrance to Comstock's old room.

"Ah, here you are. What are you doing ...?" He swallowed the rest of the sentence as the glow of the lantern fell on my throbbing cock.

"Were you so bored that you had to pleasure yourself alone? Too bad you couldn't wait for me. I couldn't get away any sooner, even though Rupert told me hours ago that you were here."

I tucked my cock back in my pants. Reluctantly, he explained what had happened.

"Yeah, I heard already. Your father came back unexpectedly."

"You can't imagine how he's been acting. I've never seen him like this before. He really gave Comstock and me hell. Something must have happened on his trip to get him really worked up. I don't know how to explain it otherwise. You must have heard about the two poor stall boys. They're the youngest in the yard. My father caught them fooling around in a horse stall, jumping around like two foals and throwing straw on each other. He completely lost it. He took a riding crop and beat the poor fellows until they were cowering in the corner of the stall. It was awful."

"Rupert told me. He was shocked by your father. The others seemed quite upset as well."

At this moment I didn't want to talk about how the stall boys had relieved their anger. They had certainly shot their wad enough for tonight. Not the worst solution for blowing off some steam, I thought. Nevertheless I took it upon myself to report what had happened to Brian when we had a quiet minute.

"Were you trying to hide from me while you took care of your cock?" he asked curiously.

I hurried up to him. His hot lips pressed on my dry mouth, he slung his arms around my hips and pulled me closer to him. Immediately, my cock grew heard, unmistakably demanding Brian's attention. His hands immediately wandered down to my waistband, seeking access.

"I watched your stall boys at their Sunday work," I whispered. "I had no idea what a well-practiced team they are."

"What nonsense are you talking, Tom?" Brian looked at me dumbfounded, then stopped. "That's right, the stall boys had to work today even though it was their free day. We pushed them so hard, they must have put down on their straw sacks hours ago. Comstock didn't give them a moment's peace until everything was spotless. He didn't want to give my father any more reason to punish the boys."

"I think you're wrong about that," I whispered. "Just look!"

Carefully I led Brian to my outlook at the end of the corridor.

"What am I supposed to be looking at?" He held up the lantern, searching. The dull light was lost in the dark distance of the giant loft. Everything was still, not a soul in sight. Just a large table standing alone in the middle of the room among a few scattered remnants of straw.

"Oh great, we've got to clean up here as well," Brian determined dejectedly.

Incredulous, I stared into the darkness. Had I dreamt it all? There was no indication that five hot men had been here minutes before, indulging their unbridled lust.

"I thought I saw something here. I was completely certain that ..." Doubtfully, I looked into Brian's questioning eyes. "Ah well, it doesn't matter. What matters is that you're here now. My little friend has been waiting eagerly for your little friend. He's completely impatient."

I pressed Brian against me again. I ran my hands through his hair, tasting his throat and sniffing my lover's unmistakable scent.

"Well then, let's see if we can't have a big celebration for our reunion," he whispered in my ear, leading me towards the room. I turned around again. The weak rays of the rising moon and uncountable radiant stars reflected in the dark wooden table. Unbelievable. Just moments ago, Robin had spread his seed on the dark surface while Bradley's cock had found a pleasure point deep in his ass. Grinning gleefully, I followed Brian. He put the light on the table and began to undress.

"Let me do that for you," I said, pushing his hands aside. Carefully, I shoved him back against the edge of the table. He smiled at me, his arms propped up and his back bent.

"I'm all yours," he whispered.

My cock throbbed against the thick package in his much too narrow pants. Slowly, my fingers removed one button after another from the loops in his loose shirt. As if by accident, I stroked his chest hairs. Brian started breathing heavier. His stomach muscles twitched as my thumbs traced after the small hills. Softly, my hands wandered back past his hips, pulling his shirt out of his pants. My beloved had closed his eyes and opened his mouth slightly. His lips searched and demanded for their warm companions. Soft moans emerged from his throat. The haze of his breath surrounded me like intoxicating fog. He was waiting for me. But I didn't want to release him yet. My lips stroked his cheeks. Greedily I sucked in his enchanting scent. As our naked torsos touched, it was like two hot suns melting together. Flashes of light danced before my eyes, my heart jumped in my throat.

"Oh Tom, what are you doing to me?" he whimpered.

"I love you, Brian."

His shirt fell from his shoulders. My fingers made their way up his back, stroking every muscle on the way to his neck. When I held his head in my hands, our glances met. Our sensual lips touched. First soft and tender, then passionate, unbridled, our tongues wrestled. His arms wrapped around me, pressing me with all their might against his heaving crotch. Hot shudders ran through my body. As our lips released, panting breathlessly, Brian took my hand without a word and led me to the bed. His pants slipped to the ground easily. He lay back on his bed and held out his hand to me.

"Come to me, Tom!"

His hard cock throbbed against his stomach. Thick dewdrops gleamed on the tip. His nipples had hardened to thick nubs, lifting and sinking along with his torso as he breathed more and more heavily. As Brian's lusty gaze met mine, I slipped my own pants off as well. My tool sprang free. Carefully, I pulled back the foreskin. My cock head filled with blood until it was enthroned above the shaft, gleaming and pulsing. Brian moaned eagerly.

"Come to me, my lover, let me feel your love pole. I've been yearning for this moment for days."

I lay on top of him. Our lips met again, and our throbbing friends found each other once more, rubbing and wrestling lustily until they were dripping and impatient for relief.

Brian spread his legs and set them on my back. Inevitably, the tip of my cock pushed against his sphincter, which opened readily. My shaft sank into his warm ass.

"Finally," he whispered. "There you are."

Moaning, I lay on top of him, thrusting my hips forward.

"Yeah, that's good! I can feel your pulsing cock."

For a while we simply laid there without moving. I heard Brian's heart beating and felt his soft hands stroking my neck. His manhood pulsed excitedly between our stomachs. My pride and joy swelled and swelled. Our tongues wrestled wildly. Brian's calves clamped around my hips. He shook as the tip of my cock unexpectedly hit his pleasure point. Carefully I pulled back, then pushed past it again. Again and again, but each time slow and cautious. Brian's body shook beneath me. Mercilessly, I continued my little torture, pulling far out of him, waiting until he cried out and pushed his calves against my ass, then sunk my shaft slowly back inside him down to the hilt. His fingers clawed at my back. Wildly, his head rolled back and forth. He reared up and snarled roughly.

"More," he moaned. "I want more!"

His manly scent rose up to my nose. My nostrils quivered.

"You'll get more, my lover," I panted, heightening his pleasure by thrusting my hips back and forth in a circular motion. Brian's face transformed into an emblem of distracted pleasure as my greedy tongue victimized his hard nipples. My teeth went to work too, pulling at the red nodes. Deep animal noises pushed from his throat as his throbbing cock exploded, spreading his hot load between us. His sphincter tightened around my tool as if it never wanted to let me go. My balls slapped against his ass one last time, then my floodgates opened as well. Hot cream flooded my angel's canal. His smiling face enchanted me, his sensual lips leading me again into paradise before I sank down against his ribcage, exhausted.

"Yours forever!" Brian's words seemed to approach me from a distance. Blood rushed to my ears like an ocean tide, a thousand bright lights dancing in front of my closed eyes.

"Yes … forever yours," I responded, not knowing if I was whispering or shouting. I cuddled up to him. Warm arms embraced me. I didn't want to be anywhere else. Just here, safe and protected at his side. His peaceful breath lulled me into dreamless sleep.

Morning came much too soon. But when the first horses began whinnying in the nearby stalls, Brian woke me with an intimate kiss.

"We need to get up, Tom," he whispered. "I have a long day of work ahead of me."

His morning wood pressed against my stomach.

"Yeah, that's how I see it as well," I joked, grabbing playfully at his hard tool. "Seems like there's a lot of work that needs to be done here."

"No, not now. I really have to go. My father must be looking for me already. Who knows what kind of mood he's in today?"

Brian escaped from my embrace and got dressed. I watched with disappointment as his magnificent, manly body was hidden by his shirt and pants.

"I can stay another two days. What am I supposed to do? I don't want to run into your father. Wouldn't you like to stay a bit longer?"

"I can't. Really. I just can't, Tom. I'll send you a message as soon as everything has calmed down again here. I have to go!"

I was standing naked in front of him. He embraced me, his strong hands grabbing my ass. His soft lips touched mine.

"See you soon."

With these words, he turned around and climbed down the ladder. "I'll send Rupert to help with your horse," he called, then disappeared.

When Rupert entered I was already grooming Dario in his stall.

"Ah, there you are, Tom." The stall boy came up to me, grinning. Then he leaned against the wall and observed me for a while.

"I heard you're going back already," he said. "That's a shame. I thought ..."

"Brian probably doesn't have any time for me in the next few days, so I'm riding back," I interrupted him. After a short pause I added: "Or were you going to say something else?"

He coughed with embarrassment as I continued to groom my horse's flanks.

"I heard your conversation last night. You'll only make yourselves miserable if you think you need to act against Lord Hamilton."

In an instant, Rupert's smile was wiped out. He looked at me wide-eyed.

"I didn't say anything about it to Brian," I calmed him. "Anyway, you seem to have found other ways of blowing off steam than trying to rebel. By the way, you've got quite a fine specimen down there."

Shamelessly, I looked down between Rupert's legs, where his throbbing cock was visible through his pants.

"Don't worry, I won't disturb your evening meetings in the future. I can keep a secret."

He responded with a broad smile and came up to me.

"Thank you, Tom." Hesitantly, he kissed me. His rough lips only touched my mouth briefly. Then he helped me to saddle and mount Dario without a word. I took a short side path to avoid riding over the yard at the main house. When I turned around for the last time, Rupert was still standing in the open stall door watching me go.

*I*t was the day Brian and I were supposed to see each other again. "Around noon," he had said, but because I couldn't wait I had arrived too early again. Our meeting place was the old cabin in the woods not far from the Hamilton estate. I remembered how I had seen it from far off when Brian showed me the view from the roof of the horse stalls. That was now some weeks ago, and this little house had become our secret love nest. Countless times, we had come here and jumped into each other's arms. After wrestling or fighting playfully we had always made abundant love. It filled me with hot anticipation every time I turned down the narrow path, only visible from the main road at a second glance, and made my way to our refuge. This time as well. Just thinking about the hours to come, I felt my pants going tight in the crotch.

In a split second I had everything prepared so we could enjoy a day without disruptions. I was just repositioning my hard shaft as the ground began to shake with the beat of approaching hooves. In a flash I opened the door to rush out to my beloved. Shocked, I saw two riders in front of me. Brian had not come alone.

"Look who I brought with me," Brian called with excitement. "James didn't want to miss out on the opportunity to visit us."

Immediately, I remembered my first encounter with the servant. Or at least my cock remembered, still trapped in my pants. James himself also seemed to remember our hot encounters.

"Hi Tom, I'm thrilled to see you again, it's been so long," he greeted me as his glance shamelessly drifted to the visible bulge in my pants.

"Well James, how do you find our little hideaway?" Brian asked, interrupting the charged silence.

James' eyes wandered appraisingly over the crooked gables, the conspicuous holes in the roof, and the partially run-down animal shacks around the house.

"My lordship's cabin has clearly seen better days," he twanged in a formal tone.

"Well, for now you will fortunately be spared the sight of the cabin's inside," answered Brian, shrugging off the dismissive commentary. Then he continued, turning to me. "James promised us a surprise for today."

"You're going to love it, Tom," the servant assured me as he saw my skeptical look. But his well-intended words couldn't really reassure me. On the one hand, I was of course glad to see James again, but on the other hand my comfortable afternoon with Brian was now out the window. The visit seemed a bit like an invasion of our intimacy.

"Don't make such a face. Get on your horse and let's go." With that, James turned to his chestnut mare and got ready to ride off.

"Where are you taking us?" I called.

"It's only a surprise if it stays a secret," was his answer. "But I promise you, you won't be complaining by the end of the day."

I was somehow relieved that James didn't want to inspect our love nest. Even if the cabin made a bit of a dilapidated impression from the outside, Brian and I were very attached to the place and the memory of the days we'd spent there together. I didn't want all that to be ruined by his snooty criticism of the rooms. So, I grabbed my things quickly, stowed them away in my saddle bags and mounted my horse.

After we had been travelling for a while, I began to grow restless. We had been following James for more than an hour over convoluted paths. We crossed small streams, galloped over open meadows or trotted through thick leaf coverings. Often it took quite a bit of effort to get through as we had to ride one behind the other or bend low-hanging branches to keep from falling off our horses.

"I hope your surprise doesn't just consist of leading us around the wilderness all day," I ventured, a mild protest.

"The young lords will only have to be patient for a little while longer. We will be there soon." came his answer from ahead.

Shortly after that, the forest cleared. Before us, a small untouched lake gleamed in the summer sun, framed by large, old trees. Proudly, James dismounted from his horse.

"Well? Did I promise too much? I discovered this place years ago. Until today, I haven't showed it to anyone else. You're the first," he called, tying the horse's rains loosely to a bush.

"Come on! It's time to swim!" He quickly began to undress. He dutifully piled his clothes together as befitted a servant. Excited, I looked out over the idyllic water, then jumped off my horse. As I ran, I freed myself from my pants and shirt. By the time I reached James I was buck naked. He was just placing his last article of clothing on top of the others when I slapped his naked ass firmly with my hand. Surprised, he bent up.

"Just you wait!" he called out loud. "You won't escape me."

Immediately, he began to chase me, and when he reached me I dove headfirst into the lake. The tingling, cool wetness felt like a fountain of youth on my skin. I felt newly born. The laborious ride had really been worth it. Swiftly, I swam a few strokes forward to stay a safe distance from James.

"The two of you seem to have some catching up to do," Brian called from the shore as James splashed loudly into the water and paddled swiftly towards me with his powerful arms. Suddenly he grabbed my foot and pulled me close. His arms clamped around me from behind like a giant brace. I tried with all my might to free myself, but I couldn't manage.

"Now I have you. You can't escape me," James panted breathlessly. I struggled and flailed like a fish in a net.

"If you don't behave I'll stick your head between my legs," threatened James playfully.

"That wouldn't be the worst that could happen to me today," I responded boldly as I made another attempt to free myself from his firm grasp. He faltered. I managed at least to turn around in his embrace.

"You'll get a special punishment for your cheekiness today," he said, grinning.

"I can't wait," I countered with glee. My cock had hardened and was pressing against the servant's stomach. James' thick shaft had risen as well. Our cocks began to battle underwater. I surprised James by giving him a passionate but aggressive kiss. He stared at me in astonishment. I used his moment of surprise to escape his clutches. Nimbly, I dove under him and swam as fast as I could in the direction of the shore. Confused, James looked around.

"Your lordship's friend is behaving most impudently," he called out indignantly to Brian, who had been watching our battle from the shore.

"Or perhaps my servant is too dumb for even the simplest of assignments," Brian replied with a smirk as he waved over to me. "Come to me, Tom. I'll keep you safe. Although it wasn't very nice of you to leave me standing here all alone."

"Standing" was definitely the right way to describe it, since Brian had been working at his fat cock while we were fooling around, and it was now greeting me cheerfully.

"I'll have to rub you dry again," he sighed, wrapping me in a large towel. Roughly, he rubbed my wet hair, then carefully stroked my neck and shoulders, and softly and thoroughly gave some attention to my ass. Finally he turned to my legs and ankles.

"Now turn around," he ordered. Crouching on his knees, Brian set to work on my feet. From there, he went slowly back upwards. Nevertheless he only reached as far as my crotch, where my cock sprang out to him gladly.

"It won't do to dry your pride and joy with a rough towel. I'll use something softer for that."

On that, his curious tongue began licking my shaft, not leaving a single spot on my tightly stretched hammer untouched. Pleasant shudders streamed through my body. When I could hardly wait any longer, Brian finally slipped his lips over my cock, exploring further down my shaft with his tongue.

"You do that really well," I moaned. My hands grabbed his head, giving more force to my demanding thrusts and pushing my shaft further down his throat each time. Brian helped me by digging his hands into my ass cheeks. At some point, my cock was swallowed easily in his mouth, which allowed me to relocate my hands to my neglected nipples. In an instant, they swelled to hard nubs. Each time I tweaked them, blood rushed to my throbbing cock. But Brian was well practiced enough to take care of that on his own.

"Let me help you with that," a voice whispered behind me all of a sudden. James pushed against my back from behind. Softly, he slipped his hands under my arms. His searching fingers kneaded my chest and his dripping hair cooled off my overheated skin. But they could not quench the blazing fire within me. Particularly since I could feel James' throbbing hammer at my ass crack.

"I told you you wouldn't be able to escape me," he whispered in my ear. "Come on, Brian, his cock is dry enough. Now it's time for you to make mine wet enough that I can give Tom the punishment he deserves. Or should I say: so he can get the surprise he's been waiting for for hours."

Brian was reluctant to let go of his tasty treat, but he obeyed. After a few pleasurable strokes his mouth finally let go of my erection.

"Here, stick your head between his legs and keep going with me," James ordered, crouching on his heels and pushing his erect mast towards Brian. "Everything you licked off of him, you can give back to me. Get my cock real juicy."

Brian kneeled down between my spread legs and sucked James' enormous bolt down to the hilt on the first try.

Invitingly, his ass wiggled in the air. The temptation was simply too great. I bent down further and stroked his white mounds. His skin felt soft and tender to the touch. I would have liked to have reached his twitching hole. But just as I wanted to push forward further, James' hands grabbed my hips and pulled me back. Unintentionally, I had put my pleasure hole right in front of his face. I should have known he would exploit my bent-over position shamelessly. And he did. Expertly, he licked in tight circles around my anus. The tip of his tongue tried to push open my sphincter. With a sigh, I pushed back against him.

I leaned on Brian's ass with both hands. With my back bent, I looked like a purring cat. My head hand down powerlessly. Between my legs, I could see my beloved forcefully blowing James' hard cock. Tirelessly, he circled his tongue. When he pulled back for a minute, only holding the tip of the cock between his lips, I saw thick veins winding down the broad shaft. But just for an instant. Then the giant disappeared down to the root again into Brian's mouth. In the same instant, James shoved his tongue even further into my hole, causing shudders to run up my spine.

"I think it's time now," I heard behind me. "For the aggravated assault of a lord's servant, Tom needs to be taught a proper lesson."

James pulled his pole out of Brian's mouth and positioned himself behind me. Brian, surprised by the sudden change in position, nearly fell flat on his face. Fortunately I grabbed on to him in time.

"But I was just getting started," he complained once he had caught his balance. "My throat had just gotten used to your thick meat."

"Then you can keep going up here," I interrupted loudly, offering my shaft encouragingly to Brian. "Afterwards, you can tell us which cock tasted better."

"Yours is not nearly as big as his," he whined, "but I don't want to be left empty-handed."

Pretending disinterest, he took my cock in his hands and began to rub it.

"I suppose I need to do a bit more work building it up. But I can manage that."

Very slowly, Brian pushed my foreskin back over the tip of my cock, then pulled it back as far it could go. After just a few times, the first drops of sweet nectar were dripping from my cock head.

"All right. Now it's time to see which treat tastes better to me."

First, Brian licked up my juice sensually with his tongue, then placed his lips around my cock. Slowly, he pushed his mouth down over my hard meat. I felt the rough side of his tongue surrounding my sensitive head.

"You'll see that my manhood has something to offer," I chided him. "You just need to please it right. Then it grows to its full size."

I muffled his answer by shoving my cock forcefully in his mouth. It would have to wait a while; I had no intention of taking my manhood out of his mouth any time soon.

"You seem to be well taken care of up there," James piped in. "Now it's time for me to take care of your ass."

With that, he embraced me from behind, lay his hands on my chest, pressed his spit-moistened cock against my ass crack and rubbed it slowly up and down.

"I need more lube," James murmured. "Come on, lick my fingers."

The fingers of his right hand pushed into my mouth. I tried to cover them with as much spit as possible. This intense sucking at his fingertips got James even more in the mood. His fat pole beat and throbbed wildly at my gate, while his left hand tweaked and tortured my right nipple. My whimpers of pleasure were lost at his eager fingers groping in my mouth.

"Why so excited?" James whispered in my neck. "The best is yet to come."

He took his moist hand and then carefully smeared my throbbing hole with it. Then I felt the thick head pressing against my ring. The pressure became greater and finally my entrance opened. Softly, James shoved his hot cock forward until his rough pubic hair was touching my ass.

He gave me a bit of time to get used to the pressure, then pulled his cock cautiously out and pushed it forward again. Carefully, he increased the tempo. But with time, it became easier for him to glide in and out of my deep canal, and he kept hitting my pleasure point, making my whole body shake. James' breath was getting quicker. Sweat dropped from his torso down onto me. His chest hair scratched against my back, while his ballsac slapped against my thighs. His left hand kept tweaking my nipples painfully. His right hand was positioned on the back of Brian's head, pushing him down onto my cock.

Glowing heat rose from my legs; my cock demanded more. Clamped between James' rock-hard pipe and Brian's mouth, my crotch swung in its own jerking pendulum back and forth. I could hardly control it. It was clear to me that James wouldn't last much longer. Wildly, I whipped my hammer into my lover's gullet. And Brian himself was rubbing his own stiff meat with unbridled lust.

James reared up, shoved his cock deep within me, and waited motionlessly for a moment. His thick cock continued to pulse, then with a last hard thrust shot hot sperm into my cave like a redemptive flood. At the same time, I reached my climax. The fire James had lit found its way from deep within me up through my burning shaft to the tip of my cock. A sudden explosion overwhelmed me, then I pumped my boiling lava into Brian's throat. I fell heavily on his back and pumped my cock empty, down to the last drop, watching my cream stream out of the corners of his mouth. James had fallen behind him into the grass, breathing heavily. I would have loved to do the same, but first it was Brian's turn. He crouched on his heels in front of me, working diligently on his cock. When his eyes glassed over and he began rubbing his swollen pole even faster, I bent over him. The first touch of my lips brought him to the threshold. Wildly, he thrust his hammer into my mouth and sprayed his sperm with a loud cry. With pleasure, I swallowed his tasty juice down to the last drop.

"You can let go now," Brian murmured, exhausted. "Nothing more is going to come out this time."

After sucking deeply once more, I finally let go of him and fell into the grass.

"I admit, that was a good surprise, James," I murmured after some time.

"But that's not everything," he answered secretively. Jauntily, he stood up and went to his horse. The low sun bathed his figure in soft light. His firm ass cheeks glowed brightly. His back muscles played with every step he took across the small clearing. His impressive shoulders, his slim hips ... he was a sight for sore eyes. Sighing, I leaned back.

"It's the same for me," Brian whispered. He had been watching me. "He's not only the best servant I've ever had, he's also a real hunk. And a wonderful lover on top of it."

I nodded. James came back fully loaded with two saddle bags. He was flawless from the front as well: his chest, his legs, those strong arms. Rays of sun gleamed in his moist pubic hair like dewdrops in grass. His thick cock dangled loosely between his legs.

"The two of you look like starving dogs," he laughed. "Before you eat me up, I'd rather give you something to bite on. Of course I planned for this as well."

Triumphantly, he pulled a bottle of wine out of his bag and held it high. Then he produced fresh bread, cheese, and sausage out of thin air. He spread everything out on a big blanket, which he pulled from the second saddlebag. Still naked, warmed by the last rays of sun, we laid on the blanket devouring our snack and enjoying the peaceful evening. We didn't leave our picturesque setting until nightfall. By the time we set off on our way, the first thin strands of fog were pulling over the water. Right where James and I had wrestled before, a small whirl of fog had built up, as if it wanted to cover the afternoon's happy memories with a veil. I hesitated for an instant. Then I let go of the thought and spurred my horse on.

That was how it all began. Time just flew by. Days passed, then weeks, then months. Brian and I met regularly met in the forest. What started as friendship and affection had grown to deep, intimate love. We could never get enough of each other, and we spent every free moment together. Summer was already coming to an end when a powerful thunderstorm surprised us one day. At first it only announced itself with harmless rumbling. But then it was followed by fierce thunder and lightning that would have turned the darkest night into bright day. That was when disaster befell our love …

"Tom. It's time for you to finally grow up," Uncle Walter said to me one evening at dinner. This simple sentence would change my life forever.

"In two weeks I'm expecting my ship, the *Margarita*, to return. When it's unloaded, you'll go on board and have your first experiences as a sailor. You'll only be travelling for a few weeks, and you'll return to Plymouth harbor with a full hold before the end of the year. Believe me, it will do you good to feel the fresh air in your lungs. After all, you'll be taking over my business one day. And without any experience at sea, you can't be a good merchant. But you know the best of all this? Ben will be on board with you. He's joining this trip to take care of an urgent assignment for me. So you won't be all alone among unknown sailors. Besides, Ben can teach you everything a seafaring merchant needs to know."

My uncle nodded contentedly. Visibly relieved to have finally spoken his piece, he leaned back and grabbed his wine glass. "To your health, my boy."

Speechless, I toasted back and emptied my full glass of heavy Italian red wine in one swallow. Walter had turned back to his meal, spearing a piece of bloody steak on his fork. With relish, he shoved it in his mouth and swallowed it down. My food, on the other hand, seemed to want to go the other way. It took some effort to suppress my urge to gag.

"You're not saying anything." Walter started up the conversation again. "I was expecting you to be a bit more excited. Aren't you looking forward to it? Your first big adventure awaits you."

"I thought … I just thought …" I stuttered. "Isn't it still a bit early for me? Maybe next year would be better …" I was desperately looking for a way out, while a single question rang out in my head: What would become of me and Brian?

I didn't give up right away. More than once I attempted to change Uncle Walter's mind. But he wouldn't listen when I insisted that I had enough opportunities on land to learn about the business. After several days of wearying conversations, many of which ended in loud arguments, I accepted my fate. I knew him well enough to know when I could talk my way out of something and when I couldn't. In this matter, it had been futile from the beginning. He had made his decision.

The only glimmer of light in this whole situation was Ben. Benjamin Wilder was an old friend of my uncle's. The two of them had often been to sea together. They had lived through many adventures and never lost touch. Whenever Ben could manage it somehow, he would visit us. At first he just came once a year for a week or two in summer. But recently he had been coming to Plymouth even more often. Last year he had spent the entire Christmas season with us. He had stayed until well into January. Shortly after Easter, he was standing in the door again, and he stayed for two weeks. After he had been living with us for another whole month, he was now supposed to accompany me on my first big trip.

"Where are we actually sailing?" I wanted to know.

"You will make a short stopover in France, then sail on to Spain. Ben will explain the rest to you. It's not good if too many people know the exact route."

I made a pained face. "Thanks for your trust, Uncle."

"Tom, please don't misunderstand me. This trip is extremely important for me. There's a lot riding on it. I really can't tell you any more at the moment. You'll understand me soon, though. Please believe me. England's future lies on the other side of the Atlantic, every clever mind knows that by now. But our queen has yet to declare war with Spain. And the public treasury is empty. As long as our ports stay open, we merchants will do business with them. The Spanish still believe they own all the world's oceans, but that will change soon. Did you know that in 1493, Pope Alexander VI split all the newly discovered lands between Spain and Portugal? Only the two of them were recognized as colonial powers. England, France, and all the other European states came out empty-handed. The Spanish plundered the West Indies. Their royal family is swimming in gold and silver. Elizabeth won't just stand by and watch them for much longer. Who knows? Maybe your next trip will be to the New World. Believe me, I envy you for your youth. By now, I'm too old for such things."

What use was my youth if I had to spend it alone? That was the only thought running through my head. Me on the other side of the world and Brian here in England. My stomach cramped up again. I felt sick. For the next several days, I avoided Walter whenever possible.

Then the next storm came. This time lightning struck on Brian's side. After a long trip, his father had returned to his estate and called his son into his chambers.

"My boy, it's time you became a real man. In the past months, I've had a chance to think about your future. Last week I consulted Court Marshal Brighton in London. We quickly agreed that an education at the Woolwich Military Academy would prepare you perfectly to serve as a royal military consultant in the future. I prepared them for your arrival next week. What do you think? Such an amazing opportunity won't come again for a long while."

"I ... I'm speechless, father. If you think it's the right thing for me to do ..."

"Yes, of course. You'll honor our family there. This path is more than appropriate for your position as future lord. I am happy for you. Now you can go and pass on the good news to James. Naturally, he will accompany you."

Outside, it had just become light. Streaks of fog still snaked through the wet grass, but the first rays of sun would chase away the last morning mist. I heard the birds singing their morning songs and dropped down onto the fresh straw bed in our forest cabin. Soon, Brian would be here. My gaze wandered past the old roof beams in the ceiling. Then my eyes grew heavy and closed.

Soft, warm lips touched my own. As he had so many times before, Brian woke me tenderly.

"Hello, Tom," his soft voice whispered. I kept my eyes shut and breathed deeply. Eagerly, I breathed in his scent. Next to a hundred other men I would have instantly recognized this intoxicating aroma. He had already settled in next to me. Cuddling his head on my shoulder, he nibbled carefully at my ear.

"Hi, Brian," I whispered back. " I was just thinking about the way you found me back then. It seems like ages ago." I paused briefly. Then I burst out: " I can't believe we might never see each other again."

A tear slipped out of the corner of my eye and rolled down my cheek. Brian bent over me and tenderly kissed the tear off my face.

"Look at me, Tom."

I blinked. Through a veil of tears I saw his beautiful, blurred eyes. His hair shone around his face like an angel's halo. Just the way it had during our first encounter on the forest path.

"We will see each other again. I promise you," he comforted me. "In a few months you'll return as an experienced sailor and you'll tell me your first stories about pirates. In comparison, my reports of my education at the academy will be dull. What's exciting about military drills and march exercises? If any of us should be upset, it's me. But we have a whole fantastic day in front of us."

As he said this he laid his full weight on me and pressed his lips on my smiling mouth. His throbbing cock pulsed in his tight pants.

"Yes, you're right," I answered, not so dejected anymore. "But it will still be difficult for me to be away from this."

I grabbed his tight ass and pulled him closer.

"Besides, there are tons of well-built men at the academy. Maybe after a little while you won't even want to see me anymore."

"James will be there, he'll look after me," Brian said, defending himself. "Anyway, that whole pile of men probably have nothing in their head but childish war games."

"Don't underestimate your little warrior's desire to play," I observed with a significant glance at his fly. "In the military they might drive it out and teach you to embrace the serious side of life."

"First I want to embrace this." Brian shoved his fingers under my shirt and tweaked my hard nipples.

"But in combat with the enemy you should attack this first," I moaned, pulling his hand to my tightly-stretched pants. Quickly, he freed my trapped cock. It sprang up, throbbing, and he grabbed it eagerly. His hands grasped the thick pole firmly until only the throbbing tip protruded from his shut fist. Slowly he rubbed up and down my shaft. With a sigh I sank back on the soft sheets.

"Now I see the first morning dew." Carefully, Brian licked the head to taste the clear liquid, still rubbing my pulsing shaft eagerly. His tongue and moist lips drew wide circles around my throbbing cock head. Meanwhile, he grabbed my balls with one hand and squeezed them softly. With his other hand, he groped back along my tight crack. Already, one of his fingers was pressing at my tight entrance.

"What are you planning?" I panted. "You're driving me wild. Don't go so fast, otherwise I'll cum right away."

Brian seemed not to hear me, as intoxicated as he was by his activity. His mouth sunk greedily over my stiff meat. I felt his hot tongue flicking wildly and passionately over my long shaft. I reared up and pushed my hips against him. My hammer shoved into his throat.

"Yeah, now this is the friend I know. And love." Brian spoke gladly. Quickly, he took my thick cock in his mouth again. Then he left a moist trace with his tongue up my stomach over my sweaty chest until he reached my mouth. Out of breath, he let me taste my own cock. Yearningly he pressed his sensuous lips against my mouth. Now he was stretched out on me so that I could feel his powerful manliness in each of his strong muscles.

"How about a little sword fight? A couple of exercises to prepare me for the academy couldn't hurt," Brian panted.

His stiff cock pushed against mine. Mercilessly our two long swords rubbed and clashed against each other. My hands grabbed at the hot skin on his back. I pressed my lover so firmly against me that it nearly took my breath away. At the same time I clasped his ass with both legs.

"Let me feel your lance inside me, brave warrior," I whispered.

I lifted my thighs higher and let go of him. With determination he grabbed my heels and shoved my legs forward. Then he lay on me again. His cock slipped against my throbbing back entrance. Brian's beaming smile seemed to transform into an otherworldly figure. I swore to myself that I would carry this moment in my heart forever.

"So, how do you like the sword practice, my love?"

I had to catch my breath as he softly increased the pressure on my sphincter, then pushed his thick cock head into my tight hole. Another small push and his lance sank halfway into my ass. I loved the feeling of lying defenseless beneath him. And I loved the way his hard spear filled my ass completely.

"Let your cock dance inside me, Brian. Skewer me completely. I want to feel it all the way to my heart when you spray your life fluid in me," I begged him.

Eagerly, Brian increased his tempo. At the same time, his stomach rubbed from time to time against the tip of my cock. The long sword within me grew and grew. Soon it actually felt as if I could feel his cock head up to my chest.

"Well? How is my lance filling you up? I notice how you're pushing your ass against me. It seems to be the perfect sheath for my thick soldier."

I was actually trying to take even more of Brian's gorgeous cock inside me. The tip of it was now rubbing mercilessly against a spot that sent powerful explosions through my body. With a loud, throaty moan he sprayed his hot cream. The glowing sword inside me continued to throb and pulse. One last time, his lance touched my sensitive spot, releasing my boiling balls of their heavy burden. Like a winding river, my hot load made its way up and sprayed over my stomach.

Exhausted, Brian sank into my arms. He rested his head against my chest. Lovingly, I wrapped my legs around his hips. I wanted to feel him inside me for as long as possible. Softly, I stroked his sweaty hair. For a while longer, we laid there wordlessly, basking in each other's warmth and closeness. Neither of us wanted this moment to end.

"Now, my weary lance-bearer. Your sword gave me lots of pleasure. But it seems to have lost its edge."

As confirmation, I pulled my sphincter tight around Brian's flaccid cock. In answer, it pulsed several times and began to swell up again.

"Don't judge a man's sword before you've experienced his power. After a little pause we'll begin the second lesson. And before the day is out there will be many more to follow."

Brian's eyes gleamed at me. His fighting spirit had been roused. The lance in my ass had already grown back to its full girth. Then the second lesson followed.

Brian held his promise. He wasn't finished proving his expertise with weaponry until it grew dark. The moment had come to bid farewell. Heavy-hearted, we saddled our horses. We rode a short section of the way together, but parted ways at a large junction.

"Here, my friend." Brian pulled the ring from his finger, took my hand, and pressed it inside. He leaned over to me. His lips touched mine.

"Don't forget me, my beloved. We'll see each other again soon."

Then he spurred on his horse and rode away without looking back.

I watched him go for a long time. Then I finally looked down at the gift in my hand. It was a smooth golden ring. Looking closer, I could make out letters finely engraved on it. They formed words that warmed my heart. There was so much more I wanted to say to him. Now it was too late. I would keep them in my heart until I returned.

It was already dark by the time I reached my uncle's yard. He was standing in front of the stalls smoking his pipe. With a lantern, he lit the way for me.

"Well, Tom, you were gone all day …"

His statement hung open between us. He wasn't expecting an answer.

"I was saying good-bye to Brian," I responded. "He's going to the military academy now …"

Then my voice gave out. I turned my head to the side to avoid looking Uncle Walter in the eye. That way he couldn't see the tear running down my cheek. Walter clasped my shoulder wordlessly.

"Let's go inside. It's going to be cold tonight. The summer is finally coming to an end."

I lived through the following weeks as if in a never ending daydream. I perceived my surroundings, but the next minute I could no longer remember what I had done or who I had spoken with.

On the one hand, time seemed to stand still, on the other hand my beautiful memories of Brian slipped through my fingers. At night, I saw his angelic face before me. His blue eyes were searching for me, but they couldn't find me. Desperately, I called his name, but thick fog swallowed up every noise around me. Again and again I called until a firm hand shook my shoulder and I shot up covered in sweat.

"You were calling for him again, Tom." Uncle Walter was standing by my bed looking down at me with a strange, empty gaze. "You'll get over it, my boy. You will."

When he turned and walked out of the room, an enormous weight seemed to lay on his shoulders. Quietly, he shut the door.

My things were packed and ready for the trip. A final dinner, then it was time. The rising sun was burning off the last of the morning mist as our coach rolled along the narrow street towards the harbor. Uncle Walter sat across from me.

"Chin up. You'll see, as soon as you breathe the fresh sea air, your gloomy thoughts will just blow away." He laid a hand on my knee and bent over to me.

"Believe me, your friend will find other friends and the same thing will happen for you. You're still young and full of drive. I would be very surprised if you didn't make new friends on your journey."

The coachmen had to take the last stretch at a crawling pace. From all sides, cars and wagons were streaming towards the harbor. Between them, a thickening crowd of people stormed about. All of them seemed to be rushing towards the same destination. Wagons clattered over the cobblestones. Heavy, iron-framed wood boxes stood on the pier; it took several men to move them. The workers' naked torsos gleamed with sweat. Four powerful men were attempting to load one of the cumbersome chests onto a horse cart in front of us as one of them stumbled on the wet stones, slipped, and fell to the side with a moan. As he fell, he nearly took his fellow worker with him, and the large box tilted dangerously. Without thinking, I jumped out of the coach and joined the men in an instant. Just in time, I pushed my shoulders beneath the hanging side as the front end touched down on the high loading surface. Soon the chest lay safely stowed in its place.

"Fucking shit," the fallen worker cursed, wiping the horse shit from his hands that had caused him to slip. With effort, he stood up and held his knee. A cluster of people had formed around us.

"Everything all right?" asked one of his comrades.

"I'll be fine. Just a little scraped. Must have had an angel watching over me today."

With that, he looked over at me and stretched out his hand, but I stonewalled him.

"Thanks a lot. First I strain my shoulders. And then I'm supposed to shake your shit-covered hand?" Annoyed, I looked at the torn shreds of fabric that had once been my best shirt. The red bloodstain on my grazed shoulder was impossible to miss. The onlookers stood back a step. If nothing else, they were at least hoping for a fistfight. But the man understood me.

"All right, all right," he said, clapping his clean hand on my unharmed shoulder and bending in. "Peter Grant. Thanks anyway for helping."

In the end, I gave in and shook the hand he was still holding out to me.

"Anyone would have done the same. My name is Tom Moore."

His powerful upper arms tensed, ready to fight. He still wasn't sure if he could trust me. The wiry hairs on his sweat-soaked chest gleamed in the morning sunlight. A fresh, manly aroma wafted from him. A contended smile slowly spread over his angular, unshaved face. He grasped my hand firmly, looked at me, and held onto my hand for longer than necessary. His eyes flashed briefly, then he let go.

After the bystanders had realized that there was nothing more to see here, they turned back to their work, murmuring in disappointment.

"Are you hurt, Tom?" Suddenly Uncle Walter was standing in front of me. He was looking at my torn shirt with worried eyes.

"Nothing bad. Just a scratch," I responded.

"You've got a strong, quick son there, sir. If it weren't for him, I'd be buried under this monster of a box right now." Silently, he looked at me again. Then he continued, looking at Uncle Walter apologetically. "No harm meant, sir, but I've got to get back to work."

As he went away, he turned around again and lifted his hand in greeting. Confused, I greeted him in return.

"Is everything really all right, my boy?"

Walter embraced me tightly. Suddenly I remembered the first time I had stood in front of him, as a young boy, more than ten years ago. Since then he had become more than an uncle or a replacement family. He hadn't just taken care of me and raised me. In the course of the years he had become a good friend. I owed him so much in life. I hugged him back. It wasn't until he complained that I was going to break his ribs that I realized how tightly my arms were wrapped around him.

"Thank you for everything, Uncle. I'm excited to get a change of pace," my voice got thinner. "Nevertheless I can hardly wait until we're anchored in the harbor again in a few weeks."

I wiped a speck of dust from my eyes and turned around abruptly. My gaze searched over the ships lying in the harbor. Ships of all sizes were moored there, barges next to little schooners, fast caravels next to cannon-braving galleons. Finally I discovered her: the *Margarita*. The stately four-master with gaff sails lay just fifty yards away. Her high masts swayed softly against the cloudless skies, all the sails were reefed. The huge crow's nest perched on the first two nests was a sight to behold. The foredeck and sterncastle, concealing artillery behind closable gunports, were sleekly built. For a trade ship, the *Margarita* was astoundingly well-equipped. The deck was bustling with activity. The air was filled with seamen giving curt orders and snappy calls. The captain seemed to have his team well in grasp.

Ben approached me over the narrow gangway. With effort, he made his way through the freight lying about. In front of the ship, barrels of salt meat, sacks of flour, and countless boxes were piled. Ben greeted me with a powerful handshake.

"Hello, Tom. I was watching your little incident from the prow. Good reaction. If you apply yourself the same way on deck, we'll have no problems with you. Are you ready to come on board? And are you excited for the journey? I can hardly wait. I've missed the stiff breeze on my nose. Seems I'm not ready to spend the rest of my life on land after all. Take your things and get on deck. I'll come in a second."

Dejected, I grabbed my bag, which held the few things I couldn't do without. I heaved the pack up the swaying planks and entered the ship through the broad gap in the bulwarks.

"Take care of yourself, Tom!" Uncle Walter called after me. I sighed deeply. To him, I was still the little boy who needed his protection. That would probably never change.

As I stood on the railing, I waved at him again with a laugh. Ben spoke a while longer with Walter then bid farewell with a long embrace. Shortly afterwards he was standing next to me on deck. A thought shot through my head: only Walter would be there waiting for Ben when we came back. Brian wouldn't be able to make it. Far away at the military academy in Woolwich, he had become unreachable to me. With a heavy heart, I brought my things on board.

A young sailor in clean, much-too-tight pants showed me the way. In the narrow, stuffy corridors I would have otherwise gotten lost right away.

"Here it is." The boy pushed open the narrow door to a small cabin. "You'll have to find the way back up on your own."

With a self-satisfied grin he turned around and disappeared. Sullen, I packed away my things in the free bunk. I would have prepared to stay down here for the whole journey. But soon I heard Ben calling out to me. When I came back on deck he was giving instructions to some of the harbor workers. The busy noise around me brought me back to the present.

"Well, everything put away, Tom? I know the cabin is quite narrow, but we'll be up here most of the time anyway. And it's enough for sleeping in, right?" I nodded in agreement. I had ended up with the smaller, relatively narrow bunk, since Ben was a good head taller than me. His bed wasn't much longer, but it was considerably wider. At least he wouldn't end up with bruises every time he tried to move. And I would just have to get used to the tight space.

Suddenly, tumult broke out behind us. The fat ship's cook was red as a crab, arms flailing wildly, screaming at a young boy.

"How many times have I told you that you need to inspect the provisions when they're delivered? We're missing two whole sacks of flour. Make sure you get them here as fast as possible. Find some idiot to help you carry them, then get lost."

The intimidated man was actually considerably larger than the beloved cook, but he didn't dare argue with the belligerent man. Curiously, I inspected the young man. His frizzled black hair and dark skin belied his Middle Eastern origins even at a distance.

"Ahmed is the cook's assistant here on board. He landed here in the area a few years ago. He was on board for my last few trips as well," Ben whispered to me. "He came to Plymouth by way of Spain and France, more than that I can't say. Just this: thanks to his help, the cook manages to cook enjoyable meals. Sometimes I almost believe Ahmed is the better chef."

"Can I accompany him?" I asked Ben out of the blue. "I've never been around the port district much. And I'm supposed to learn everything. On board I'll just be in the way anyway."

At the sight of the young cook's assistant, my cock had promptly filled out the crotch of my pants. The most fascinating thing about him was his even, dark skin. With his smooth skin, his proud, aristocratic facial features, jet-black hair, and deep brown eyes, he looked simply ravishing.

"Ahmed, come here!" Ben called out to the intimated man, pointing to me. "Here's the help you need. Tom will go with you. But don't waste any time."

"So, you're the new guy." The seaman inspected me suspiciously from the side. "Tom, the land rat. Already seen enough of the ship that you want to get back on land? Or you just can't wait to carry heavy sacks of flour? My name's Ahmed, by the way."

With that, he hurried off. I could barely keep up with him.

"I just wanted to explore the port area. This was a good opportunity to get off the ship."

"It's all right. I didn't mean it that way," he said with a smile. "I'm just furious at that incompetent cook. He was the one who ordered the provisions wrong and now I've got to take care of everything. But we'll take our time. Once I'm back on the ship, the old slave driver will have a thousand other tasks for me. Come on, come with me. I'll show you a view you won't forget for a long time."

Casually, Ahmed slung his arm around my shoulder and pushed me forwards. His fantastic body was so close to me that my mouth was watering. But Ahmed pulled me further away from the quay bulkhead. Around us, a new world suddenly opened up. Wooden sledges hauled by oxen or horses were being pulled through the soft mud of the streets. Handcarts with oversized wheels threatening to break beneath their weight pushed along the narrow streets past wide horse carts. Fibers, balls of twine, and wood planks were stacked everywhere. Wiry man with naked, sweaty torsos heaved heavy packages on their broad shoulders and carried them from the landings into storehouses or into the hold of a tugboat waiting impatiently to ride out with the next tide. Among all this, street merchants praised their wares loudly and boys in torn rags chased wildly screaming cats.

With a sleepwalker's certainty, Ahmed led me through the narrow, winding gullies of the port district. I had lost all orientation by the time we slipped through a small passage that was just barely wide enough for two adults to go down it side by side. Now it was noticeably quieter. A few kids were playing at the other end of the street. Houses piled up askew next to one another. On the second and third floors, built up on top of the others, the gables seemed to be only a few hand widths apart. Few rays of sunlight managed to reach the sludgy ground. And even on this beautiful, clear morning, it smelled wet and stuffy down here. Ahmed stopped at a small dilapidated door. He thrust his shoulder against the weakened gate, which swung open reluctantly with a loud squeak. Carefully, Ahmed climbed over the unsound threshold, waved me in and closed the entrance carefully behind us again.

"This building has been empty for quite a while. I'm sure you can imagine that this area is not the most desired place to live in the city."

We climbed several floors up a dilapidated staircase. The old wood beams creaked dangerously beneath our weight. I stayed close behind Ahmed and was relieved to reach the top landing unharmed after countless stairs.

"This is my kingdom," he said proudly as we entered the spacious attic. "I discovered it by chance when I was looking for a place to sleep. When the ship is on the quay and the other sailors go to the whores in the harbor at night, I'm undisturbed here. Come, Tom, you have the best view from here."

Ahmed waved me over to a small, round bay window. The view was incredible. From the window, we could look out over the entire harbor area. I saw the huge ships anchored tight to the quay bulwarks. Trade ships, fishing boats, freight barges … a vast array of masts, rope,s and halyards. At some distance from the mighty barges, several men of war were anchored. The multitude of sounds and calls were muffled by the time they reached us. It was almost completely still up here. A light breeze blew salt air up to us.

"The *Margarita* is down there. On the left, next to the big storehouses. Do you see her?" Ahmed's voice bubbled over with excitement. "And far off you can see the open sea. Isn't that a great view?"

He had laid his arm around me and pulled me close so we could both see the small window. I had to hold on to him to stay balanced. The view was actually breathtaking. But what confused me even more was the wonderful manly smell emanating from Ahmed's body. Appreciatively, I sniffed the hairs on his neck and closed my eyes. When I opened them again he looked at him curiously: "Are you afraid of heights? Are you dizzy?"

"You make me dizzy," I admitted.

Ahmed ignored my answer and pointed to a shadowy corner beneath the roof tiles.

"Come, lie down here. It's just an old sailcloth I found, but it's quite comfortable. I'll open the main roof hatch to let some fresh air in."

He lifted a long beam beneath the heavy hatch. Then he lay down next to me. He looked at me in the eyes for a long time, his head propped up loosely on one arm. Through the hatch, a reviving gust of wind blew over the attic.

"So, you wouldn't go to the whores with the other seamen either?" he asked uncertainly.

"No, definitely not," I whispered. Slowly, he bent over to me. Shivering, his soft lips touched my mouth. I put my arms carefully around his shoulders and pulled him closer to me. His tongue pressed against my mouth. And his hard cock pushed against my stomach.

"I was hoping to make love you," he whispered after a long, deep kiss. "Ever since you got out of that coach and came on board, I've been longing for you."

In response, my cock beat against his. My arms slipped under his shirt and pulled it over his head. I stroked his back softly. My hands slid eagerly over his smooth skin. I could feel his hard muscles as I glided over his broad, strong shoulders down to his firm ass cheeks. Ahmed pulled his pants over his feet, then slowly pulled mine down as well. My cock sprang gladly out of its dark prison. Ahmed grabbed it fearlessly and rubbed my hard-on with a firm fist.

"You like that?" he wanted to know.

Relaxed, I sank back on the large sailcloth. With his free hand, Ahmed stroked my stomach, then wandered gradually upwards to my protruding nipples, circling them one after the other then pressing them softly with his fingertips. He continued this for a while.

"Yeah, very good," I moaned. "But I want to be of use, too. That is, of use to your beautiful cock."

I sat up and looked lustily at the thick pole between Ahmed's legs.

"Nothing's simpler," was his answer. In the next instant he had swiveled around so his mast landed right in front of my face. Excited, I grabbed his stiff meat. It was a bit longer than my own cock. As soon as I squeezed it, the head throbbed dark red. And just like the rest of his skin, his shaft had an even dark tone. Blue veins protruded markedly. But what stuck out the most was that his pubic hair was shaved. Even his soft sac was completely smooth.

"You don't have any hair down here?" I asked in astonishment.

"Lots of men in my culture don't just shave their chest hair. They also find it cleaner to be shaved between their legs as well," Ahmed explained.

"But isn't it dangerous to fool around with a sharp blade near your balls?"

"No, not at all. You just need a bit of practice. And a cock feels great when there's no hair getting in the way. The best way, of course, is if a friend helps. If you want we could try it out right now," he offered with a smile. "I'll be very careful. You'll be astounded how it feels afterwards. And if you don't like it, just let it grow back again."

Eagerly, he pulled at my curly pubic hairs. I breathed in deep.

"All right, get to it before I think better of it," I said bravely. My cock, which had been rock hard moments before, had returned rapidly to its flaccid state. Small and frightened, my balls pulled together tight at the base of my cock.

Ahmed was already holding a small knife in his hand. The sharp blade gleamed triumphantly in the sunlight.

"Lie down and just look at the ceiling. Or wait … here, you can try it out and feel what a hairless sac feels like."

Legs spread wide, he crouched his ass over my face. His naked sac dangled directly above me. Hesitantly, my tongue reached up to his balls. I could only feel the clipped, soft hairs when I licked very

114

intensely. More courageously, my tongue began to explore every corner and finally reached the underside of his stiff cock. Softly, my tongue slid upwards until it had come to his mushroom head.

"Tom, think about the fact that I have a knife in my hand," Ahmed warned me. "If you keep going like that it will be hard for me to work carefully."

Immediately I pulled my tongue and responded quietly. "It feels really amazing. I couldn't resist. But now you can keep going."

Skillfully, Ahmed slid my manhood through his hands. Soft scratching and barely perceptible tugging was all I felt. Every now and then he licked a spot in exploration, then took the knife and continued shaving carefully. Suddenly one of my balls was in his mouth. His tongue rolled over every surface, testing the shaved skin. Now my second ball was subjected to an oral examination. This tongue test continued at the base of my cock and ended at the tip of my once-more raging hard-on.

"But I never had any hair there," I observed with a weak moan.

"I'm just feeling here for comparison," Ahmed explained cleverly. "Besides, I've earned a bit of a reward after this hard work, right?"

"Of course, I can see that. Take what you want. I'm not miserly when it comes to these things," I answered flatteringly.

"Miserly would not be the right description for the giant beast I've got in front of me," Ahmed responded with amazement. "After shaving, it doesn't just seem bigger, it feels better too."

His full lips slipped over my mushroom head and greedily swallowed my cock. His tongue wandered over my smooth shaft searchingly. The sight whetted my appetite. I snapped lustfully after Ahmed's stiff rod, bent it softly back and ran my tongue over the cock head.

"As a little thanks for your efforts you can have this extra reward," I murmured, swallowing his cock deep in my throat. Without any hair to get in the way, his balls and thick meat did feel better. I sucked in his manhood appreciatively. My hands made their way to his back entrance. My fingers reached his tight ring with determination. At the first touch, his cramped muscles relaxed. Gingerly, I massaged the soft area until Ahmed pushed his ass back against me with a sigh. I pushed a finger carefully into his tight hole, exploring his hot insides. In a quick rhythm, Ahmed sucked at my cock, leading up and down my pulsing cock. I matched his beat and let my finger work just as steadily at his hole. When I added a second, the cock above me began to twitch. Clear liquid dripped from the thick shaft onto my chest. Ahmed tried eagerly to push my finger in deeper. He threw his head back wildly.

"I can't take it much longer," he gasped. "Didn't you say you were generous? I need this giant here," he grabbed my hammer cheerfully and pointed it straight up, "in my ass. Desperately."

Ahmed bent his knees and led my moist cock to his twitching hole. Without waiting, he pressed down on my stiff mast and pushed it into his expectant entrance. Then he bent forward again, relaxed. Knees bent down next to my legs, he leaned his hands against my upper thighs.

"Oh yeah ... I needed that. You're really very generous, Tom," he panted.

"I keep my promises. My cock is completely at your service."

Ahmed took me at my word. My manhood sank to the hilt in his warm hole. Slowly he raised and lowered his ass. The sun had long ago passed its highest point. Its rays fell through the small bay window and bathed the room in warm light, shining on Ahmed's muscular back. Small beads of sweat gleamed on his skin. I stretched my arms behind my head and observed the play of light and shadow on his back, intoxicated.

Ahmed's breath was noticeably faster now. He seemed to be prepared for a long ride, and he clearly had a lot of stamina. I liked this slower pace. Again and again, my mast shoved deep inside his ass. Several times I even let the tip of my cock slide all the way out, then pushed it back in with soft pressure. My nipples pulled together into tight nodes. My hands massaged and tweaked them compulsively. Soft contented roars escaped from my throat. Irresistibly attracted by Ahmed's bright ass, my hands stroked over my quaking abs down to his tight mounds. Quivering, my fingers felt his silky skin. My hands stroked further until my arms were stretched wide and could go no further. I held myself tight to his torso and pulled myself up, pressing myself against his sweaty back.

"Hello, Tom," whispered Ahmed.

"Hello, Ahmed," I whispered back. My arms clasped tight around his ribcage. I kissed his neck lovingly. Almost motionless, Ahmed knelt onto me. My hammer throbbed within me. His sphincter twitched unconsciously at every slightest motion.

Calm yet befuddled, we sat there. Time seemed to stand still around us.

Ahmed's throbbing cock danced heatedly on his crotch, demanding my attention. First I kneaded his firm nipples once more. Then my hands slid down to his urging erection. Clear nectar flowed down from the tip of his cock. I couldn't grab his swollen meat in one hand, it was so thick. So I grabbed it with both hands. Ahmed panted out of pleasure. At the same time, his sphincter tightened around the base of his cock. I stroked him mercilessly. His asshole pulsed more forcefully.

"What are you doing there?" he asked in confusion.

"I'm going to make you explode, slowly but surely," I assured him.

My cock was longing for release. Without letting go of his fat hammer I bent down and pulled Ahmed with me. We landed on the soft blanket. The beautiful chef's assistant laid his back against my stomach with his legs spread wide. My cock was still skewering him from beneath.

"Are you crazy?" he snarled, thunderstruck.

"No. Just wild to shoot my load inside you. I hope you're comfortable like this. Because my giant, as you called him, has finally reached his full size. We'll see if you like it when he lets loose inside you."

I had been waiting long enough—there was no holding back. I pushed my ass up wildly, driving my shaft all the way into his hole. Yes, it was better this way. All I needed to do was tilt my crotch and my greedy cock rubbed against Ahmed's pleasure gate on its own. As well as I could, I kept stroking his cock with one hand. My other hand alternated between his navel and nipples. It was fantastic to feel his full weight on me and nevertheless to be able to move without effort. His gleaming skin seemed to have caught fire. In the dancing rays of sunlight, I saw how a fine steam was rising from his body. The moist air in the spacious attic was filled with our manly sweat. I sucked this reviving aroma deep within me. My giant cock swelled further and tortured Ahmed's ass even more wildly.

"I can't hold back any longer. It's boiling within me, I'm burning. Uhh ... yeah ... now!" he howled suddenly. In a high arc, his sperm shot over his stomach. His cock pumped relentlessly. His sphincter pressed tight around my stiff pipe.

"I can quench your fire," I called out excitedly. I thrust mercilessly with all my strength. My thick hose sought out his hottest point, then sprayed my overflowing cream into his hot crevice. I cooled his inner heat as best I could until the two of us collapsed next to each other, exhausted and breathing heavily. I·stroked Ahmed's skin gently. Then he rolled away from me, turned around, and looked at me seriously.

"In these next weeks, we won't be able to see each other often, Tom. The captain is pretty strict, he doesn't tolerate any loafing. And the cook is a real hard-ass. I will try to come to you as often as I can. We have to find some place where we can meet undisturbed. There aren't many quiet corners on the old clipper."

He stroked a few wet strands of hair tenderly from my face and laid his warm hand on my cheek. "I will never forget this past hour with you."

He gave me a long, tender kiss. His sad expression weighed heavily on my chest.

"Chin up," I encouraged him. "I'm just glad not to feel alone on this long trip. Even if we can't be together very much. The trip will certainly be a fantastic adventure. I've never been to sea on such a big ship. You'll see, everything will be all right."

We lay together for a while, contented and happy to have found one another. As we headed out, it was already growing dark. We picked up the missing provisions quickly and carried the heavy bags to the ship. On deck, Ben received me with a somber look.

"Did you grind the flour first or something? We've been waiting for the two of you for ages. This is a great start. Get below deck, you good-for-nothing! I suspected you would be nothing but trouble!"

He turned away abruptly and left me standing there. In an instant, my good mood was wiped out. Annoyed, with grinding teeth and balled fists, I entered the cabin. How could he be so rough with me? Why was he so furious? Just because we had come back late? My anger didn't abate until I was sitting in my bunk. I would have preferred to slink off board and simply disappear. Then I could finally live my life the way I wanted. No one would tell me what to do or who to love. I thought about Brian. Why had everything turned out this way? Hopelessly, I sank down.

Suddenly the door banged open and Ben was standing there, looking at me guiltily.

"I'm sorry," he said softly. "I don't know what came over me, Tom. But please try to understand my position. I promised your uncle I would watch over you at all times. After he told me you had been attacked some weeks ago, I was just worried."

This hulk of a man sat carefully next to me and threw his arm around me in consolation.

"Yes, I was really worried," he repeated.

"It won't happen again," I answered. "It's not like I can just run away on the ship." I looked at him apologetically. He took my chin tenderly in his hand and wiped a tear out of my face. He looked at me contemplatively. It was a short look, yet it somehow lasted too long. What did this confused look mean? Was he trying to tell me something?

"We'll be late," he rose up hastily. "The night before setting off, the captain traditionally invites the crew to dinner. His agitated mood won't be any better if we make him wait. So, come on!"

He held out a hand to me genially. Hesitantly I grasped it and used his arm to pull myself up from the edge of the bed.

"All right. You're even smiling again. You'll see, everything will be all right."

Strange. I had just been reassuring Ahmed with the same words.

"What's wrong?" Ben tore me from my thoughts. He stood in front of the door impatiently.

"I'm coming," I answered. Wordlessly, I trotted after him. His broad shoulders almost filled the narrow corridor completely. At times he needed to bend his head down to keep from hitting a low beam. His firm ass was clearly framed in his tight pants. In spite of his size, his stride was light and soft as a cat's.

The way he stroked my cheek so softly, and the worried look on his face: Was he really just worried about me? Or was there something more? I had never seen Ben like this.

A suspicion was growing within me that this trip was going to be much more eventful than I had expected. But this wasn't the right moment to think about that. In front of me, Ben opened the door to the captain's cabin. A loud hubbub of voices rose up to meet us.

"There you are finally," an older man in a captain's uniform greeted us.

That evening, I drank more than was good for me. And a whole lot more than I could handle. Maybe an unconscious attempt to drown the past. In any case, it was in vain. With each wine I swallowed down, Brian's face appeared more clearly in front of my inner eye. At the bottom of the next mug I suddenly saw Ahmed's features floating before me. Then Brian appeared next to him. To top it all off, Ben's contemplative face joined them as well. He nodded significantly to the other two, then stared at me with sad eyes. I pushed the wine away. I felt sick.

*C*lear the deck to cast off. Anchor up!"

The order rang through to my left ear as if penetrating a thick wall of fog. Glumly, I moved to the other side, where the sharp wail of the boatswain's whistle reached my unprotected right eardrum. Creaking boots hurried across the planks of the deck. Rumbling curses broke out every time someone else was standing in the way of the men rushing to their places at the anchor windlass. The ship shook and shuddered as the anchor was hoisted. I looked up in shock, then slammed my head against the low ceiling of my berth. I would have to get used to that. Dazed, I rubbed the painful spot on my forehead. That would turn into a thick bruise. The others would be certain to make fun of me. Everyone on board knew the signs of distinguished "landers," as they called newcomers on board.

I tried to sit up again. This time a rolling motion of the stern knocked me back into bed.

"If this keeps going, I won't be on deck until we've reached the high seas," I cursed. After my third attempt I finally stood up, though a bit wobbly, on both legs. Ben's bed was of course already empty. Surely he had gone up on deck early in order to witness the hoisting of the anchor. Lucky for me that he couldn't see my first awkward attempts at walking on board. I hastily attempted to pull on my pants, but the floor heaving beneath my feet repeatedly upset my plans. I was overjoyed when I managed to even get one of my legs in, but I had put it in the wrong pants leg. The ground swayed again and I landed hard on my ass. At some point I finally managed to slip into my unruly pants. My head was buzzing uncomfortably, but I knew where that came from. My feeling of dizziness wasn't just coming from the alcohol and the unfamiliar movements of the ship, I was also hungry. Impatiently, I woofed down a few bites of the breakfast already standing on the table. A good start couldn't hurt.

I didn't bothering washing up, so I reached the stairs to the deck a few moments later. When I came to the top, I was welcomed by massive chaos. A swarm of bees wouldn't have been more hectic. The whole crew was busy casting us off. Hastily, ropes were loosened and tied fast in other spots. Orders rang out and echoed, sailors ran up and down. But everything seemed to be following a secret plan. Everyone seemed to know exactly where he was needed. Except for me.

"Out of the way, landlubber!" called a sailor bearing down on me. Just in time, I jumped to the site. Cursing, he rushed past me.

"Come over here, Tom," called Ben. He stood somewhat off to the side, observing tensely as the ship was prepared for its long journey.

"I thought you were going to sleep through the big moment," Ben said. "Look, they're just untying the bow and stern lines from the posts on the pier."

Amazed, I watched as powerful port workers loosened the arm-thick rope from its anchoring. With a splash it fell in the water and was quickly pulled up by sailors. I tensed up as the jib and topgallant sails inflated above me with a loud snap in the gusty morning wind. The ship shook. Then the distance between ship and quay grew noticeably larger. My first big ship journey had begun.

"It's finally starting." Excited and nervous, I looked at Ben.

"Yes, the first time is always an exciting experience. Ever since my first trip, seafaring hasn't ever quite left me. I hope it will be the same for you. But don't tell your uncle I said that. He'd much rather have you at home in his business so you can relieve him of his work in the coming years."

"What does 'landlubber' mean?" I asked him.

With a laugh, Ben put his arm around me. "You'll have to figure that out for yourself."

The strange mood he was in yesterday seemed to have disappeared. He was in the best of spirits, like a new man. Those unmistakable laughter lines played around his blue eyes once again, and he was as excited as I was to finally reach the open sea. Side by side, we stood at the railing and watching the ship pass the entrance to the harbor. Some children were standing on shore waving farewell. In the east, the sun was just rising over the roofs in the harbor district. Its warm rays drove away the cold night air. More sails were unfurled. Gleaming white, the giant stretches of fabric stood out against the cloudless blue sky. Gradually, we set into full motion. The ship leaned slightly to the side. It swayed a bit, as if it was glad to finally by sailing out onto the sea.

We stood at the railing for a long time, talking about the daring sailors who had discovered the New World not all that long ago. Then suddenly Ben was giving me a questioning look.

"Your face looks so pale. Are you all right? You're not getting seasick, are you?"

I must admit, I did actually feel as though my stomach had not yet gotten used to the ship's turbulent rocking. At first I had observed with fascination as the foamy waves had splashed against the side of the ship. But now I wished that the water were smooth as glass and that we would stop being thrown about until my stomach had calmed down again. My hands grew clammy, sweat covered my forehead. A few seconds later I leaned far over the railing and vomited up my entire hastily consumed breakfast. Behind me, I heard mocking laughter. But Ben comforted me.

"First I'll bring you below deck. Believe me, it's easier to handle it lying down. It will pass soon." Unable to resist, I let him lead me down the steep stairs into our cabin. As soon as I was lying down, the dizziness and nausea abated. Ben lay a moist, cool towel on my forehead and looked at me sympathetically.

"This happens to a lot of men who've never been to sea. But for most of them it only lasts a few days, then disappears forever. So don't worry. You've just got to keep eating, otherwise you won't be able to stay up on your feet. For now, shut your eyes a while. Later, I'll send Ahmed over with a little something to eat."

On the word "eat" I made a grimace and my stomach rebelled again. Ben clapped me on the shoulders genially, then left me alone.

I must have fallen asleep. Suddenly Ahmed was standing next to my bed.

"Are you feeling better? Stay lying down." He pushed me back softly as I tried to sit up.

"There's no shame in being seasick. It takes time to get used to the ship's rocking. The best way is to stay lying down. I brought you something to eat. You don't need to make such a face. Believe me, it will be easier for your stomach if it's not completely empty."

He sat on the edge of the bed, dunked his finger in a bowl of sticky broth and brought it to my mouth.

"Try it! I cooked it just for you," Ahmed said, smiling proudly at me. Without waiting for an answer he shoved his finger in my mouth. His big dark eyes looked at me expectantly. Reluctantly I licked off the broth.

"Not bad at all," I murmured as I chewed.

"I took some honey from the cook's supplies. Even the worst seasickness tastes much better that way. You've got to admit that much!"

As he spoke, he spooned more of the sweet dish from the bowl. This time he shoved two fingers in my mouth.

"I can't take anymore. Otherwise I'll throw up again," I protested.

"You just need a bit of distraction, my friend," was his snappy answer, and he kept feeding me. As he did this he slipped his free hand beneath my shirt and began stroking my stomach, drawing small circles around my navel. This actually helped my cramped stomach relax. Softly, he stroked upwards. In the middle of my chest, he paused hesitantly for a moment, then approached my right nipple slowly, circling it and pressing it passionately. A relieved sigh emerged from my throat. His fingers in my mouth played sensually with my tongue. My lips trapped them tight, eagerly sucking the last sweet drops and not wanting to let go.

Alternating right and left, Ahmed rubbed his flat hand over my chest muscles. My cock inevitably reacted by pulsing impatiently. Slow and steady, Ahmed worked his way down to my throbbing erection. Without touching it, he stroked the insides of my upper thigh and freed me skillfully from my narrow pants. Tenderly, he took my balls in his hand and rolled them carefully like two marbles. He pushed his thumb firmly against the smooth crack leading to my sphincter. When my cock sprang up he started skillfully with his mouth and slid his firm lips along it.

What a magnificent feeling. His tongue licked along my firm shaft, leading back up to the tip of my cock, surrounding my throbbing head and finding the way back down again to the base. Frantically, I sucked the fingers in my mouth. Ahmed's strokes grew wilder and faster. He had found the way to my back entrance, groping around it with his soft fingertips. Then he shoved two of them into my tight hole. Eagerly, he explored my narrow canal. Instinctively, he started rocking me back and forth, like a ship rocking on the waves. There was something calming yet arousing about this rocking motion. My crotch shifted between the demanding fingers in my ass and Ahmed's hungry mouth. I couldn't decide whether I should thrust deeper into his throat or rather feel his finger deeper inside me. I loved being trapped at three points simultaneously. I couldn't let go of his sweet fingers filling my mouth either. Impatiently and unstoppably, my pleasure paved its way. Hot trembling waves rolled over me. My panting breath almost overwhelmed me.

"Yes, deeper, deeper," I cried out encouragingly, thrusting wildly and pumping my sperm down his throat in prodigious spurts. Just at the moment his fingers rubbed my pleasure point most intensely. Ahmed tried in vain to swallow down my entire load. It was just too much for him. When he finally let me go, he greedily licked the rest from my stomach. Then he pulled his finger out of my still twitching ass. He bent over me. Intoxicated and passionate, he kissed my lips.

"And how do you feel now?" he asked softly.

"My nausea has just been blown away," I admitted with a smile. It was true. I felt so much better. Ahmed had done good work.

"Now you should try to sit up," he said. Carefully I lifted my head, held both hands firmly on the bed, slid my legs over the edge and finally reached a sitting position. I closed my eyes. I felt everything start to spin again, and the contents of my stomach rose up. Moaning, I wanted to fall back on the bed, but Ahmed held me energetically by the shoulders.

"Stop, stop," he called out. "That's the wrong direction. I had a feeling this lesson wouldn't be enough. But let me take care of it. Keep your eyes closed. You just need to feel. Your senses will gradually get used to the unfamiliar motion. Spread your legs wide and put your feet firmly on the planks. Give me your hands. And hold on tight."

Ahmed stood between my upper thighs, took my palms, and pressed them onto his hips.

"First I'll try to distract your taste buds," he explained.

Curious and expectant, I opened his mouth to suck on his fingers again. To my astonishment it wasn't sweet broth that met my tongue this time, but a thick syrup with a strong, tangy taste. But the most delicious part was how it was served. To my glad surprise, it wasn't Ahmed's fingers pressing into my mouth but his hard throbbing cock. I didn't dare open my eyes; instead I concentrated on this new sensation and the huge shaft filling my mouth completely. Curiously my tongue bathed in the erotic scent. Ahmed's cock head pressed softly against my palate, rubbing his juice over my taste buds. The fresh, slightly tangy ingredients filled my mouth with pleasant warmth that spread deep down into my stomach. The more I sucked his stiff rod, the more intensively I felt this fiery glow. It spread further, reached my legs and then finally my cock. Unfortunately I couldn't take care of that myself at the moment, although it was tingling excitedly between my legs and demanding a firm grip. But I simply didn't dare remove my hands from Ahmed's hips. I knew that as long as I held on tight here, I wouldn't get dizzy again. Better to leave my hands where they were, even if it was difficult.

"Don't be influenced by the movement of the ship. First you have to find your own rhythm," Ahmed said encouragingly.

I followed his instructions eagerly. Without hesitation I sucked faster and harder at his manhood. My hands wandered back around his firm ass cheeks. Beneath his skin I could feel his muscles tensing, offering me a secure hold and allowing me to control how deeply I wanted to swallow his shaft into my mouth.

"You're just getting better and better, Tom," Ahmed praised me with a gasp. "This hot meal seems to be working wonders. Yeah … uhh … harder. Keep going. I'm heating up as well."

I ventured a shy glance upwards. Above me, Ahmed was tweaking his nipples like a madman. With his head thrown back wildly and his mouth wide open, he gave in to the ecstasy of the moment, bending further and further back. It was hard for me to keep hold of him. As soon as my fingers found his twitching sphincter, his eager gate opened at first light touch. Moist heat surrounded the bold invaders. I only needed to move them a little and Ahmed shoved his hammer forcefully in my throat. His legs shook lightly. Searching for support, he grabbed the edge of the upper bunk with both hands. His uninhibited lust was uncontrollable. Thrusting heavily, he pushed his steadily swelling shaft in my mouth. My tongue rubbed mercilessly along his hard meat, even though his wildness made it more and more difficult. Ahmed's balls slapped roughly against my chin. He thrust his hips wildly and sprayed his full load without warning, deep in my gullet, accompanied by a throaty moan. I was treated to a new taste. It was delicious. Long after Ahmed had pulled his cock from my mouth I continue licking my lips eagerly.

"Is Sir content with his meal? Are you full, Tom? This meal cost me a lot of effort. I hope you liked it."

"You taste quite good," I said, nodding excitedly and gazing contentedly into Ahmed's dark brown eyes.

"Looks to me like you're ready for the last course." He looked lustfully at my thick meat. I had begun to rub it unconsciously.

"Your refreshing cream was not enough to quench the fire you've sparked in me. I desperately need another cool-down," I admitted.

"Then come here." Ahmed pulled me to my feet and positioned me in the middle of the room. He stepped close behind me.

"Now you will learn to stand on your own two feet."

His whispered breath on my neck drove tingling shudders down my back.

"Stretch your arms out backwards," he ordered. With fast, practiced strokes, he bound my hands together.

"What are you doing?" I protested.

"Trust me. This is the only way you will be able to finally journey on the sea without fear. After this test, nothing will keep you from standing on your own two legs. But now for the desired cool-down."

He pulled a small bottle out of thin air and poured some of its contents in his hands. He stood in front of me and rubbed the fluid on my cock. A pleasant, refreshing feeling spread through the whole shaft. He spread the rest on my nipples. Smiling expectantly, he blew on it forcefully.

"Cold enough now?" he asked superfluously. My traitorous nipples had formed hard nodes in the cold gust of air. I breathed deeply.

"Don't make such a fuss, my friend. Listen to me," he continued, somewhat more seriously. "You have to try to feel the ground beneath your feet. Position your legs a bit further apart. Yes, that's better. Always stand upright. Don't bend forward. Focus your eyes on a fixed point."

"But where am I supposed to look?" I asked, annoyed.

"You see this little birthmark on my back. Look at that, no matter what happens." He turned around and showed me a dark spot on his neck. Nevertheless, without being able to steady myself with my hands, my legs began to shake uncontrollably. Again I felt the ship rolling beneath me and felt dizzy. With small, uneven steps I strained to keep my balance.

"Yes, you're doing it just right," Ahmed spurred me on.

"Bend your knees a bit more, then it will be even better."

"I'm going to fall and crack my head open. Please untie the knots," I begged him. "I need to hold on somewhere."

"Then I'll give you a bit of help instead," he sighed. Bent over, he propped his hands on the table in front of him and pushed his ass towards me with a gleeful grin.

"You can dock here and cast anchor if you're losing stability."

Between his tight white mounds, his small moist jewel gleamed.

"I knew you were a true friend. I'm all too glad to take the offer of a secure harbor in these stormy times." I thanked him profusely and led my upright mast purposefully towards my rescue. Outside the wind had picked up again. I could clearly hear the individual gusts thundering in the sails. But I had other concerns now. On my first attempt, my cock slipped up between Ahmed's ass cheeks.

I crouched down further on my knees and tried again. This time, the oily balsam on my shaft made it slip down and hit his loosely dangling balls.

"Not bad," he said. "But you've still got to practice this entrance maneuver. Try it slow. Feel the way the ship is going to move in advance."

I exhaled deeply, felt the floor of the ship beneath my feet, heard the storm, focused on the spot on Ahmed's neck, and drove my throbbing cock head to its target. At the same time, the whole bow shook, followed by a jerky thud. Without me having to move, Ahmed's ass had swallowed my cock halfway. The astonishment took my breath away. Ahmed purred contentedly.

"Very good. Welcome on board, Tom. Now become one with the ship. Let your mast sink deep into my ocean the way the bow of the ship plows the water."

Now nothing could go wrong. Fearlessly, I thrust forward until my balls touched his ass. At the next wave peak, our tight connection released on its own and I slipped almost completely back out. Just the tip of my cock was still surrounded by his tight sphincter.

"Make sure you don't get off course," Ahmed warned. He had turned his head back and was looking at me with longing. "Your anchor found just the right place. A true seaman practices until he masters the use of his tools flawlessly."

As we suddenly sunk into the next wave, he was abruptly silenced. A drawn-out moan was his only utterance as my rock-hard schlong thoroughly massaged his insides. Gradually I got used to this back and forth rocking, since I had a firm base. My cock was eager to explore all the depths of Ahmed's ass. Keenly, I watched his back muscles tense and release as he tried to withstand my powerful thrusts. His whole body was constantly in motion to make things as easy as possible for me. My only guiding light was to imagine the way the prow of the ship split the waves the same way my stiff mast was splitting Ahmed's ass cheeks. When the foredeck dove deeper into the water, I sank my shaft in deeper. If the ship tilted to port, I leaned starboard to balance. Tingling ran through me from head to foot. Suddenly I understood: a ship and the sea always belonged together. They were indivisible and passionately connected to one another. The way I was now connected with this man. Ahmed had noticed the change in my motions.

"Now you're ready to take charge," he said, spurring me on.

"Show me who the captain is, take the rudder in your hand. Or should I say: how you push your prow forward?"

I didn't need to be told twice. I thrust mercilessly, attacking his ass with increasing fury. My balls beat wildly against his thighs. Yes, I was finally the helmsman on the rolling seas. Around me the ship heaved and rocked, thudded and creaked. But I stood there like a rock in surf. Indestructibly bound to the ship's planks, rock-hard and securely connected to the most beautiful mooring I could imagine. My powerful spear pushed forward boldly into unknown depths, then back to the surface only to dive again with the next wave.

"Do you feel the storm getting stronger?" I called to Ahmed. "I love the wild roar."

Suddenly my floodgates opened. Seething up, the spray flowed out of my delta and into Ahmed's sea.

"I am the lord of the seas," I cried out, beside myself, pumping wave after wave of sperm into him.

Ahmed straightened up abruptly, pushed his ass down on my hard pole and leaned in close to me. His whole body shook. His tight gate clenched up suddenly. With a moan he laid his head on my shoulder and grabbed onto my ass with both hands.

"Here comes my storm flood," he roared. He shot his sperm in a wide arc onto the floor. The rolling waves that ran through him seemed to not want to let up. Curiously I looked over his shoulder.

"You wasted the whole dessert," I whispered in his ear.

"Don't worry about that," he reassured me. "I'd be happy to bring you a new one tomorrow."

With a smile, he shut his eyes and leaned his head back on my shoulder. I couldn't resist nibbling lovingly at his ear.

"Would you mind untying me finally? Even if I'm not about to fall over anytime soon, my hands are growing numb."

Ahmed let go of me immediately and turned around. His arms embraced me. Carefully, he undid the knot and pressed his hands to my ass. Trustingly, I laid mine on his back and pulled him in close. I kissed him tenderly. My lips touched his mouth with longing.

"Thank you for your help, my friend," I murmured.

"I hope you will take advantage of it more often," he responded.

Fresh morning air welcomed me as I walked out onto the upper deck the next morning. The first rays of sun were wandering over the topgallant sail, shining on shrouds and ratlines until they hit the top of the mizzen mast. In the east, the blazing disk reigned over the horizon and illuminated the new day. Up front to starboard, the night fled to the west into the new world. The vaulted sky radiated a pure light blue, and the sea mirrored the rising wind and first strands of cloud in dark colorful splendor. In the coming days I was excited for every storm that popped up on the horizon. I started to enjoy the rolling and rocking on deck. I ran proudly along the planks without holding on. Even the old seadogs on board were amazed at my newly-gained confidence. Of course Ben had also noticed that I had gotten back on my feet very quickly and was no longer disturbed by the movement of the ship. Curiously he asked: "How did you recover so quickly? You really seem to be enjoying the rough weather."

"Ahmed took good care of me," I answered, chuckling. "He gave me a hearty meal. His desserts are particularly nutritious. And he showed me how I need to move in order to not lose the ground under my feet."

A strange smile flitted across Ben's face, then he nodded understandingly.

"I understand! I think this landlubber is turning into a true seaman."

I quickly grew accustomed to the unconventional rules of seafaring life. Again and again, the sailors had to report on deck. The day's orders were given loudly. Bad work or laziness were punished severely. But there were also sociable moments onboard. Sometimes the captain sent around a round of rum. Old seafaring stories were told and bold sailor songs were sung. In the evenings, I often sat on deck with the crew and simply listened. The rum—which I, of course, also tried—tasted disgusting at first. Bit by bit I came to enjoy it, and I could even soon sing along with most of the songs. But committing to this rough arduous life forever was something I couldn't imagine. True, living only among men wasn't a difficulty for me—quite the contrary—but I had yet to be taken up among the sworn community of the ship's crew.

One night, I had emptied my mug a few too many times. Probably also to escape the loneliness that had become my constant companion. I hardly ever saw Ahmed. Since our last escapade I hadn't spoken to him. The ship's cook always had new tasks for him. And since I was no longer sick, visits to my cabin were no longer a part of that. Grumpy and drunk, I lay in my cabin, tossing from side to side until I finally fell asleep uneasily.

In the middle of the night I woke with a shot. My eyes gazed out into impenetrable darkness that swallowed all the contours of the room like black ink. No sound could be heard. Even the otherwise calming splash of the waves was muted. Bathed in sweat, I pulled back into the farthest corner of my bunk, trembling like a frightened weasel. I had had a terrible nightmare: Ahmed had disappeared without a trace. I had turned the ship inside out looking for him. I had searched for him everywhere, called loudly after him, stumbled up and down countless corridors. I couldn't find a soul to ask. In the ship's quarters my steps echoed through the oddly blank, empty between-deck. At the stations for night watchman and helmsman, which assured security on board, icy wind crawled over the abandoned planks. Had the entire crew left the ship? I clasped the railing dizzily. Half-reefed sails flapped above me on the topsail and topgallant halyards. The unsecured anchor chain dangled over the foredeck. Somewhere beneath me, a cabin door creaked, then slammed shut with a bang. Eerie stillness filled the ship, long shadows crawled at me from all sides, and bone-chilling cold clawed at my throat. I panted, scarcely able to breathe. Cold sweat ran down my forehead. Then a realization hit me like a punch in the stomach. I was alone onboard the ship. Alone on the vast ocean. I sank to my knees. Alone ... alone ... alone.

My head was buzzing as if a swarm of bees had made it their home. The bed seemed to lurch unbearably. The air in the narrow cabin was so thick I could have cut it with a knife. Carefully I sat up and held fast to the edge of the bed with both hands.

"Just a dream, just a silly bad dream," I kept whispering to myself. Gradually my shaking subsided and my eyes became accustomed to the darkness. Relieved, I ascertained that Ben was lying in his bunk breathing peacefully, his face to the wall. His blanket had fallen to the ground and his waistband had slipped down lightly. Unavoidably, I stared at the top of his bright ass cheeks.

A clear line ran over his slim hips where his habitual broad belt normally blocked all sunlight. As always, he was sleeping without a shirt. My eyes wandered up his tanned, brown back. I would have loved to cuddle up to him. With a light sigh, I stood up, lifted the blanket and covered him carefully. No, the thought budding up within me was not one I could allow any room. Nevertheless, I couldn't ignore the sudden pressure between my legs. Grumbling, I pushed my throbbing erection into a more comfortable position, slipped softly through the next ladderway up on deck. A little bit of clear air would clean my head out and drive away those dark illusions for good.

I breathed in deep, sucking in the cool night air. The moon hung at half height behind the mizzen mast. Thin cloud strands covered the bright disk, gleaming spectrally in front of them. Far back on the afterdeck I made out the helmsman. Behind him, the watchman patrolled carefully back and forth.

Without attracting their attention I squeezed into a dark corner. A carelessly tossed-down piece of tarp served as a bed. It was even big enough to wrap around myself. The fresh starboard breeze did me good. My thoughts were calmed and I decided to stay out here until dawn. Soon I fell asleep.

I was awakened by the soft moaning of a man's voice. Curiously, my eyes searched the deck. A mere twenty feet away from me, two sailors were wrestling with each other. One of them lay stretched out on the planks, the other was bent over him. In the moonlight I saw a knife blade gleaming. I was about to jump up to fall upon the assaulter when I realized it was only a silver belt buckle reflecting the moonlight. Just in time I stopped and watched the supposed attacker tearing his pants from his legs in one motion. Then he fell on his knees and buried his torso between the legs of the man lying beneath him. The next thing I saw was his head eagerly bobbing up and down on the other man's stiff meat. I realized it wasn't any normal fight I was witnessing. Excited and curious, I leaned back and watched the forbidden show. Between the steps of the stairway in front of me, I had an unhindered but protected view.

The sailor working on the thick pole had stripped off his own pants as well. He kneeled down next to his comrade, his large hands greedily exploring the other man's tight body as it moaned and reared up under his firm touch. His muscular body gleamed as the cloudbank broke upon for a moment and both men were bathed in pale moonlight as if onstage. As a fine spray of watery fog splashed over the dock, the sailors' skin glittered like silver dust. The man underneath stroked his hand over the other man's ass crack. His huge paws pulled him closer until his comrade's swaying ass hovered in front of his face. Roughly, he spread the mounds in front of him and darted the tip of his tongue into the tight entrance. Taken by surprise, the other man released the daredevil's cock and threw his head back, moaning wildly.

"You drive me wild," he hissed softly before sinking his mouth down again over the thick plank.

Neither of them were perturbed by the rising swells of the sea. Instead they continued fumbling around. They slapped their cocks against each other's ass cheeks until they glowed red in the moonlight. One of them stood up, bent over a waist-high barrel and stretched his steaming ass against his comrade. He looked over his shoulder demandingly.

"Come on. I've been waiting all day to finally feel your mast," he grunted.

The other man brought his pole into position immediately, grabbed his friend's ass, and shoved his giant erection against his rosebud. Hard and fast, he shoved his cock in the man's ass. He was standing with one foot on the box next to him, his hand rubbing his comrade's pole fiercely.

"Yeah, I like that. Harder, Mark. I know you can get it in deeper."

"Just don't complain if you can't walk again tomorrow," was his curt answer. "Hold on tight. Here comes my storm crusher."

The salvo that broke out rivaled the forceful storm tide. Mark held his companion by the shoulders with both hands. At breakneck speed, his cock dove in and out, throbbing the other man's cock against his stomach. Both sea dogs' muscles strove wildly in the moonlight, offering an impressive view. Moaning and panting as if they had the ship to themselves, the two of them drove on towards their climax.

By now I had pulled my own hard-on from my pants, stroking it in time to the pair in front of me.

"Now," Mark howled suddenly, throwing himself down on his friend's back, thrusting wildly a final time. His ass shook as he shot out his sperm like roaring surf. After he had calmed again he began to massage the shoulders he had been clawing at only a moment before, as if in restitution.

"You'll have to think of an excuse for the red scratch marks, Harry," he said with concern.

"That's my problem," was the answer. "And you don't need to keep going on my shoulders. I have a much more urgent task for you to take care of."

Harry stood spread-legged in front of Mark, who was leaning back relaxed against the ship's planks, rubbing his thick shaft.

"Then bring your task over here," Mark demanded. A second later, Harry's sausage was in his mouth. Without hesitation, the thick tool sunk deep into his greedy gullet. This time it was Harry who thrust his cock forward brutally hard at a breathtaking pace. Mark was already stroking his cock back to its imposing size. Then with his left hand, he squeezed Harry's balls tight and slid his hand into his ass crack. Without resistance, he pushed two fingers into his still-moist hole. Harry moaned as he was skewered. His tight ass twitched exuberantly back and forth. I would have loved to position myself behind him and my anchor my hard pole in his moist cavity, which was still overflowing with Mark's juice. My cock head shimmered wetly, streaming pre-cum. I could feel a tingling, rising warmth in my stomach. I bit my lower lip to keep from crying out. Like a cannonball, fiery and hot, silky cream suddenly shot from my barrel. At the same time, Harry fired his load in Mark's mouth, while Mark reached a second climax and sprayed sperm all over his stomach.

"Who's there?" the watchman called suddenly, leaning suspiciously over the railing of the afterdeck.

"Just me, no one else. It's Harry. Had to piss real quick. I'll be gone in a second." Thinking quick, he pulled up his pants and positioned himself next to the barrel so that the watchman couldn't see Mark. Then he made his way nonchalantly towards the crew cabins and climbed down the ladderway. Mark waited a while in the shadow, then snuck down to the stairs I was hiding behind, to my horror. I pressed myself deeper in the dark corner. He had already taken the first step when he stopped and smiled down at me.

"Well, young man," he whispered slowly. "I hope you enjoyed the show. It would be best for you if you keep our little secret to yourself. Then you won't need to worry about your own little secret."

He put particular emphasis on the word "little," starring unabashedly between my legs and grinning. Then I remembered that I was still holding my fat cock in my hands. I was about to snap at the insolent man, but he had already disappeared. Worked up and nervous, I stayed still until the watchman on the afterdeck turned his back to me. Then I made my way back to my cabin. I opened the door noiselessly. Pale moonlight fell through the open hatch. On tiptoes, I slipped into my bunk. Unfortunately as I was doing so I missed the chair standing in front of the table and fell flat on my face. Cursing, I pushed myself back up as dull candlelight broke the darkness.

"What happened?" Ben stood next to me, helping me up.

"I was just on deck for a minute because I couldn't sleep. I'm sorry I woke you."

"It's all right, I wasn't sleeping very soundly. To be perfectly honest, I didn't get any sleep tonight at all. Come, Tom, sit by me. I need to tell you something you should have known long ago."

Ben sat with his back against the wall of his bunk, waving me over.

"You're bleeding. Your lip is torn. Here, take this towel," he said with concern as I stepped into the light. Worried, he bent over me. "Let me see. Doesn't seem to be too bad. You must have bit your lip when you fell." He sighed, embarrassed. "How can I begin?"

Was I going to find out another secret tonight? As far as secrets were concerned, my needs had been more than met already. A thought that reminded me of my "little secret," as Mark had called it. I sat next to Ben in the cabin, pulled my knees in for security, and waited. Even though the weak light barely illuminated his face, I could make out the deep worry lines on his forehead.

"Tom, it's not easy to tell you this. I promised your uncle I wouldn't say anything. But I believe it's not right to you to continue this journey with a lie."

"Is it so awful?" I interrupted him uncertainly.

"You have to try to understand that your uncle only wanted to do what was best for you. And I wouldn't want you to be unhappy. So ..." Ben made a long pause.

"Six weeks ago, Lord Hamilton paid an unexpected visit to your uncle. He made it clear to him that your friendship with his son was inappropriate. Your frequent meetings had made him suspicious and an informer had reported to him about your hideaway in the forest."

I felt hot. Sweat ran down my back. I slid away from Ben into the corner of the cabin.

"Lord Hamilton suggested to your uncle that he should send you off on a long trip. Otherwise his business, he threatened unashamedly, would suffer severely in the future."

Ben laid his hand softly on my shoulder.

"I'm so sorry. Really ... Walter and I tried everything to change Lord Hamilton's mind. But in order to be completely certain, he even sent Brian away to military academy, as you painfully had to learn."

"No!" I cried out to Ben and approached him with balled fists. "No, that can't be true. It can't be. Uncle Walter would never do that to me."

I punched all around me, but Ben's strong arms stopped me effortlessly. I kept hitting him. He let me continue.

"Your uncle couldn't do anything, Tom. Lord Hamilton would have sent Brian away either way."

My rage generally subsided, my punches grew weak. Finally I began to accept the reality of this admission. Ben grabbed my arms and looked me sadly in the eyes. "I'm really sorry for your long love," he said.

When he let me go, I collapsed. My world was falling apart again. Tears of sadness ran down my cheeks over the loss of my lover and so much injustice. After a period of oppressive silence, Ben said comfortingly "I feel for you, believe me. I know what I'm talking about."

Defenselessly, I fell back into his arms. Brian and I had been torn apart because our love was not recognized. Life could be so cruel. Suddenly a flash of realization shot through my head.

"Are you in love with my uncle?" I asked him, unabashed. Ben held his breath in shock.

"He's always so different when you're around," I continued without waiting for an answer. "He's so much warmer and more cheerful. When he sees you he even laughs out loud. I know that feeling. And I saw you kissing once," I ended my shameless suspicion. Ben said nothing for a long while. He sat absently on the edge of the bed, his head propped in his hands. With a sigh he straightened up and looked me: "Yes, I love Walter. We've been in love for many years. A long time ago, when things were just as bad for me as they are now for you, he was there for me. Since then, we've been together."

"So you haven't even lost your love the way you just claimed," I said, balling my fists again in rage.

"Calm down, Tom. When I met Walter I was as sad and furious as you are now." He leaned back. "The reason was Jaschir. He was the oldest son of the chief of an Arabian desert tribe."

Ben laid his arm around me and pulled me closer. I felt his pleasant warmth and saw how he was trying to lessen my sorrow with his comforting words.

"Jaschir was my first love. When I was a young man, about your age, I went along on an expedition as a scribe. My father was thrilled by my thirst for knowledge and encouraged my curiosity. So I came to Alexandria in Egypt with that same expedition. Tom? Tom ...?" Ben shook me awake. "We should sleep now. Stay with me. You don't have to be alone tonight."

Deep fatigue overcame me. I thought about Brian. How was he doing? At the same time I felt Ben behind me, his strong arm resting on my shoulder.

When I opened my eyes again it was pitch black. The candlewick must have been doused with wax. At first I didn't remember where I was. But Ben's peaceful breath at my back reminded me that I was still lying in his bunk. My throbbing cock had awoken me. Thoughts of Brian wouldn't leave me—or my manhood—alone. Cautiously, my hand groped for my pulsing meat. If only it were Brian's hand giving me relief. I bit into the fabric of my shirt to keep from moaning out load. My cock quivered madly in my hand. Just imagining that my lover was lying next to me, his sensuous breath stroking my neck, his hand groping my chest and squeezing my thick shaft softly, brought me to the edge of an explosion. Then suddenly Ben's strong arm was wrapped around me. His resolute hand loosened my firm grip on my pulsing cock.

"Let me do that for you," he whispered in my ear. "Just imagine a good friend is helping you out."

My initial shock disappeared quickly. I had come to trust Ben so much in the last few weeks that I gave myself completely to him. His warm hands eagerly stoked my long-suppressed desire. His searching fingers burned on my skin like glowing coals. Or were they quenching my inner fire with their fleeting strokes? Somehow, both seemed correct. For an eternity, he stroked my skin. Then it was no longer just his hands awakening my senses, but his arm resting on mine. His stomach at my back. His feet at my ankles. His lips on my shoulder. And … his throbbing cock at my ass. He rubbed his hard shaft against my back demandingly as his hand heated my glowing steel. I moaned out loud, "Ahhh! Ben, what are you doing to me? I can't take it much longer."

Ben rolled onto his back and pulled me on top of him, letting me feel his hairy belly beneath me.

"Grab the back of your knees," he growled to me while pulling my ass cheeks apart. His thick cock head pushed against my hungry entrance. In a few forceful strokes, he pumped a flood of pre-cum from his shaft. I felt the cool nectar on my quivering rosebud. Then he grabbed my twitching shaft roughly and coaxed a bit of clear fluid from it as well, then rubbed it on his own cock. His hands grasped my hips and held me tight. He began to rock his hips back and forth, shoving me down on his hard mast. With a relieved moan I welcomed the throbbing tip into my ass. Ben pushed eagerly through the tight ring of muscle. Now I was hanging on this fat line like a fish on a hook. I twisted and turned, as a big catch should. Not that I was trying to escape: instead, I was trying to slip deeper onto the fat hook. Again, the sea came to my assistance. A large wave shook the bow of the boat, causing Ben to release his hands from me. With a single jerk, his giant stake sunk deep inside me. I caught my breath. But as the tension released, I was filled with wonderful, pleasant warmth flooding through my deepest center like a warm, reviving bath.

"Ohhh … yes … That's right where I've wanted you for so long," I sighed with relief and fell onto him. My head rested on Ben's shoulder. His breath was fast. With a hesitant voice he asked softly, "Well, Tom, how do you like that? I've seen the way you've been looking at me for weeks. Maybe you've noticed that I couldn't keep my eyes off of you."

"Oh yes, I noticed all right, even if I didn't admit it to myself right away. But what I'm feeling right now exceeds any fantasy I've had about you in the past."

I couldn't see Ben's face in the dark bunk, but I knew he was smiling. Exhausted, I propped my feet against the sides of the bunk while Ben moved his hips back and forth rhythmically. I enjoyed the fantastic pressure of his hard cock thrusting through my narrow gate. With one hand, Ben stroked my chest as he gripped my pleasure pole with the other.

"I could stay like this forever," I groaned lovingly.

"I'm afraid I have to disappoint you, my friend." Ben's quivering breath flowed over my neck enticingly. Stormy waves of unbridled lust shook through me. Hard as the breakers in a storm flood, his crotch beat against my ass. The hammering tool inside me took no mercy; with wild thrusts, it brought my own cock near the edge of explosion. Helpless under the force of my hulking sea god, I tried to hold tight to the bed. But that was unnecessary. Ben's strong arms were wrapped tightly around me like a giant octopus holds its prey. He used my cock like the rudder of an old sailboat, keeping me securely on course.

"You've learned a few things about sea traveling, Tom. I wouldn't have thought you could hold tight during such a storm," he laughed suddenly.

"Is this how you test every novice's abilities?"

"Only men who learn the seafaring craft with determination, strong will, and courage can hope to become true seamen. And you are certainly on the right path."

"Then I hope there will be many more tests. I'm quite enjoying this one," I cried as Ben suddenly thrust my cock upright and slid his hand rapidly along it. At the same time he rammed his pole into my ass like a madman. His hips thrust swiftly up and down, and then with a last wide thrust and a loud moan he shot his load. His hot juice spread within me full force; it seemed to push all the way to the tip of my cock. Pulled along on this wave of lust, all my dams broke loose. The pressure became too great, I began to quiver from head to toe, then finally climaxed, spraying a white fountain from the tip of my cock that flowed over my hot body like sea foam.

Later, as I was cuddled up to Ben's belly while he held me in his arms beneath the warm blanket, I couldn't resist asking the question that was running through my head: "What would Walter say if he saw the two of us lying here?"

Now it was out in the open. How would Ben react? For a moment, it was still in the cabin. Then a deep breath. "Your uncle is a wise man. As we left the harbor, he said to me: 'Take good care of my boy. I want him to enjoy this journey so much that he forgets his heartbreak. It should be a real adventure for him. Show him the wide world. And show him that there are other men who are worth loving and living for. As long as you are by his side, I'm not worried.' Then he took me up in his arms and I knew what he meant. So you can rest easy, Tom."

"You mean this was all planned beforehand? You intended to seduce me so I would forget Brian quickly?" I asked, both sad and furious.

Ben must have heard the injured tone in my voice.

"No, that's not true," he reassured me. "If you hadn't wanted it, nothing would have happened. Nevertheless I wanted to show you that life goes on, even after your first great love. You will certainly meet other men who are worthy of your love."

"But I can't just forget Brian. I miss him so much."

"Give yourself time, Tom. When we're back in a few weeks, you'll see him again. You will find a way. His education at the military academy won't last forever. Everything else will work itself out."

"Thanks, Ben."

"For what, exactly? My words?" His tongue seductively drew a moist trail down my neck. "Or for my actions?"

He pressed his thighs against my ass and grunted seductively. His half-hard cock slipped between my ass cheeks.

"For both, of course." I snuggled closer to him. Then I sighed. "I'll jump into whatever adventure life offers me."

"You don't sound so excited. But if you allow me, I will support you with all my strength. You will see, there are often more surprises on a journey like this than one would like. This night was just one among many."

"The rest will have to wait until morning. I'm more than happy with the start, but my eyes are getting heavy."

Ben's answer sank already into a thick fog mixed with restless dreams that tortured me throughout the night. More than once I shot up without knowing where I was. But Ben took me in his arms again and again, pressed me close and covered me with the blanket again. Finally, by dawn, I fell at last into a restful sleep. When I opened my eyes the next morning, I was lying alone in Ben's cabin. I hadn't even noticed him getting dressed and slipping off. Breakfast was standing on the table. The warm aroma of fresh bread wafted to my nose. My mouth watered. I decided to approach this day with new courage. Maybe today would bring my first great adventure. I didn't know what it would be. But I was ready.

*M*y hopes were not fulfilled. The next days passed without much incident. But my narrow bunk was empty most of the time. There was plenty of room for me at Ben's side. Here, we found time for long talks—and some other things as well.

A few days later we reached the port of La Rochelle in France. Ben wanted to visit some business partners here. The ship was supposed to pick up fresh provisions and set out to sea again in two days. The *Margarita* sailed into the port with a Union Jack flapping proudly from the mizzen gaff. A few spectators had gathered on the jetty to watch the foreign ship arrive. A quick glance around the ship convinced the captain that everything was in its proper place. He undertook the difficult maneuvering in the packed harbor himself.

"All hands on deck!" he turned towards the upper deck. "Clear sails to furl! Leave the jib, mizzen, and topgallant sails flying. Go, go, you loafers. Get to work."

The well-drilled sailors reacted immediately. Like weasels, they sprang up the masts and climbed back down while the men on deck grabbed hold of the ropes to furl the sails. Then the first staysail rolled up, and the surface of the square sail rapidly grew smaller. The ship gradually approached the pier. As in every harbor of the world, workers were standing by the water to pick up the lines. First, a throw line was tossed from stern onto land. Then the heavy aft line followed. A large man in a colorful, half-open shirt picked it up and expertly tied it to the nearest post. Once all lines were tied, the gangway was laid out. Shortly afterwards, the first harbor workers brought new provisions on board. The trip was well-planned, and Ben's business partners had been awaiting the *Margarita* for days.

"Can I go explore the city with Ahmed?" I asked Ben excitedly. "He told me that some relatives of his live here and he really wants to visit them."

"First I would like you to watch over the first loading with me. I wanted to explain to you what you need to watch out for. Handlers in foreign ports always try to pull a fast one. Then you can head off with Ahmed. But be back by dawn at the latest. There's lots to get down in the next couple days. But I can understand that you'd like to feel firm ground beneath your feet again. Even after all these years at sea, it's still the same with me."

Ben was in a good mood, I could see that. Maybe it was because the heavy of burden of his lie was no longer wearing down on him.

In the afternoon, I followed Ahmed through the winding city streets. When we reached a long, white wall he suddenly stopped and knocked at an inconspicuous door. An instant later, a small hatch opened at eye-height. After a brief nod on Ahmed's part, a few words I couldn't understand, the door opened. A man in an Oriental-seeming robe bowed deeply and let us enter without a word. I was amazed. Behind the white wall, a whole new world had opened up. We walked through a blooming garden to the entrance of the house, which was somewhat set back. Exotic flowers exuded intensive, sweet odors; around me I saw flowers in every color of the rainbow. Giant trees offered cool shade. Nearby I heard a fountain splashing, but I couldn't see it through the thick blooms.

In the entrance hall, a tall broad-shouldered man with a short beard was waiting for us. He wore a white robe decorated with fancy embroidery. Around his throat, the material was cut wide, allowing a view of his dark, curly chest hair. His eyes gleamed affectionately as we approached him.

"Hello, Ahmed. It's nice to have you back in the city." Ahmed was greeted with an affectionate embrace. "Who did you bring with you today?" he asked, turning around to me.

"This is my friend, Tom. We just got into the harbor a few hours ago. As soon as we could, we snuck away. And of course, you were my first destination. Tom, let me introduce Karim. He's part of my family from back home."

"I'm glad you've come. Has your journey been peaceful so far? Have you seen any pirates?" Karim asked. "You hear all sorts of frightening things ... but how impolite of me. I'm badgering you with my curious questions and you haven't even properly arrived yet. Make yourselves at home. Ahmed, you know your way around already. We'll see each other later."

At that, he left us alone, beaming. Ahmed took me down a corridor to the washroom.

"First we need to get rid of all the dirt from that long trip."

He pointed to two large wash basins standing by the wall. In a split-second he was stripping off his clothes and rubbing his body from head to toe with water and soap. The firm mounds of his ass gleamed at me, the same dark brown as the rest of his even body.

"Don't you want to get all the muck off you? Where I come from, cleanliness is very important. Your people don't seem to think much of water sometimes." He wrinkled his nose.

He had turned around and was applying ample soap to his cock.

"You like what you see?" he grinned. "Now would you get undressed? I'll help you wash up."

Encouragingly, he stroked his stomach and slid his hand deliberately up and down his erection. Sunlight fell through the window. Countless drops of water gleamed like tiny colorful gems on Ahmed's moist, glittering skin. I drew my tongue across my dry lips and slowly pulled my shirt over my head. I took my time deliberately so Ahmed could get a good look at my powerful arms. My stomach tightened, showing off small mountains of muscle. I stretched my arms as far as I could upward so he could see the rough hairs in my armpits. I knew this view would turn him to butter. Then I turned around, pulled my pants slowly down over my ass cheeks and bent over. Once my hands touched the ground, I gave him a roguish grin through my spread legs. Suddenly, Ahmed had a pail of water in his hands. Before I could stand up straight again, he tilted it over me in one motion. I shot up with a snort, tripped over my pants, which were still at my ankles, and landed just in time in Ahmed's spread arms. Then I slipped from his soapy body and landed roughly on my knees.

"That's not what I meant to do," he laughed. "Get up. Otherwise we'll never finish."

But I wasn't planning on standing up. His hard cock was much too seductive, dangling in front of my face.

"Or I could keep going right here," I said, grabbing his pulsing shaft and rubbing it. Thanks to the soap, it was easy to slide through my hands. With a firm grip, I rubbed his stiff tool from head to base.

"No ... ohh ... not yet, Tom. We've got time for that later."

He pulled me up and gave me a tender kiss on the mouth.

"We've got plenty of sweet hours in wait for us here. Karim has prepared some surprises that are waiting for us now."

Expectantly, but unhurriedly, we washed each other until the last grain of sea salt was stripped from our skin. As I dried off Ahmed's back and massaged his round ass cheeks, I would have loved to sink my pole into his ass right then and there, but Ahmed was unfazed. He was already grabbing one of the broad traditional robes that lay waiting for us. Expertly, he pulled the ankle-length, sack-like dress over his head, filling out the long sleeves. Awkwardly I tried to imitate him, but was unsuccessful. Ahmed, amused, helped me to fit my head through the right opening. The fabric was light and pleasantly cool on my skin. Our habits were decorated with ample embroidery as well. It gave me a comfortably tingling feeling to be completely naked beneath this strange dress and to feel the fabric softly rubbing at my skin.

"You look good," Ahmed observed, looking at me from all sides. "Now we're presentable. But we shouldn't keep our host waiting any longer. And I'm hungry."

As if in agreement, my stomach rumbled softly. Laughing, we set off on our way down the corridor; at the end, two servants were holding a wide door open for us. As we entered the room behind it, I couldn't contain my astonishment.

"You've probably never seen anything like this, have you?" asked Karim, who was lying stretched out on soft cushion in the middle of the room by a low table. He clearly enjoyed my amazement. And I was actually speechless. The walls of the room were covered with the finest ornaments in every possible color. Light, dark-red streams of fabric hang from the high ceiling. On one side of the room, elegant columns and arches led out to a bright courtyard filled with greenery. Behind low bushes, the calming splashing of the fountain could be heard again. The floor was entirely covered with soft rugs.

"You're not the first to be at a loss for words," Karim said, waving us towards him at the table. "But everyone has managed to find their voice again. At least our delicious meal will loosen your tongue."

Hungry and completely overwhelmed, I fell onto a soft cushion. Steaming bowls of strange dishes I had never seen before stood on the table.

"Simply try what you like. You can eat with your fingers. Just be brave," Ahmed said, encouraging me, then turning to Karim and speaking to him in his native language.

I bent over the countless bowls, sniffed the strange delicacies one after the other, brimming with curiosity. Another surprise awaited me. Some of the dishes were spicy and fragrant, while others were sweet, heavy and sticky as honey. Karim and Ahmed advised me.

"You absolutely must try this here," Karim said, grabbing a bowl and passing me something yellow. Curiously I opened my mouth and he pushed the stuff cautiously into my mouth. I sucked Karim's fingers with pleasure for a minute before he pulled them out.

"Really incredibly tasty," I asserted with a hungry look in his eyes.

"Your friend seems to enjoy our way of life," Karim said to Ahmed.

"I'm sorry," he said. He stood up rapidly. "I will leave the two of you alone again for a while. My servants will clean up the dishes as soon as you're done. They are at your service for anything else you may need."

Ahmed lounged on the cushions once Karim had left.

"Isn't it fantastic here? Almost like paradise."

"But a little something is missing for my completely happiness," I purred and rolled on top of him, softly squeezing the visible bulge between his legs.

"I have to show you something," Ahmed said, ignoring my seduction attempt. He jumped up and walked in the direction of the courtyard. Excited, I followed him and watched him undress and dive into a small pool. It was actually a giant washtub dug into the ground, filling out the entire courtyard. I had never seen anything like it. The edge of the pool was decorated with Oriental ornaments, while the bottom showed an artful mosaic picture of naked, wrestling man. Ahmed snaked in the middle of the glass-clear water, waving to me.

"And now for that little something. Come in, it's fantastic. The pool is fed by a warm spring."

I undressed myself and slide into the water. Pleasant warmth surrounded me. After two powerful strokes I reached Ahmed. He was lying flat on his back in the water, holding on to the edge of the pool. His fat cock swung between his spread legs under the surface of the water. I dove under and swallowed his erection in my mouth. My tongue surrounded the pulsing head. With soft leg motions, Ahmed swung his hips to shove his shaft in further. Just before I saw black in front of my eyes, I let go of his cock and gasped for air, panting.

"Good job, Tom. But you can have it a lot more easy."

Ahmed pulled himself up by the edge of the pool and sat on the edge. His legs dangled loosely in the water. I snapped greedily for his fat meat as it danced back and forth in front of my mouth. Aroused by my previous work, Ahmed pressed my head firmly to his throbbing cock.

"Suck harder," he moaned. "As deep as you can. I've been waiting so long for you to finally conquer my cock."

Spurred on by his words, I took its whole length in my mouth down to the hilt. Ahmed had leaned back on his elbows, throwing his head back, relaxed. With wild thrusts, his hips came towards me. His balls, which I was kneading forcefully in my hand, had already pulled up in his sac. The inside of his thighs began to twitch lightly. His stomach muscles tightened together. Then he shot his cream deep in my gullet in forceful shots, accompanied by loud moans. I sucked until I had squeezed out the last drops from the tip of his cock. Then I let him go, slipped into the water, and swam on my back while looking up at the radiant blue sky.

Next to me, I saw Ahmed entering the water and whispering, "Thank you, my friend. For a brief moment, I was really in paradise."

Suddenly a shadow fell on our faces. Two dark figures stood at the edge of the pool.

"My lord instructed us to prepare the two young guests for the great evening event. Everything is set up in the main room."

It was Karim's servants who had interrupted our intimacy so unexpectedly. I had already noticed these two well-built men on my arrival. They had both changed and were standing at the edge of the pool with just a narrow towel around their waists. Their powerful arms were crossed over their naked chests, shaved as naked as their gleaming heads. Powerful upper thighs and tight calves rounded out their perfectly formed bodies. They waved us invitingly out of the water. Wet and naked as we were, we followed them.

The low table and cushions in the inner room had disappeared. In their place, there were two waist-high lounge chairs. We were requested to lie down with our faces to the ground.

"Do you know what's going to happen now?" I asked Ahmed nervously.

"Don't worry," he answered. "Just try to stay relaxed and enjoy it. After the festival dinner tonight, we'll probably need to work more, but first you can relax a while."

The lounge chairs were comfortable and soft. On the spot where our faces were positioned there was a large hole to allow room for our noses and mouths. Our sensitive manhoods had also been considered. In order to avoid squishing them, there was an opening in the lower area to let both cock and balls hang down loosely.

"My name is Umar," said the servant next to me. "Now I will attempt to release all tension in your body. This relieving massage will make your work tonight so much easier. My brother Walid will take care of your friend Ahmed."

Slowly and evenly he began to spread oil on my back, ass, and legs. With skillful hands he loosened my cramped neck. Working down my back, he touched every muscle fiber and vertebra. Under his skillful strokes, I sank deeper and deeper into the lounge chair. I shut my eyes and entrusted myself to Umar's giant, incredibly sensitive hands. He paid particularly diligent attention to my ass cheeks, giving them a powerful massage. Steadily increasing pressure, he rubbed first my right, then my left cheek. My cock gave an excited twitch. It filled firmly with blood, beating against the lounge chair from below. Umar bent down to see what was wrong. When he glimpsed my hard-on, he nodded approvingly. "That's good. The more relaxed you get, the harder your cock will grow."

Umar continued working down my thighs towards my feet.

"Soon you'll see the effects. Don't be afraid," he warned, pressing painfully on individual spots on my foot soles. Suddenly, hot waves shot up my legs through my whole body. Small drops of sweat beaded on my skin. My mouth began to water and my cock twitched. Short, vibrating waves flowed up to the tip of the cock. I felt more pre-cum dripping from the tip with every wave. Umar was stroking the inside of my legs, moving upwards. Once his hands reached my ass he pulled my ass cheeks apart carefully. His fingers worked intensively at my rosebud.

"Now this the only part of you that's not relaxed," he observed with a chuckle, pressing a finger slowly and cautiously into my hole.

In soft circles, he spread my hole. Shivers ran up my back from my ass all the way to my neck. Then I felt a second finger. After a few cautious strokes, it was joined by a third. Together they inspected my hot cavern thoroughly.

"Breath nice and deep to relax your muscles," Umar explained. But his fingers were expert; after a short time they slid within me without any difficulty. Amazed, I observed that my body was actually growing more and more relaxed, while my throbbing cock was getting harder and harder.

"Are you ready, Walid?" Umar asked, looking over to the other table. I had completely forgotten that Ahmed was receiving the same treatment on the other lounge chair. I turned my head to the side and saw Walid nodding with a contented smile. He spread Ahmed's legs apart and knelt behind him on the lounge. His imposing cock stood straight upright. Gleaming like a polished scimitar, his voluptuous weapon darted out from his black loins. His dark nipples stood out firmly. He had a wild gleam in his eyes as he bent forward, placed his hands on either side of my friend's torso, and slowly sank his erection into Ahmed's ass crack.

Almost at the same time, I felt a pleasant pressure at my back entrance. Umar shoved his hard tool down to the hilt in my widened hole without resistance.

He lay his muscled torso heavily on my back.

"Do you feel completely relaxed now?" he growled in my ear, thrusting his hips back and forth in slow, circular motions. I felt his hard meat deep and warm within me. Then he pulled it all the way out only to sink it back even deeper. Each time he hit my pleasure point. Sparks shot along my rock-hard shaft.

"Do you know what Umar means in your language?" he asked me suddenly. "Umar means 'he of long life.' And I promise you: my joystick lives up to the name."

Immediately, my cock began swelling even more. The prospect of feeling his thick meat inside me for even longer—to helplessly submit to his powerful thrusts even longer—was almost too good to be true.

"Yes, now I really feel totally relaxed. You have fantastic hands, Umar. But what I really love is your magnificent massage rod in my ass," I sighed.

My words spurred him to work ever more tirelessly on my willing ass. A glance at Ahmed showed me that he was enjoying his treatment as well. Walid slid up and down his well-oiled back as Umar's hard stomach muscles rubbed upwards from my tailbone. Now the two of them increased their tempo. Under the table, my cock throbbed harder and wilder. I would have loved to take it in my hands and rub it, but the chair was simply too wide to grab around. It had become a kind of mischievous torture instrument, letting the tingling at the tip of my cock grow almost unbearable.

Umar started panting heavily. His fast thrusts became harder and bolder. With a last wild attack, hot syrup flooded from his cock, streaming deep inside me. Throbbing, he filled my hole with his fluid. I bucked and reared beneath him. The tingling and burning in my own cock was becoming unbearable. I tightened my ass cheeks to pump the last drops out of Omar, keeping his cock inside me. Walid had reached his climax as well. Moaning, he thrust his pelvis forward. His buttocks tightened and he let out several moaning roars. Then he slung his load deep into Ahmed and lay down on him, exhausted and powerless.

In the next minutes, all I could hear was our breath as the four of us calmed down. Contented silence reigned, undisturbed by the quiet splashing of the fountain in the courtyard. Then a loud gong interrupted our cozy intimacy.

"The evening feast is approaching," whispered Walid. "Come with us, we'll lead you to an out-of-the-way room where you relax a bit more and get composed again."

"Hopefully you both liked your massages and will stay relaxed all night," Umar added with a broad grin. His white teeth briefly flashed on his dark face.

We used the time to wash ourselves thoroughly. Much to my regret, Ahmed wouldn't let me rub him dry. And he didn't make any offers to help me out of my uncomfortable situation. My throbbing cock was still tingling mercilessly along its whole length, all the way up to the fatly swollen head. So I massaged my thick meat myself.

"Knock it off," Ahmed snarled at me. He grabbed my hand and pulled it indignantly off my erection. "There's no more time for that."

"I'll be real quick," I pleaded with a submissive smile. "You have no idea how nimble my fist can be when necessary."

And it was necessary. Without even touching myself, I was hard as a rock. Just thinking of giving my stiff friend some quick work with my hands nearly made me blow my load.

"I said no, Tom!" The resentful undertone in Ahmed's voice allowed no contradiction. What had gotten into Ahmed all of a sudden?

"Get dressed. They'll come for us any minute. And our host doesn't like to be kept waiting."

His irritated mood and obvious unease ruined my good mood. He was suddenly acting as if we were standing at the top of an important guest list.

Ahmed held out a colorful, artfully designed tunic to me and I pulled it over my head morosely.

"The inhabitants of my native country call it 'galabiya,'" explained Ahmed. "It is only worn for special feasts."

Gradually his unease was becoming contagious. What awaited us tonight? Ahmed was silent. He kept adjusting his tunic without ever seeming content with the result.

"How do I look?" I asked uncertainly.

"You look fantastic," he answered. In this fancy outfit I felt like the son of an Arabian ruler. I grabbed him firmly by the shoulders and pressed a long kiss on his sensual lips. I didn't dare to pull him close to me. His carefully smoothed tunic would have become twisted, and he would have felt my throbbing torpedo. My throbbing meat was still clamoring for attention. At least Ahmed was beginning to relax again. A small smile flashed over his face; I couldn't get enough of it. His large, dark eyes looked at me seriously.

"I hope you'll like the evening. Enjoy the good food and the show."

"What kind of show is it?" I wanted to know.

But at the same instant, Umar appeared in the door.

"Well? Ready, sirs? Karim would like to introduce you to his friends."

Silently, we followed the giant man. My impatience grew at every step down the long corridor. Finally we were standing in front of the main room. The two heavy doors opened.

"Ah! There you are, my friends." Karim bowed before us and turned around to his guests. He clapped loudly three times. The clamor of voices was stilled. All eyes in the room turned to us.

"My dear friends. I would like to present to you our special visitors tonight. Ahmed, who some of you already know, and his friend Tom, who undertook a long journey from England just to be with us here tonight."

Karim told a wild story about how we had fought with dangerous pirates and barely escaped with our lives. I gave Ahmed a questioning look as he softly translated Karim's words in my ear.

"This is all part of this special festivity. I will explain it all later."

Karim had finished with his introduction. He led us to a table with six men who already seemed to be expecting Ahmed, receiving him with loud cries. Then the master of the house led me jovially but firmly to a seat further back in the room.

"What am I supposed to do?" I called back to Ahmed, alarmed.

"Enjoy the meal," he called after me. He waved reassuringly.

I was received with loud, exuberant greetings and friendly embraces, and offered a seat. Thick cushions were spread around a low round table in typical Middle Eastern fashion, more inviting for lying down than for sitting. Legs crossed, I got as comfortable as I could in this unusual position. The other men at the table had already sunken back into their conversations. I had the opportunity to look around a bit. In the weakly-lit room there were twelve tables surrounded by loudly gesticulating men of all ages. A few young men, but also many of Karim's age. Without exception they had all appeared at this feast well-dressed. As my eyes wandered from table to table, I noticed how the man sitting to my right kept inspecting me with brief glances. He was excitedly talking to another man in his native language. Then he suddenly laid a hand on my shoulder and pointed to the table. To my astonishment, he said in nearly accent-free English: "Wouldn't you like to try the delicious dishes? Karim will be upset if he learns you haven't eaten anything all night."

"Oh, yes, of course," I answered, dumbfounded. "But I don't know what any of the food is. And my friend Ahmed is over at that table there, so he can't help me right now."

"If you allow me, I'll put together a few things together for you. I know Englanders' tastes very well. Trust me."

He had already started preparing a large plate for me from the overflowing bowls.

"I'm sorry, I haven't introduced myself."

He placed the dish in front of me and bowed.

"I'm Ṣaif Rahman from Kadif. I am glad to meet you, friend of Karim and Ahmed."

"My name is Tom—Tom Moore—and I'm from Plymouth, England."

"I know Plymouth," said Saif, excited. "A few years ago my travels took me there. I lived there for almost a whole year. You come from a very beautiful city, Tom. I learned your language there from a good friend. It took a lot of effort, but it was worth it. Otherwise I wouldn't be able to explain the show to you, and you wouldn't understand the most magnificent part of the evening. It was a good idea on Karim's part to seat you next to me."

I must have given him a wide-eyed, confused look.

"I understand," he said with a friendly smile and nodded contemplatively. "You don't understand at all, do you? You have no idea what to expect tonight. Well, then enjoy the surprise. Here, first try some of this."

Saif took an oblong, sweet-smelling fruit and placed it in my mouth.

"It's going to start any second now, I'm sure. I'll sit closer to you and explain all the particulars."

He slid close behind me. I felt his breath on my neck. He positioned his legs loosely left and right of my thighs.

"Look, the lights are already going down," he whispered in my left ear.

Only the candles on the tables were now bathing the room in dim light. In the open courtyard area, right next to the large pool, diligent servants lit several large torches. Soft music rang out, and a tender man's voice sang a ballad. The voice grew louder and stronger. Suddenly two men entered the lit area. Each of them carried a scimitar in their right hand and a short dagger in their left. They were completely naked. Their back and chest muscles were clearly visible as they circled each other with grim gazes at some distance. Their sturdy legs carried out a kind of dance in time with the music. Then their swords met, clashing loudly above their heads. With their short daggers, they tried to stab their opponent's thighs. Less than a hand's width from their bodies, the sharp knife blades whizzed through the air. Again and again the two men came at each other with loud cries. As they raged, spectators cheered them on. Names were called out, and the excited onlookers quickly formed two groups, each supporting their favorite. Both opponents, surrounded by a wave of commotion, dove more spiritedly into their duel. I twitched involuntarily as a saber nearly split one of the men's heads. Saif clasped my shoulders reassuringly.

"These two are the best fighters out there. Sometimes even I think one of them is about to get cut open by a dagger. But don't worry. All their steps and thrusts are carefully planned out and well-practiced. The show and the song are telling a very old story of something that supposedly happened long ago in my homeland."

While the two fighters devoted themselves to their bitter duel, Saif explained the dance's true meaning to me:

"A long, long time ago there were two enemy kingdoms. For many years, the rulers' armies had fought one another. But no armed forces were enough for either kingdom to conquer the other. Finally, the warriors were supposed to meet for a final great battle. All available soldiers from both kingdoms gathered together at the frontiers in a broad, empty valley. The armies had travelled all day to get there. Before the last battle, which would decide between victory and defeat for one of the kingdoms, both commanders decided to let their men rest for a day.

Early in the morning on the next day, it was time. The kings headed up their armies at either side of the valley. The high mountains on either side made escape impossible. In spite of the size of the battlefield, the valley could barely contain all the soldiers. When both kings saw the vast array of soldiers, they stopped. In their wisdom, they realized that if one land was victorious, the other would be destroyed. But the victor would not be able to rule both lands. Too many men would die. Hunger and disease would break over the new kingdom. No king should do that to his people. So the two kings met alone in the middle of the battlefield. They spoke together for three days and three nights. Then they made their decision known: their beloved sons Mikrin and Serur would decide the battle through a duel. The two young men would be sent to a high mountain, armed only with a saber and a dagger. The winner would only be allowed to come back once the fight had been decided. Unclothed, equipped only with their weapons, the young men climbed the mountain. After hours of climbing, they reached a broad plateau. The sound of their scimitars clashing together could be heard all the way down in the valley. Hour after hour passed. After two days, the battle was not yet finished. On the morning of the third day, there was silence on the mountain."

At that moment, the two warriors in the courtyard had set their swords and daggers aside. Out of breath, they stood in front of one another. It was clear they had given their all. Sweat ran from all their pores, washing over their bulging muscles in gleaming pearls. Their chests rose and fell. Powerless, they jumped into each other's arms, fell to their knees, then began rolling on the ground in a desperate struggle.

"Time passed, but neither of the two were seen. Every now and again, a loud cry or moan was heard. Moaning and roaring like wounded lions. Then the voices died out as well. In the evening, when neither of the sons had come down into the valley, messengers were sent out to look for them. But just as they reached the foot of the mountain, both young men came down to meet them. Astounded that both kings' sons were returning, they were brought before their fathers.

'We fought for two days and wrestled one another for a whole day,' said Mikrin.

'Neither of us was strong enough to conquer the other,' confirmed Serur. 'So we fell upon each other and crossed our manly swords.'

The two of them looked down at each other and their large swords flashed stiffly upward, ready to fight.

'Each of us took the other the way only men can. But neither my sword nor his were dulled, no matter how often they met,' Mikrin continued. He looked earnestly into his father's eyes.

'Both our people are strong and proud. We have both fought for our lives these last days. Through fighting, we learned to value and love one another. Because of this, our people should learn to value and love one another. Never again should there be war between us as long as we live.'

In front of their fathers' eyes, the two kings' sons embraced and kissed, crossing their manly swords without hurting one another. The old kings could see that their children were much wiser than they were themselves, and appointed them the new rulers of their lands. The two kings visited each other as often as they could. Trade between the two lands flourished like never before, and the peace between the kingdoms gladdened the people to the depths of their hearts. When the time had come, after both kings had ruled long and wisely, Mikrin and Serur passed their titles on to their sons. The two of them then passed their remaining years on the solitary mountain where they had first fought, until one day they disappeared and were never seen again. Their graves were never found, despite a long search. Even today, travelers passing through the valley report that when the wind blows down dust from the high mountain on stormy days, they can hear a roar like lions and the moan of fighting men."

One of the two wrestlers was pressing his opponent's face against the floor. Then he laid his full weight on the man's back, clasped his wrists and spread the other man's thighs with his powerful legs. His throbbing cock pushed towards his enemy's defenseless gate. Slowly, the bulging torpedo sank into its quivering target.

It had become strangely quiet in the large festival room. Here the quiet murmur of individual voices, there a suppressed moan— otherwise the ritual in front of us was accompanied by still- ness. The tip of his cock softly touched the quivering ass. Slim hips pushed upwards. The vanquished man's relieved sighs were overwhelmed by his assailant's loud cry of victory as he shoved his powerful sword into his opponent. Nestled together, the two manly bodies lay in front of the pool. Now all we could hear was their heavy breathing. The two warriors were completely spent. But the victor wanted more. The muscles on him twitched vis- ibly in the shine of the surrounding torches. His hips rose and fell boldly. Lustily, he shoved his fat meat into the conquered flanks beneath him. The vanquished warrior only defended himself briefly against this treatment, then began to moan in enjoyment of this loving torture. But after a short time, the loser seemed to have gained new strength. With one motion, he shoved his ass up- ward. His surprised opponent lost his balance and fell backwards. In a flash, the previously vanquished man was sitting on his rival, grabbing his cock and shoving it voluntarily into his ass. Pressing his enemy's torso down with both hands, he set the tempo now. His ass slid rapidly and up and down the other man's thick scimitar, as if he wanted to sharpen the hard steel inside him. His own cock danced out from his crotch until his enemy's hands grasped them expertly and held them as well as they could. The wild ride became more merciless.

The moaning and panting around me grew louder and louder. On all sides, Karim's guests were busy conquering foreign cocks, investigating hidden entrances or fending off assaults of enemy hands and greedy jaws. I wasn't spared from these attacks either. Saif's throbbing cock beat eagerly against my back. Curious hands shoved beneath my shirt, stroking my chest hair.

"How do you like this old story?" Saif whispered in my ear.

"It's too beautiful to be true. The two kings' sons must have been wonderful, fearless men. And even though they came from different races, their love united them forever."

"We are very different from one another as well. When I look at your light, smooth back ..." Saif had slipped the broad tunic over my head and set it aside. He drew twisting patterns on my skin with his fingertips.

"... Then look at my own dark, hairy chest." He pressed me close. A shiver ran through me as his hair touched my back. His hands wandered over my stomach deep into my crotch. Contented moans rang from my throat as his hands grasped my twitching shaft. I leaned back against him and enjoyed the arousing sensation.

"We'll soon find out whether the difference between us is really that big," I whispered, thrusting.

I released myself from his embrace and turned around. For the first time that night, I looked Saif in the eyes. They gleamed mysteriously, and his sensual mouth and full lips smiled at me seductively. His teeth flashed as I wandered my hands up his inner thighs and grabbed his thick meat. A surprised moan escaped his opened mouth. I couldn't resist bending down to him and kissing his sensual mouth. Greedily I pressed my lips to his and greeted his moist tongue wildly. I fell upon him with my whole weight. We landed softly in a tall mountain of cushions. Expectantly, I rubbed my cock against his hot shaft.

"Are you trying to challenge me to a sword fight, Tom?" Saif grunted after freeing himself from my lips. "Our little show must have aroused you quite a bit?"

"I'd much rather find a sheath for my sword," I answered, out of breath.

Without hesitating, I grabbed his legs behind the knees and lifted them up. My quivering cock head found the right spot immediately.

"Stop, stop, my young friend," Saif halted me. "Your sword should only enter its sheath well-oiled. Proper weapon care is good for sword and sheath alike."

Saif grabbed a round fruit from a large bowl on one of the tables. He squeezed the red pulp with his powerful hand and dripped the sweet-smelling juice first on my shaft, then on his own throbbing manhood.

"This will make things so much better. Try it."

He put the rest of the fruit between his teeth and grinned at me. I didn't know what he meant by that. Did he want me to try sticking my dripping cock into his ass or was he referring to the fruit beneath his lips that was giving out such a seductive aroma?

Still kneeling in front of him, I bent down uncertainly. First my cock touched his tight entrance, then I tasted the fruit between his lips. My cock sank noiselessly into his warm ass. The sweet fruit delighted my gums, the sticky juice dripped from my chin onto Saif's chest. My curious tongue followed the red trail.

"We call this fruit mahniuc," Saif explained, breathing heavily and swallowing down the rest of the fruit. "My ancestors brewed an aphrodisiac with it. Your stiff friend will give you lots of enjoyment tonight. This juice has a very particular effect. Can you already feel a tingling at the tip of your cock?"

I had already started thrusting my shaft impatiently in Saif's ass. Now I felt a light itching that spread over my whole cock towards my balls. It wasn't unpleasant, but as soon as I stopped my movements for a second, the seductive tingling became a powerful burning that made sweat form on my forehead. I could only hope Saif knew what he was doing with this infernal stuff. Perched on my knees, I pulled his ass against my steaming crotch and shoved my hot iron in his tight hole. The pleasant feeling returned, forcing me to continue.

"Yes, that's what I was hoping for, my friend. From the minute I saw you this afternoon I wanted your giant sword inside me," Saif moaned, relieved. My shocked moans no longer concerned him. Now a broad grin spread over his aroused face.

"A few selected guests were allowed to watch your preparations for this evening from a proper distance. Small eyeholes are built into the ornaments on the walls."

My eyes searched among the serpentine carvings for suspicious holes. But it was much too dark to make anything out. Instead, my eyes became aware of what was going on in front of them. All around the room, Karim's guests lay spread out on soft cushions. Naked bodies rubbed together. Faces contorted with pleasure revealed unbridled lust. Greedy lips sucked on fat cocks. Hard shafts pried open hidden entrances. Loud moans and manly, throaty sighs rang out in the night. The sweet aroma of fruit hung over the entire scene, mingling with the sweat of hungry men.

"I can't anymore," I called out as my legs cramped up and my crotch refused to obey my demanding cock. Immediately Saif sat up and bent over my tense torpedo.

"Wait, I'll help you."

His sturdy legs were now supporting his entire weight. Nevertheless, his ass raised and lowered light as a leaf in the wind. Relieved, I sank back and closed my eyes. From a distance, I thought I heard Ahmed's bright voice. Saif's rapid ride coaxed unknown tones from my mouth. Desperate, I pushed my hips against him.

Early in the morning, I was awakened by the first rays of the sun. Saif lay sleeping peacefully in my arms. Lost in thought, I observed his fine facial features. Memories of the night before drifted through me like a bank of clouds: I was grasping his throbbing cock in my hands, rubbing his hot tool firmly while he rode my cock. My raging loins wanted to explode. But Saif always stopped at just the right time to catch his breath, and the moment passed.

We reached dizzying heights. He cried out and turned when I grabbed his balls in my fist, squeezing them tight. Finally, after many hours, his tortured sword shot out hot seed in a wide arc. He reared up, moaning, shoved his finger in my twitching hole, and put my own pleasurable torment to an end. Like a dam bursting, my sperm poured into his narrow canal. All my tension abated. He kissed me contentedly and we fall asleep. The whole thing still seemed like an intoxicating dream.

Suddenly Ahmed was standing in front of me: "It's light out," he whispered softly. "We have to get going." He had already donned his old shirt and ankle-length pants. He held out my things to me. I carefully slipped away from Saif without waking him up. When we were standing in the door, I looked back again. Saif was leaning up on one arm looking at me. He nodded farewell. I bowed and flashed him an intimate smile.

On the front steps of the house, Karim awaited us.

"I hope you enjoyed our little festival. Shame that you've got to go. Next month, a troop of travelling acrobats is going to visit us. Their performances will be very exciting." At the last word, he winked conspiratorially at us.

"If your travels bring you here again, you're of course welcome at any time. I packed some extra provisions for you. Here, Tom, find a safe place for this."

Our host gave me a small copper jug sealed with wax.

"As I've seen, you know how to make good use of this."

Suspicious, I eyed the vessel. As I sniffed it cautiously, a familiar sweet odor rose to my nostrils. I couldn't conceal a grin.

"Use the fruits sparingly. As you know, they can be dangerous. Pleasure and torment are closely related," Karim added in warning.

He took Ahmed in his arms firmly and pressed the guy so hard he flinched.

"Yes, yes, I'll come back. Don't worry, my journeys may take me all over the world. But I will always come back to this heavenly place."

"And I certainly won't let Ahmed travel alone," I agreed, bowing low. "Thank you for the unforgettable feast."

"Now get going, it's getting light out already." Karim ushered us to the wall with its narrow gate. "Otherwise this will be your last trip on shore for a long time."

I cast a last glance on the small garden with colorful flowers and blossoms. Wet dew on the closed buds gleamed in the first light of day. The cool night air hung over the flowerbeds.

Then we were suddenly standing in the narrow street and the city welcomed us with early morning hubbub. Women with dirty laundry slipped past us. Drunks leaned against the narrow walls of houses, sleeping off their hangovers. Seamen hurried past them, cursing loudly when they stumbled against stretched-out legs or when washing women barred their way. But Ahmed and I were walking on air. We made our way through that obstacle course quickly and unharmed.

There's our ship," called Ahmed in front of me as he left the narrow streets and reached the open harbor. Without my friend I would have gotten hopelessly lost in this foreign city, but now I too saw the *Margarita* moored in the harbor. From afar I recognized Ben because of his large stature. He was standing at the railing talking excitedly with a man in an officer's uniform.

"Thank you for the news, Colonel," he was saying as we came on deck. "I will tell the captain right away."

The officer saluted and left the ship without even stooping to glance at us. But Ben's chastising look as we tried to slip past him more than made up for it.

"Would you please explain to me why you're just showing up onboard now? You were supposed to be back by dawn. And now it's the middle of the day. The cook has been searching for you, Ahmed. He has been sharpening his knife for hours, cursing so loud that no one dares come near him. And the two of us are going to have to have a serious talk about your responsibilities onboard, Tom," Ben snapped at me.

"But we have a good reason for being so late," I said, hoping to escape the impending lecture.

"It was because of the pirate ship that's planning to attack us," Ahmed blurted out.

"What nonsense!" Ben's voice grew louder. "I just heard from the colonel of the local prefecture that no pirates have been seen here for months."

"But that's a tactic," Ahmed insisted. "I know that the pirates have been waiting for our ship for weeks."

The sailors rushing past had stopped out of curiosity to listen to our argument. Ben's face had grown red and I was awaiting a further onslaught from him.

"Come to my cabin!" he hissed between clenched teeth. "And get back to work, you lazy bums," he snapped to the staring sailors.

"Are you out of your minds to say something like that?" he screamed at me as the cabin door slammed shut behind us. "If the captain hears that you're spreading such rumors and making half the crew turn on their heels and run, you'll spend the rest of the trip in chains below deck."

Ben went to the cupboard, took out a flask and drank a few powerful draughts. I have never seen him so worked up. He sat down in a chair and gave us a penetrating glance. He didn't speak again until his breath had grown calmer.

"Try again, one at a time. And I want to hear all the details."

Ahmed told Ben about our visit to his uncle, about the evening festival and all the visitors he had spoken to. When he mentioned the name Karim, Ben perked up his ears.

"Karim ... ah, yes ... I've heard of a Karim here in La Rochelle," he said, lost in thought. His eyes seemed to be searching for faded images behind the thick wall of the ship.

A smile flashed over Ben's face. Suddenly I saw him as the young, radiant man he once had been. But the impression disappeared as quickly as it had come. Years on the rough seas had drawn fine lines over his face, and several deep worry lines were unmistakable.

Ahmed continued his report: "One of the guests found out that we had come into harbor on the *Margarita*. Karim told us of the last reports from his scouts. A pirate ship has been lurking in a nearby bay for some time now waiting for a ship. Their sights weren't set on any old cutter, they were aiming for a particular English ship. It cost the scouts a good deal of effort to discover its name. But in the end, under extraordinary circumstances that the visitor didn't want to explain in detail, one of the pirates revealed the name of the ship. It was called *Margarita*. That was the ship the pirates have been waiting for. But I couldn't find out why the pirates are so interested in our ship in particular. What's certain is that as soon as the *Margarita* has set out a few miles on the open sea, the pirates' plan on capturing and boarding the ship with their quick schooner. And the scout learned another important detail."

Ahmed made a significant pause.

"The pirate captain was particularly determined to find out if a certain Benjamin Wilder was actually on board."

Ben sank down in the chair. All the color had gone from his face.

"After so much time ... the old scoundrel!" he stammered.

"All right," he said shortly in a firm voice. He stood up and stamped around the tight cabin agitatedly.

"Of course, this excuses your lateness. I will go to the captain and talk to him about the situation. Wait here until I come back. Don't talk to anyone about what you just told me. Understood?"

Ben's tone had become penetrating and authoritarian again in the last sentence. Nevertheless I could clearly hear the unease in his voice. As his heavy steps echoed away, I looked inquisitively at Ahmed.

"Do you know what this all means? Why would a pirate captain be asking about Ben, of all people?"

Ahmed shrugged his shoulders. "All I can tell you is what Karim already found out from his visitors. I don't know anything more. Ben seemed very unsettled. It almost seemed like he knows these pirates somehow. All we can do is wait for now. That's at least better than running into the cook's arms."

Ahmed looked around the cabin. "Maybe we can make ourselves a bit more comfortable?" He pointed to Ben's wide bunk. "I barely slept last night. And I'm sure you didn't either."

"You left a few little details out when you were telling him about last night, my friend," I scolded Ahmed jokingly.

"Wel,l for one thing, those were by no means little details that I had to report to him, and secondly I didn't want to bore Ben with the particularities of an old warrior dance," he contradicted.

The look on Ben's face when he heard Karim's name made me doubt Ahmed's words. Maybe Ben even knew the old story. But for the moment, I kept this thought to myself. Anyway, Ahmed had already jumped into the bunk, and his even breath made it clear to me that he was already sleeping sound and deep. I laid next to him. But for a while, thoughts of our conversation ran through my head: Did Ben know Karim? That would mean he also knew Mikrin and Serur. But finally sleep overcame me, too. Suddenly I felt a strong hand shaking my shoulder.

"Tom, wake up. I just spoke with the captain. I'm supposed to thank you for this report which could save all our lives. I promised him you would receive a fat reward. Now it's wake-up time. I know you've been waiting for this. Look."

With effort, I sat up on the edge of the bed. I felt dizzy. The first thing I saw were two hairy legs in rough sailor boots standing in front of me. Tree-trunk thick, muscular thighs grew up from the boots. A giant hand was stroking an equally giant cock. Clear fluid was already dripping from the throbbing head onto the floor, where it ran in dark streams. The other hand fondled his thick pubic hair, stroked his flat stomach, circled his navel seductively, and then followed the dark line of short hair up to his imposing chest muscles. When I looked into Ben's eyes, they were overflowing with a shower of warm sparks of lust and desire. All traces of the past were wiped from his face. He looked young and incredibly attractive. Wordlessly, he held out his hand to me. As his powerful arms embraced me I was already completely naked. His hot skin unlocked a passion within me like none I had ever known. Sensual lips met my dry mouth. Delicious nectar flowed down my throat. Suddenly I felt very light and lost the ground beneath my feet. Ben grabbed my hips, spread my legs, and positioned his giant phallus between my ass cheeks. I sank on this gift from the gods with a loud, relieved moan. Light as a feather, he raised and lowered my ass on his throbbing torpedo. My arms clasped to his broad shoulders. My lips sucked the sweet juice from his mouth. Waves of indescribable joy flooded through my entire body.

Carefully he bent over the broad table and laid me down cautiously on my back. Reluctantly, my mouth released his lips.

"I never thought you could be so gentle," I whispered. Ben straightened up, grabbed my heels and shoved his hard shaft deep inside me. Now it was his turn to express his lust with a contented moan.

"I hope my gentle side also does you good." He pulled his cock far out, then drove it back through my tight entrance. His balls slapped against my ass. The table creaked dangerously under his wild thrusts.

"Yes," I panted, surprised. "That's at least as good. I can't get enough."

Ben went to town. There was no more gentleness to speak of. He rammed his hard torpedo in my tight canal with increasing fury. The rubbing sensation alone set my ass on fire. Then suddenly Ahmed's voice rang out from the dark corner of Ben's bunk.

"You two are giving me quite a show from this angle. But I have to admit I'd rather be at your side." He was already standing next to us. "I've got a little problem here … or I should say, a big problem." Ahmed's thick shaft was pointing up, pulsing impatiently back and forth.

"You're in the right place. Come here," said Ben. He pulled his cock out of me. But before I could protest, Ben had grabbed Ahmed by the hips and shoved his manhood into my ass. Ahmed's cock felt cool and hard. It wasn't quite as long as its predecessor, but it was at least as thick. Completely confused by Ben's actions, Ahmed nearly lost his balance and landed on my stomach. Ben was already standing behind me, rubbing his meat between his dark mounds to keep warm.

"Then I can give you your part of the reward you've earned."

Suddenly I felt Ahmed's cock jerk forward inside me. My friend let out a shocked, throaty moan.

"What the hell is he doing?" Ahmed managed to pant.

"He's on orders ... from the captain ... to give us a fat ... reward," I responded, gasping. Now Ben was thrusting as powerfully into Ahmed's ass as he had just done with me. The pulsing cock inside me was an unmistakable sign that Ahmed appreciated this kind of reward. He clearly enjoyed Ben's treatment. True, he had made the largest contribution, so it was only natural that he received the lion's share of the reward.

While Ben's thick meat continued to warm Ahmed's ass, Ahmed's cock dove deep within me. And while Ben's fingers tweaked Ahmed's nipples forcefully, Ahmed grabbed my throbbing shaft so tightly it felt it was about to burst. Loud moans and grunts filled the room. Three men intoxicated by their senses, all on a wave of ecstasy. Ben's floodgates were the first to open, spewing his seed in wild thrusts. Howling, he threw his head back, clasped Ahmed's chest and flung his hips forward one last time. Ahmed's cock fired his load into my hot ass in seemingly never ending thrusts, while my torpedo, tightly clasped in his hands, sprayed sperm all the way to my throat. I closed my eyes and gave way entirely to this sensual pleasure as it spread through my whole body. Warm hands stroked my face. Then a hand shook my shoulder.

"Tom, wake up. I just spoke with the captain. He would like to thank you for the report that might just have saved all our lives. I promised him I would give you a big fat reward. Now wake up, Tom. I know you've been waiting for this a long time."

With effort, I swung upright on the edge of the bunk. I felt dizzy. The first thing I saw was Ben standing with his legs spread in front of me.

"Now look at this fat piece of meat."

I had to look twice to understand what he meant. Leaning forward, I arduously tried to hide my hard cock, which had slipped from my wide pants. Once I had gotten everything halfway back in order, I stood up.

"You don't seem exactly excited," Ben said, reading my facial expression. "Just take a good look at this magnificent fish. Doesn't it smell fantastic. The cook could hardly believe he was supposed to prepare this fine cut especially for the two of you."

A brown-seared fish lay on a silver platter filled with fresh, steaming vegetables. A pleasant aroma filled the cabin.

"Or were you expecting something else?" Ben asked, looking attentively down at me.

My cock was still clearly visible in my pants. But what was even more visible was the big moist spot on the bright fabric. Had I dreamt all that? I looked around me. Ahmed was sleeping tight in the bunk, Ben was standing in front of me, fully dressed. His face suddenly looked older again. Yet his eyes were gleaming more than usual. But then who had stroked my cheeks softly before Ben woke me up? I could still feel the warm hand on my skin. I looked into Ben's eyes. Ahmed stirred behind me in the bunk. He rolled over and vaulted up onto the edge of the bed.

"That smells fantastic. My mouth is watering. Is there something to eat," he interrupted the silence.

"Yes, the captain would like to thank you for your report, so he's sent you this special meal. And this bottle of wine is on me."

Ben pulled a bottle of fine French wine from his broad jacket pocket. As we ate, Ben explained to us the captain's surprising plan. During the coming night, two full days before the planned departure, the *Margarita* would slip out of the harbor onto the open sea, taking up its journey toward Spain with full sails by the first morning wind. Wherever the pirates were hidden, they wouldn't be expecting us at such an unusual time. By the time they followed us, we would long have disappeared beyond the horizon. As security, our companion ship would only follow us a day later. In case we couldn't escape the pirates, the *Amelia* and the *Providence* would cut off the pirate ship's escape route in a skirmish and sink it.

I only half-listened to the plan, while Ahmed eagerly asked Ben for details. My thoughts kept wandering back to my dream of the two of them.

"Tom ... Tom, were you listening? What do you think of the plan?" Ahmed asked suddenly.

"I hope it all works the way Captain Finch thinks it will," I answered skeptically.

"In any case there are all sorts of things to prepare before we can set out tonight." Ben was already standing in the cabin door. "Ahmed, don't keep the cook waiting too long. And Tom, come up to the afterdeck soon. We have some things to discuss."

Ben stomped away with heavy stride.

Hastily we ate a few more delicious bites while standing, took a last swig from the wine bottle, then hurried to the upper deck. But not without pressing a long kiss on Ahmed's lips, which were still salty from the fish.

"Mmmm ..." Ahmed whispered softly. "I could use more of that, my friend."

"If we survive the next few days without getting sunk by the pirates' cannonballs, I promise you a giant fried fish and then more than my warm lips afterwards," was my honest answer.

For two days, a storm had been raging constantly. A harmless-seeming cloud bank pulling by on the horizon had transformed into a powerful storm front. No one had been counting on that. Unluckily, two mainsails tore with an earsplitting din when they couldn't be pulled in soon enough. The captain had to look on helplessly as only the tattered remnants could be salvaged. Finch never stopped cursing, loudly berating his crew's incompetence and the first officers, the weather, and last but not least the cook, who couldn't prepare his beloved English tea without a firepit, since all open fires on the ship had to be put out during the storm for safety. To the chagrin of the crew, who could only attempt to avoid Finch's constant, coarse maledictions, there were no exceptions.

Each time the waves beat with a loud crash against the side of the ship, a shudder ran through the ship down to the last plank. Spray clouds high as houses wet the deck through. There was scarcely a single dry spot left on the *Margarita*. Even the ladderways and paths beneath the deck were repeatedly flooded with barrels of water. In the bilge, two troops of eight men each worked like mad. Nevertheless they were standing in water up to their knees.

Everyone did their best to defy the wild attacks of the furious sea god. We still had yet to see the pirate ship. Some time before, our two companion ships had appeared in our field of vision, only to disappear shortly after.

"We're losing the *Amelia* and the *Providence*. Now we've been out of contact with them for hours," the captain screamed at Ben. "I can't send anyone up to the crow's nest in such terrible weather."

Agitated, he searched the horizon with his telescope. Even though Ben was standing directly next to him, the storm made it almost impossible for us to understand one another. Both of them had made their way up to the afterdeck in the hopes of sighting our escort. I stood tight at Ben's side, grasping the railing desperately. After tossing and turning for sleepless hours in the bunk, I had followed Ben up here. Gazing off into the distance I could see every mountain of waves, but the two schooners had disappeared. Suddenly the *Margarita* careened and tilted dangerously to port. I held tight to the bulwark as a giant wave flooded over the whole aftercastle.

"Damn this storm!" Finch raged, leaving the deck with further curses.

I was already regretting having exchanged the half-dry cabin for this stormy position. My clothes, which had already been moist, were now soaking. Icy wind drove through the wet fabric and made me shudder.

"Come on, let's go below deck," Ben called sullenly. He grabbed my arm and we attempted to reach the ladderway safely without being washed off board by the next wave. The sea had already taken two sailors this way. Anyone who lost his footing on deck without being roped up would be washed irrevocably into the depths by the next big breaker.

"What will happen if our escorts don't show up again?" I wanted to know as we stripped off our wet clothes in the cabin. "Do we have to turn around?"

"We've agreed that we will sail on and that the other two ships, as long as they've withstood the storm, will make their way back to Plymouth. As soon as the storm abates, we will continue on our way to Cadiz. Even if they haven't caught up with us by then. It's still not clear how far off course we've gotten, but Finch is an experienced captain. We can trust him."

"What are we going to do in Cadiz?" I asked him curiously.

"Officially we are delivering the requested wares to your uncle's business partners," Ben grinned. "But we're also going to be looking around a bit on our own. What I'm about to tell you has to remain in strictest confidence." Ben had lowered his voice to a barely audible whisper. He pushed me down on the bunk and sat next to me. "Our scouts in Cadiz report that the Spanish fleet has been equipped with new ships. I've been active for years as a … let's say a source of information for an important English figure."

"You're a spy for the Crown?" I gasped out of shock.

"We prefer to think of ourselves as Her Majesty's scouts, if you will."

"Is my uncle a spy as well?"

"Scout, please!" Ben corrected me with a stern look. "Secret agent would also be an appropriate description. We are the good guys, Tom. Protecting and preserving the kingdom. Your uncle is my contact man in Plymouth. He used to do more field work. As the black sheep of your family, he could take liberties that served his duties well. But by now—partly thanks to your unexpected appearance—he's settled down. He's my first contact point when I'm finished with a mission."

"But what are the Spaniards planning? They wouldn't want to attack our fleet, would they?"

"That's exactly what we're supposed to find out. And I was planning on taking you with me on this little reconnaissance mission. What do you think?"

"Me, as a spy—sorry, as a scout—with you in Cadiz? It would be an honor to protect our kingdom from the enemy." I stood upright and proud in front of Ben with my hand on my heart. "Am I supposed to swear an oath now or something?"

Ben laughed out loud, "No, no. Later perhaps. But now it's time to get out of these wet clothes. And don't breathe a word to a single soul about this."

Ben had already taken off his jacket, moist shirt and completely soaked pants. Quickly he grabbed a large towel and rubbed his cold skin dry. He was so intent on what he was doing that he didn't notice me watching him. Carefully, he rubbed his arms and legs, kneading and pressing the skin until it glowed red. It took him a bit more effort to reach his long back. His muscles stretched and tensed. Several times, the towel slipped from his hand. Suddenly he looked up at me.

"Well, you've stood there gawking long enough. Would you help me with my back?"

I set about the task gladly, grabbed the towel and rubbed his skin dry. I was just about to dedicate myself intently to his white ass cheeks when Ben took the towel from my hand.

"You're still wearing all your dripping things. Come on, take them off, otherwise you'll end up with the flu. The last thing I need is an agent sneezing and coughing, betraying our presence at every street corner."

"Yes, Doctor." I followed his instructions dutifully, but I couldn't suppress a grin. I had scarcely shed my soaking clothes when Ben wrapped a large towel around me and rubbed me dry. My arms were surrounded motionless in the vast swath of fabric, placing me fully at the mercy of Ben's careful attention. I had to hold tight as the stormy sea shook the ship with a powerful shudder. Suddenly as he stood behind me with his legs spread, I felt his hard cock rubbing my ass through the towel. His strong hands settled on my hard nipples as if by accident, pulling me into his torso. A soft sigh escaped me.

"Are you dry all over, Tom?" he asked softly, slipping his hands down further.

"Not all over yet," I answered truthfully. "My cock feels so wet all of a sudden."

My stiff mast had in fact found an exit from the large narrow towel, twitching excitedly to be freed. Ben turned me around in one go. Shaking his head, he looked down at my magnificent piece.

"I see your manhood has indeed resisted my efforts. But no more." Ben sank down on his knees in front of me, licking the first drops of pre-cum from my the tip of my cock. Slowly, his lips explored my whole shaft for leftover drops of water. His tongue searched delicately along the throbbing veins.

"Keep looking," I encouraged Ben. "I think my cock is wet again."

"It's true!" he exclaimed, astounded. "There must be a hidden spring here."

Now he put his hand into action, pulling my foreskin far back and then forward again. Each time, new drops gleamed on my throbbing cock head which he licked off with his tongue. Meanwhile his hand stroked up and down my shaft.

"Yeah, that feels good. More ... more!" I pleaded.

I grabbed Ben's head wildly and forced him down on my cock. My balls pulled together rapidly. Ben's tongue surrounded the throbbing base. A warm wave washed from my hips up through to the twitching tip of my cock. Like a long-dammed river, sperm shot from my bursting pipe into Ben's open mouth. He boldly swallowed down my full load and licked my torpedo from top to bottom. Then he looked in my eyes. "I think you're all dry now."

"I can't say the same for you, my friend." I glanced down at his neglected meat twitching upright between his legs, begging for release. A few clear drops were visible on the ground in front of him. Still kneeling, Ben shoved his hips eagerly towards me.

"I'd be glad if you could help me out of this misfortune," he grinned at me.

Then we suddenly heard the sound of the signal bell ringing through the loud roar of the storm. Alarmed, we looked at one another. That couldn't mean anything good. Hastily, we climbed into our moist clothes, which had simply refused to dry for days. Ben had trouble shoving his stiff cock back into his tight pants.

"I guess I'll have to rub you dry later," I called after him as he rushed up the ladderway to the afterdeck. Then I followed him

"Attention on deck! Sail in sight!," the call rang down from the re-manned crow's nest on the top deck.

"What bearing?" called the captain.

He was standing in position with his telescope drawn.

"Three mils forward on the starboard side," was the prompt answer.

He stared into the glass for a long time. He kept opening his mouth as if he was about to say something. Then he closed it wordlessly. Ben and I waited next to him, impatient for his answer.

"It's not ours!" Now it came out. Long silence followed.

"We'll see," he said softly to himself. Then clear and loud to his first mate: "All men make sail. Prepare the artillery. By noon at the latest, she will catch up with us. Our torn mainsails make us a sitting duck. I want to be prepared for anything."

The shrill tone of the boatswain's whistle echoed across the deck. Orders thundered through every corner of the ship. In seconds, all the sailors were at their proper places. The sails were tied carefully. A fresh breeze filled the creaking sail. The masts moaned under the pressure of the wind and the *Margarita* took on speed. Under full sail—though the sails were still damaged—the steaming ship plowed the foaming crests of the waves.

After three more hours, we were as prepared for an attack as we could be. Then the ship's alarm bell rang.

"Pirates ... pirates ... they've hoisted the Jolly Roger! A three-master. I can see down to the second reef of their topsail."

The sailor called several times from the crow's nest. The cloud bank had opened and the sun was even illuminating small stretches of the gray sea with white rays. The shrouds were teeming with sailors. Repairs would still take a while. Without the missing sails we couldn't escape those devils of the sea. Finch cursed again. The pirates' caravel drove through the waves towards its prey with the ease of a dolphin. Suddenly there was a loud thundering crack. Muzzle flashes blazed on the pirate ship. Then an ominous hissing filled the air. Just a ship's length behind the stern, cannonballs crashed into the water in a seething fountain.

"Aft deck, load the artillery! Bombs away!" called Finch.

"Let's see how they like a taste of their own medicine."

The entire ship shuddered as the blazing fuse reached the powder, slinging the cannonball out of its steel pipe with the force of the explosion. This sudden release of a full range of cannons was the captain's decisive answer. But these shots hit empty air, falling far short of their target.

"I want full sails at once, Brington," Finch called to his first mate.

"Aye, Sir. I'm doing everything I can." He turned around, yelled a few loud orders and hurried away. Ben and I stood a bit aside on the aft deck, following the attack agitatedly. By now we could see the pirate ship well. All sails set, spray blasting over the bow, the ship pressed towards us, revealing its imposing form to the eyes of the enemy. The lower part of the ship's wall was painted black, with a narrow red stripe running through it. The towering masts, spars, crossbeams, caps, and even the blocks were painted snow white. Midship between fore and main masts, a long twenty-four pounder was secured to a gun carriage turning in a circle. On every side of the deck, narrow-gauge artillery were mounted.

"Stay here," Ben said suddenly. "I'll be back right away."

He ran off in the direction of our cabin as the pirates' next cannonball whizzed over our heads, splashing into the water portside, a hair's breadth from the ship. I cringed. Cold sweat suddenly ran over my forehead. When would the captain finally run up the surrender flag? Or could we still escape them? Images of bloodthirsty pirates boarding the ship played out in my mind. Bearded sea robbers jumped to the foredeck with drawn knives and sabers, a fight to the death began. But it hadn't come to that yet. The enormous pirate ship slipped next to us with its horrible black flag. Its artillery shot out another salvo at the *Margarita*.

"Here, Tom," Ben's voice tore me from my rigid, staring horror. "Here, take these things. Your uncle gave them to me. In case something happens to us you should make sure to hold on to them. I'll hang the key around your neck." Ben held a chain in his hand with a small gold key.

"I will strap the map tight over your chest. I hope we can hide it in the cabin tomorrow when all this is over." The case was bound in expensive leather. Heavy gold rims decorated its bejeweled lock. Ben drew a broad leather belt—secured with Uncle Walter's secret—around my waist. His hands were shaking. He could barely manage to tie the right knots. I could scarcely perceive the sound of splitting wood. Out of the corner of my eyes I saw the giant masts falling on us, rigging and all. Wrapped in the sail fabric, everything flashed bright white for an instant, as if the rays of the sun had finally caught our ship. Bright flashes shot through my head. The cries of the others reached my ear from a distance, as if through thick fog. Then suddenly all was black and still around me.

swarm of hornets seemed to be raging in my head. Everything in and around me buzzed and roared incessantly. I even briefly smelt fresh grass and a particular kind of flower whose name I could no longer remember. My hands were playing in the shallow water of a small stream. My feet dangled in the reviving water. Then suddenly the air tasted salty. *Strange*, I thought, and then I heard a rough muffled voice entering my consciousness.

"What have we got here?" the voice asked, but I couldn't see anyone. The meadow was still empty. The sun bore down on my face.

"Look at the gold key around his neck. Would be a shame if that went overboard with him."

"Leave it. The dead should be left in peace," a second voice cut in.

"But the key won't be of any use to him down there. And look. He's got a leather case wrapped around him. I bet a share of rum he's got more gold in there."

The rough voice was nearly breaking from excitement.

"All right, the bet is on," the second voice enthused. A little bit later, I was lifted up roughly by my hair and dragged from the soft meadow with the bubbling brook. I protested and tried to defend myself but my arms hung heavy as lead at my sides.

"That man is still alive," a third voice cried suddenly above me. It sounded threatening and energetic. "What is going on here? Why are you standing around when there's work to be done?"

"Look, captain, he was knocked over starboard onto our ship. Lucky for him he was caught in the ropes of the shattered mast. Otherwise he would be swimming with the fishes. He must have gotten caught yesterday during our little skirmish. We thought he was dead. But then he started moving and moaning something awful."

"Then bring him onboard. What are you waiting for? Bring him below deck. As soon as he's back on his feet I want to talk to him. Maybe we can make this little birdie sing."

The men laughed out loud.

"And ... bring the chain and the map to me, just the way they are. Understood?" His droning voice faded off with heavy steps.

"Shit, damn it. Now the old man is going to pocket everything for himself, yet again. If only you hadn't squealed so loud," the rough voice hissed furiously.

"Come on, grab on. We've got to lift up this wet sack and bring him below deck."

I couldn't open my eyes, even though the light was flickering bright red in front of my eyelids. I was pushed and dragged around and then at some point left to fall. The voices around me grew softer, then silenced completely. I was on the green meadow again, smelling the fresh grass. I wanted to stay there.

Were my eyes still closed? Had I suddenly gone blind? Or was it just pitch black around me? Something hard chafed against my cheek. A foul-smelling thick piece of fabric was covering my face. It was difficult to breathe, I could hardly gasp enough air. And my stomach couldn't take the stench for much longer. With effort, I managed to suppress my gag reflex. My arms felt as if they had been pierced by a thousand thin needles. I was sitting with my back leaned against a wall. My wrists were wrapped in something firm, then tied together over my head. Even the slightest movement caused flashes of pain to shoot through the back of my head. I could barely move my legs, which were stretched out in front of me on the ground. My ankles were tied together—and to my horror, I could not feel my toes. But I was alive. I hadn't gone overboard, drowned and become fish food. But that seemed to be the only positive thing about my current situation. The ground beneath me wobbled. So I was still on a ship. But which one? Certainly not among friends. Then I had to be with the pirates! A thought shot through my head: their caravel was probably on its way to the next slave market. These kinds of stories were often heard from the pirates' victims who managed to escape. Pirates didn't generally take prisoners. They only took survivors onboard when they could sell them as slaves in the New World. Very few of them had ever been seen again, and no one made an effort to try to find them. In the face of these hopeless prospects, the last remnants of my courage faded. A worse fate than death awaited me. I let out a desperate sigh.

Suddenly, I heard a crass manly voice muttering: "Seems to be still alive, the little one."

"That's a shame, I would have let the sharks have their meal," another voice said.

I hadn't heard anyone come in, so the two of them must have been standing there for a while.

"I don't think he'll last very long. But maybe he can still make himself useful before we throw him overboard. Let's look at what we've fished in," said the first man. Then the rough sack was abruptly torn from my face. Unprepared, I was blinded by the harsh glare of a lantern. I blinked, trying to make out the men behind the voices. Gradually two silhouettes formed vaguely against the bright light. A sudden coughing fit shook me. I heaved and gasped for air, panting desperately. With each involuntary movement, stabbing pain shot through my tormented muscles.

"Look at that, not a bad catch. Handsome boys fetch a good price on the slave market." By now I could make out the two pirates more clearly. Licking his lips greedily, the larger of the two approached me grinning. A broad scar ran over his entire face. A black leather patch covered the spot where the scar reached his eye. His face, like many seafarers, was wrinkled and rough. His greasy, half-open shirt revealed a thick bush of dark chest hair. Spreading his legs wide and strutting cockily to show off the fat package between his thighs, he walked towards me and bent down. Terrified, I cowered back against the wall and turned my head to the side. In one go he tore my shirt open. The rascal pawed my chest roughly. Then he reared up lazily in front of me.

"Look at this boy! He's about to wet his pants," he said, looking triumphantly over at his companion. "The two of us will have to pluck this fruit the next chance we get. I did bag him with my own hands, after all. Yeah, I bet that shocks you, little boy. You owe your life to me. The others thought you were already dead and wanted to toss you in the sea, but the little package you were defending so desperately caught my attention from the very beginning. So I grabbed it. And you as well! So you belong to me. But of course I'll share you with my best friend here."

A rough, croaking chuckle broke from his throat. He bent over me, grinning.

"I'm sorry, how impolite of me. I've forgotten to introduce myself. My name is Stevenson—ship's mate Stevenson—and this scoundrel here is Mr. Hawkins." He shoved his boot between his legs probingly, then rubbed my cock roughly with his boot sole though the fabric of my pants. "If the rest of you is as promising, we're going to have a lot of fun with you."

His giant mouth contorted into a derisive grin.

"Hey, ship's mate," a voice called suddenly from further back. "The captain wants to know what's going on with the prisoner. What should I tell him?"

"He'll survive," he called back. And then somewhat quietly, with a wink to his companion: "For now, at least." Then louder again: "First we've got to nurse him back to health and then get him back on his feet. Tomorrow we'll bring him back above deck." The other pirate stomped back up the ladderway jangling loudly.

The ship's mate looked after him briefly. Then he turned back around to me and examined me with a lustily look in his eyes. A wild, hungry smile spread over his visage, making him look even more demonic.

"Send for Noah," he said to his partner. "Our prey stinks to heaven. We can't send him to the captain like that. We'll come back later and bring you up, my boy."

Again, he playfully pressed the tip of his boot against my balls. Then the two of them turned around, laughing loudly.

"Where are the others?" I could barely manage to pronounce the words. My lungs rattled loudly. And my quivering voice had become a powerless whisper. But the ship's mate had heard me. He looked back. His eyes narrowed to small dark slits.

"What do you think? We shot your ship into a thousand pieces. It sunk like a stone." Again he came very close to my face.

"It went under without a trace. You're the only one who made it out."

With that, the door slammed shut. A heavy bolt was thrust in front of it.

All of them dead. The whole crew. Ahmed, Ben. A black shadow weighed upon my heart. I could scarcely breathe. My arms and legs wouldn't stop shaking. Then it went dark around me again. I wished for death to take me. But it wasn't to be.

Pale light slipped through a small barred opening in the door. Now I could just barely make out the extent of my prison. I was in a small room just large enough for me to stretch out fully. Fear and desperation rose within me, gradually transforming into sheer panic. I tried to scream but my mouth was completely dried out. It wouldn't have been any use anyway. I was trapped. I pulled in my legs, aching terribly, pushed my feet against the ground and propped myself up bit by bit on the back wall. Maybe if I could stand up I would be able to untie the straps on my hands. My confidence was returning. But when I had nearly gotten to my feet, one of my legs gave out and I slipped sideways on the planks, tumbled, and fell on my face. The leather straps on my hands shielded me from an overly rough impact. However, the fall pulled the straps tighter, sending stabbing pains through my shoulders and wrists. I let out a blood-curdling scream. Then I completely lost my balance and fell back with my face against the wall, completely twisted. Tears of rage, grief, pain, and disappointment ran down my cheeks. It was hopeless. Nearly at the same instant, the door burst open.

"Why you scream loud?" a deep manly voice asked reproachfully. I had no more strength to answer and merely whimpered softly.

Powerful arms turned me around. At first, all my tear-stained eyes could see was a giant black shadow approaching me. I felt someone straightening my legs out carefully on the ground. Nimble hands loosened my straps.

"Thank you," I babbled, hesitant and awkward. "I can't feel my feet," I added softly. The shadow loosened the chains around my ankles a bit more. Relieved, I leaned back. Slowly, life came back to my toes. I sighed. Finally I realized why I hadn't properly seen the puzzling figure in front of me. The man's skin was deep black—blacker than I had ever seen. Strong muscles stood out from his body, which gleamed like a frosted chocolate cake. The giant was wearing nothing but a pair of much-too-tight pants that barely left anything to the imagination. He looked down at me, full of compassion. Involuntarily, I winced. Two rows of snow-white teeth beamed down at me.

"You no fear me. Noah wash you."

His unusual pronunciation drew a small chuckle from me. He took that as confirmation and continued rubbing my legs.

"Now you stand," he ordered. "I help you."

Noah grabbed me under the arms and lifted me up. I seemed to be light as a feather to him. Cautiously, he put me on my feet. And I was actually able to stand on my own two feet—though a bit wobbly and leaning on his chest. Noah was nearly a head taller than me. He wrapped his powerful arms tightly around me and at the same time untied the rope securing my hand straps to the wall. My arms rested like enormous weights on his back. As they hung there, leaden, I could feel the strong muscles tensing beneath his skin. While he kneaded my shoulders gently, a strong manly scent emanated from him. I had never smelled a black man before. I sucked in the magnificent aroma with leisure. My cock reacted immediately, throbbing gently against the crotch of my pants.

"You thirsty?" Noah interrupted the quiet moment.

"Yes, very," was my pleading answer as I looked into his eyes. Deep, dark seas surrounded by shining white seas stared back at me. But this tender moment was interrupted by Noah, who pushed me abruptly into the middle of the room. Before I realized what he was doing, he had lifted my arms up and knotted the leather straps to two rings in the ceiling. Shocked, I looked at him.

"What are you doing?" I whimpered.

"So you no run away. I go get water. You stink!" he countered roughly.

"Where am I supposed to run away on a ship, you dimwit?" I yelled at him with my last strength. A resounding slap to my face was the answer.

"You not swear at Noah. We not friends."

The door slammed loudly behind him. His stomping steps echoed below deck. Then it grew quiet again. It became all too clear to me that my situation had become drastically worse. I had received help, then squandered it rapidly. Sure, I was standing on my feet and the chains weren't as tight as before, but my arms were stretched out on these damn rings on the ceiling. When my legs grew weak, which was only a matter of time, I would be hanging here miserably like I was in the pillories. Suddenly, the door opened with a creak. Noah came in carrying a pail in each hand. Without hesitating, he poured the first bucket over me. Cold water splashed over my entire body.

"Now wash. You still smell."

I was about to snap again, but I noticed him observing me with an iron gaze. I understood. If I didn't want to completely spoil it for myself I would have to show regret.

"I didn't mean it that way. Really." I spoke quietly.

"Then ... it good," was his monosyllabic answer.

Noah came up to me and tore the dirty shirt off my body. With a single tear, he ripped my short pants right and left and threw them in a corner. I stood across from him completely naked. To my surprise he had a piece of soap with him and began lathering me up. Only rich nobles could afford such expensive French soap. And anyway, most of them still believed that washing with water would make them sick. But I knew better from my uncle who had undertaken many travels in foreign countries. "In the Orient there is a distinctively cultivated and deeply developed bathing culture. Regular washing is taken for granted there. No one ever got sick from clean water," Walter would always say. And thanks to Ahmed I had been able to experience the hospitality in a bathhouse firsthand.

Noah must have noticed my astounded glance. He gave me a significant look and said, "Last ship boarded full of soap."

Since I still didn't know how I was supposed to behave, I let him continue without speaking. But how long would I be able to stand the rubbing strokes of Noah's soft hands working over my whole body? Bold and afraid at the same time, I got myself under control. My cock only twitched up once as Noah stroked along the inside of my thighs. But then when he stood close to me and circled my chest muscles with his enormous hands, I couldn't help myself any longer. My shaft jumped up straight as an arrow, slapping loudly against my stomach. An unavoidable moan escaped from my lips.

"Here. Now soap here?" Noah asked with a grin, grabbing my throbbing erection.

"Yes ... please," I begged. Immediately he bent my manhood down and pulled my foreskin back slowly. With his other hand, he spread soap over the trip of my cock. Then he washed my hard shaft with both hands, stroking slowly up and down. He took his time, slowly soaping up my stiff mast. His hands worked thoroughly and continued rubbing while I let out softly whimpering moans. Then Noah let go of my cock unexpectedly and stood behind me. I felt his firm nipples on my back. His powerful arms embraced me and he pressed his hard torpedo against my ass. Now it was his turn to let out a passionate moan. As he slid his stomach up and down my wet back, his erection slipped forcefully between my ass cheeks. At the same time, his hands stroked between my stomach and my upright cock.

"I can't stay on my feet any longer, Noah. You need to untie my arms," I begged.

"No, not allowed," was his merciless answer.

Visibly sobered, Noah let go of me. It was then that I finally saw the giant torpedo that had been sliding along my ass. It was even darker than the rest of that muscular giant, towering up like the foremast of a galleon. Its thick head exceeded the mast on all sides, gleaming a deep dark red. In my astonishment, I nearly slipped on the wet planks, but I caught myself just in time. Cursing loudly, I stared at him.

"Damn it! These straps are going to cut off my wrists!"

The answer to my unrestrained behavior was a second volley of water. But to my surprise, it was pleasantly warm this time.

"You should not complain so loud. Now I make you dry. Then help you. With this."

Noah pointed to my arms. *Finally*, I thought with relief, but said nothing just to be safe. With a soft towel, the hulk dried me off. As he did this he made sure to thoroughly rub my chest. My nipples reacted to this torture by sticking out firm and hard. And since my cock seemed to be directly wired to those sensitive pleasure nodes, it did the same. Without Noah even coming near it, it reared up again and throbbed heavily, as if to attract attention. To my great disappointment, Noah paid no attention to this clear offer. Instead, he wiped the last drops from between my ass cheeks with fastidious exactness. One hand spread my naked mounds apart while the other shoved the fabric in my crack.

"You're going to rub me raw. That's enough. Come in front instead. There's something waiting for you here." I tried to focus his attention on my increasing problem. Finally, he let go of what he was doing, stood in front of me and looked down at my throbbing cock with a smile.

"Nice mast," he said, impressed. Then he looked around and went up to the weakly burning lantern hanging from the ceiling. He tipped it to the side and dripped some of the lamp oil onto his thick torpedo. Then he pleasurably rubbed the warm liquid into his veiny shaft. In the feeble light his magnificent cock gleamed like a polished, pitch-black wooden club. I watched Noah, amazed. He rubbed his shaft firmly. His angular chest muscles pumped up a bit with each stroke, and his tight ass twitched slightly. Reluctantly he lifted his hands from his pleasure pole and a soft moan slipped from his lips.

"First get ready back there," he turned to me with determination.

Before I realized what he meant Noah was spreading my legs and leaning on my shoulders. The leather straps on my hands pulled painfully for an instant, but before I could cry out, he had already shoved his powerful paw beneath my ass cheeks. Then he held me light as a feather in one hand. With the other he grabbed the towel again and began rubbing my crack dry. This task seemed to excite him. It seemed to take an eternity before he was content, saying, "All right, dry now. And your arms better this way."

He pushed his second hand beneath my ass and lifted me up a bit higher. My whole weight was now held in his powerful hands, and my arms could now relax. I was enjoying this feeling of weightlessness when I suddenly felt a strong pull between my spread ass cheeks. My guard had positioned the tip of his cock directly at my back entrance. Slowly he lowered my ass down onto his oiled mast. He paused for a second, then his hammer pushed through my muscle ring. Beads of sweat formed on my forehead. I wasn't ready for this. Desperately I tried to pull myself up again to escape the unbearable pressure, but instead my shifting movements brought me further down on the giant tool.

"You're killing me," I cried out. "Your monster cock is too big for me."

"If you think? Then I free you."

I could hear disappointment in his words. Nonetheless he lifted me up again—though much too slowly. Then he bent his head far down and took my throbbing cock in his mouth. His teeth slid down to the base. Cursing, I gasped for air. My asshole cramped up and clamped around his cock directly beneath the head. When he released my cock from his mouth, Noah briefly loosened his grip. This time I slid down full force on his pole.

"Don't do that again, you barbarian ..." I threatened, breathless. But the gleeful grin on his face left me no hope that the rascal would take my words seriously. I wouldn't be able to escape him. After all, pirates were known for taking what they wanted. Grabbing my ass firmly, Noah played with it, pushing me faster up and down on his cock while his hungry mouth swallowed my manhood to the hilt every time he lifted me. Wild lust spread through my crotch. I wanted to feel this cock deeper in me. And I wanted Noah to swallow my cock even deeper in his throat. I pulled myself slightly higher with the chains above my head only to increase the torturous pleasure when I fell back down. When I felt my torment-er's cock growing thicker I knew he wouldn't last much longer. I tightened my sphincter and pushed my cock as deep as I could in his mouth, bringing him to the point of exploding. Noah bent back and stood on his toes, shoving his throbbing sword in me down to the hilt. With a loud howl he shot his load in my tight gate. His final thrust brought me past the point of no return. My sperm flew onto his chest in a wide arc. The white splotches looked like snowflakes on black ebony. Panting, I sprayed my load onto his chest in spurt after spurt. The hot cream in my balls had been wait-ing for that moment so long, not running dry until the last drop shot from my quivering cock. My asshole twitched slightly around Noah's softening cock. Slowly, his breath began to calm. Streaming sweat, he stood in front of me.

"Now I need to wash you," I said boldly.

He pulled his thick cock from my ass and slipped my legs off his shoulders wordlessly. But I wouldn't let him go.

"But you've got to free my arms first," I said, trying to convince him. "Then I could at least rub you dry."

Noah actually pulled a knife from his pants, which were lying on the ground. He came up to me, took me in his arms and cut through the damn straps. Powerless, I sank into his arms. "Thank you, you strong pirate."

His sensual lips embraced my dry mouth in a long kiss.

"Now drink, then sleep," Noah ordered. Without letting me go he pulled a small flask from his pants and directed it to my mouth. Cold sweet wine flooded down my throat. An act of kindness. Then Noah pulled a hammock from the corner and stretched it across the room. Carefully, he set me down inside it.

"I come tomorrow," he promised, then shut the door behind him and locked it. As soon as I was alone the wine took effect. Before I could even think what the next day would bring I fell into a deep, strong sleep.

"Come on, wake up, boy." Someone was shaking my shoulders roughly. "Here, put this on and come with me."

A pirate stood in front of me, grimacing. You could tell his pirate's honor was injured by having to deal with a worthless prisoner.

"Is the captain already waiting for me?" I asked hopefully.

"Bah, the captain has more important things to do than deal with beach rubble." His eyes gleamed mockingly. Then a grin flashed over his face and he made an ironic face. "But the whole deck is waiting for you."

As we left my prison I was blinded by broad daylight. The sudden brightness made me wince involuntarily.

"It's better if you look down anyway," my guard mocked me. "Here's a brush and pail. Start scrubbing the deck. That's your first task. And when you're done you can start all over again."

He kicked me in the ass. Awkwardly, I stumbled over the pail. I tried to hold tight to the railing but I slipped on the wet wood planks. A second later I landed roughly in a puddle of dirty water on the ground. The pirates standing around howled and roared gleefully at my misfortune. Accompanied by their disdainful cries, I started scrubbing the ship planks.

"What's going on here," a thunderous voice called from the aft deck.

"Nothing, Master Jack. I just brought the prisoner on deck to work as you ordered. As we expected, he's quite useless. This fine gentleman clearly isn't used to scrubbing the deck on his knees."

The man who was speaking cast me a derisive glance then disappeared again. For the next hour I scrubbed the cursed deck. Driven by uncontrollable rage, I set to work with determination. I gained strength from my rage over my fate as a prisoner, rage over my friends' fates, rage about losing the valuable things Ben had entrusted to me. Then there was my wild fury about the humiliation of having to scrub planks for these pirates. Once I had worked of all my resentment I began to look inconspicuously at my surroundings. The busy hubbub around me had abated. Here and there individual orders were bellowed out, but in the midday heat most of the sea robbers had retreated to the shade. All the sails were set. The ship flew along the light waves. I felt as if I was being observed.

When I turned around I saw a young man standing on the aft deck in the glaring sun. For a few seconds his gaze rested attentively on me. Then he looked out towards the sea again. Now I was the one observing him. The sight of this magnificent man made me speechless. Upright, unflappable as a rock, he stood there. His broad knee-length pants didn't conceal his powerful legs. His broad shoulders were covered by a white, half-open shirt. Dark hairs curled on his chest. His face was lean and shaved smooth, his skin bronzed by the sun, his dark eyebrows set apart from the clear sea blue of his eyes. His nearly black hair was bound together at the back, blowing in the wind. Was he the captain of this pirate ship? No, he was much too young to be the captain.

He looked over at me again. He had probably noticed me staring at him intently. He flashed me a friendly grin. Confused, I lowered my glance and continued to work. Now it was no longer rage driving me forward, but a pleasant tingling between my legs. Then I suddenly felt the tip of a boot roughly hit my ass.

"Well, boy, scrubbing hard? You seem to be a real expert. I can think of a few other things I'd like you to scrub." I turned around. Stevenson and Hawkins were standing behind me. The ship's mate leaned lazily against the railing, still pressing his boot against my ass.

"I'll get you, little one, you can depend on that," he grinned. Turning to his companion he continued "Tonight, the boy is going to get it."

"Ship's mate, do you have nothing better to do than pestering the prisoner?" the beautiful man called from the aft deck.

"Aye aye, Master Jack. Just wanted to make sure that this dandy here makes the ship properly clean."

Then he kicked me again, this time so strongly that I fell flat on deck. Bored, he turned and slinked away. I could hear him whisper to Hawkins. "Wannabe-master-vice-captain-fine-Jack is acting like an admiral again. It stinks around here since the captain's bastard son is on board. Time for him to pay a visit to the fish. But first pleasure, then work." With that, the two scoundrels disappeared below deck laughing gleefully. What were the two of them planning? I was already dreading my return to that stuffy prison. I looked over to the man on the aft deck again. So his name was Jack and he was the son of the pirate captain. He was busy observing the execution of a turning maneuver in the halyards. His determined tone when giving orders, his confident behavior and decisive facial features as he drove the others on to work made him seem older than he really was. I could understand how experienced sea men would have a problem with having such a young man as a deputy. But at the same time I could recognize that the captain had found in his son an excellent, conscientious seaman who knew how to run a ship.

As I continued scrubbing the planks, I didn't work as thoroughly as before. I kept looking up at Jack. I simply couldn't get enough of his fantastic body. When it began to grow dark a pirate brought me back to my cell. A meager dinner stood ready. A jug of stale water stood on the ground next to a piece of hard bread. To my surprise, there was also a half-glass of wine standing next to it.

"With greetings from Master Jack. He was pleased with your work," the pirate said as he saw my astounded face. Then he closed the door from the outside and placed the lock over it.

The pale light of the sinking sun fell through a few narrow cracks in the wall. My arms and knees were in pain from the unusual strain of the day. Hungrily, I swallowed the food down. But I savored the wine leisurely in my hammock. The cold drink was a blessing for my dry throat, loosening my tense muscles. As they had numerous times that day, my thoughts strayed to Jack. Tomorrow I would try to talk to him to thank him for the wine.

*T*he loud creak of the door and bright light flooding in made me sit bolt upright. I had tried to stay awake to avoid being surprised by the ship's mate's threatened visit, but fatigue had overpowered me. Before I realized what was happening, someone was grabbing me by the feet. I was pulled roughly from my hammock. A second later, Stevenson's roguish grin appeared in my field of vision.

"Sleep well, boy?" he hissed at me. His breath smelled of fatty food and rum. Thinking quick, I pulled my fist back for a quick uppercut. In the middle of the motion it suddenly stopped. Held tight by an invisible force, it hesitated motionless in midair. Then I noticed that Hawkins, the ship's mate's comrade, had taken position behind me. With an iron grip he clasped my arm and smiled derisively at me.

"Who would give such an unfriendly greeting? We just wanted to see if you're all right, and if you've got everything you need," he murmured in an exaggeratedly obliging manner.

"Exactly. We need to reassure ourselves that you are doing fine. It's my responsibility you don't collapse tomorrow or stink like a fish when you're brought past the captain," Stevenson added self-contentedly.

"But when you come at us like that … then we really have no other choice but to teach you a little manners."

He nodded briefly to Hawkins, who had already begun tying my hands up. With secure seaman's knots he fixed my outstretched arms to the side braces of the hammock while the ship's mate tied two rough loops around my ankles, pulled my legs up high and secured the ropes on metal hooks built into the low ceiling. Now my back was the only part of my body still touching the protective fabric of the hammock. My head hung over the edge, sinking lower as they worked. On the other side, my ass jutted out unprotected past the fabric.

"So let's begin with the inspection. Check if the man still stinks."

Hawkins pulled my hair and rubbed it between his filthy fingers.

"Completely rank, ship's mate. And there are definitely lice in here as well. Looks like it's got to go."

"Don't you dare touch my hair …"

I didn't get any farther. My voice failed when Stevenson flashed his knife. He approached slowly. His eyes gleamed threateningly.

"The captain doesn't like it when vermin are dragged on board his ship," he hissed. "I would advise you to keep very quiet now. Come on, hold his head tight, Hawkins."

He came closer to me and whispered directly in my ear: "We don't want to shave the young man's scalp off his skull, do we?"

Then he started to shave my hair indifferently. The scraping noise of the blade pierced me to the bone, but I clenched my teeth and didn't dare move. I held my eyes closed. Memories rose in me of how my father had always stroked my brown locks. How my mother had tirelessly combed them with a brush when thick clumps of dirt had gotten caught in them after I had been out playing. How long ago had that been? And how far away? Again and again, Stevenson applied the blade without mercy. I heard locks of hair falling to the ground left and right. And gradually I felt the cool breath of sea air on my naked skin. Then a rough hand followed, examining my bald skull. When I opened my eyes cautiously I was staring directly into the shipmate's spiteful face.

"Well, how does that feel? Look at that, Hawkins, the little boy is about to blubber."

Both men laughed out loud. With glassy eyes I tried to meet their derisive gazes.

"You will pay for this," I snarled.

"Those are awfully tall words, boy. Seems it's time we stuff your cheeky gullet." Stevenson put his knife away. Then he bellowed over to his companion: "Come on, keep going!"

Immediately, Hawkins bent over me, his nostrils widening loudly as he sniffed eagerly at my armpits. My body twitched lightly as his rough tongue suddenly licked my inner arm softly.

"Everything seems to be clean," he stated neutrally. He switched to the other side. Again, his tongue stroked my delicate skin. The rascal stuck his nose among my short chest chairs and licked my nipples tentatively. Then his tongue wandered down in the direction of my navel, still standing behind me with legs spread. The bulging crotch of his pants hovered over my face, and I could clearly feel his thick pirate cock throbbing against my forehead. Hawkins seemed to enjoy the pressure on his manhood. His rough pants rubbed unrestrainedly against my face. Unfortunately, my own tool could not help reacting to this particular treatment. First hesitantly, then boldly, my plank rose up. In seconds my cock head was swollen thick, pushing eagerly out of my foreskin.

"Ah …" grunted Stevenson with a contented glance at my erection. "Here's another spot that tends to get forgotten during washing. I'll have to take care of this all by myself."

His hand clasped my shaft firmly and pulled my foreskin down.

"Looks quite all right," he murmured in appreciation. Then he bent my hammer back. Next I felt his tongue exploring the tip of my cock. Leisurely, the shipmate tested every inch of my rapidly pulsing manhood to make sure it was clean. Then my thick shaft disappeared unexpectedly into his large mouth. The pirate swallowed my sword down to the hilt. He sucked dutifully, as if he actually wanted to test it.

"I'm still not sure," he turned to his comrade. "Why don't you try?"

He was already pushing my cock towards Hawkins encouragingly. Hawkins, who had been licking my navel thoroughly, shifted downwards. His tongue was much softer and more cautious than the first mate's. But his lips, which were now slipping over my cock, were even more demanding and firm. Different tongues feel so different, I thought. The next instant I was ashamed of the thought. These two men were inspecting me like merchandise, and all I could think about was how their tongues felt different. I must have gone crazy. Up until this point, I had let them examine me without moving. Not just because I was still chained hand and foot, but because I was afraid that any movement would make the two rogues turn malicious with me. Even though my cock had been following its own laws for some time now. Hawkins let my meat slip from his mouth.

"At least his equipment is fully clean now," he grinned at Stevenson and licked his lips. "The boy really has a gigantic rod. Even yours isn't that long, shipmate. And if anyone can judge that, it's me."

His hands began to knead my nipples.

"And if I press a little bit here ..." He squeezed my hard nipples painfully. "... The thing jumps like a dolphin out of water."

"We'll see whose is longer," Stevenson retorted defiantly. He had taken his pants off already; now he threw his shirt carelessly in a corner. I lifted my head and looked at the first mate's angular, thickly-haired chest. Even his muscled upper arms were covered with thick fur. Together with his black beard and scarred face he was a quite fearsome sight. But what was even more terrifying was the giant bulging shaft towering out of the thick bush between his legs. The first mate pushed up tight against my ass and placed his cock on top of mine. His torpedo was actually slightly longer than mine. As he squeezed the two cocks together in his fist I could feel the blood pulsing in his thick pirate meat.

"I've got to get a closer look," said Hawkins, bending over me again. Then he sunk both our cocks halfway into his massive mouth.

"I should have known you were trying to trick me, you deceptive rascal," panted Stevenson, who had seen through his friend's bold trick. "But if that's the way you like it, help yourself. You can even have more if you like."

With that, he grabbed the back of his buddy's head and thrust his cock deeper into his throat. I felt the first mate's hard shaft rubbing up and down on mine as he sensually slipped in and out of Hawkins' mouth. The pirate's lips pressed our throbbing masts tightly together. Not every mouth would have been capable of taking on such a considerable task, but Hawkins seemed to truly enjoy working over two thick cocks at the same time. His tongue circled tirelessly around the pulsing tips of our cocks, wandering down one shaft then the other. Stevenson's torpedo had gained even greater length, and my manhood made it up for what it lacked in length through increasing girth. Hawkins had visible difficulty taking us both in his throat at the same time. But he didn't give up yet. Snorting, he grasped my ass cheeks with his hands and shoved my plank deeper into his throat. The first mate's paws pushed his friend's head down on our two throbbing masts. Hawkins' lips were stretched to the breaking point, but he still managed to push them down further over our poles. When the tip of his nose was finally digging into the first mate's thick hairs, he gave a contented grunt despite his full mouth.

But my awe didn't last long. Shortly after that, when Hawkins spread my ass cheeks with his hands and shoved two fingers through my tight entrance, I cried out loud in shock. Up until now,

I had suppressed every movement out of fear for more torture, but now I thrashed about wildly in my rage and pain.

"Take your filthy fingers out of my ass," I cried. "And I'm going to choke on your reeking pants if you don't stop pushing your bull balls in my nose, you goddamn hellhound."

To my surprise, Hawkins actually let go of my ass. He even let our cocks slip from his dripping mouth, then slipped off of me and stood up. With a grin, he looked down at me, then over to Stevenson. The two of them laughed out loud. I knew that was not a good sign.

"Well, well," Stevenson grunted. There was a spiteful undertone to his voice. "So you're insulting the man who rescued you? That's not very grateful of you. We just want a bit of compensation for the work we've done. Without us you would have landed with the sharks a long time ago. And maybe you'll actually get to be acquainted with the lovely animals quite soon."

His giant hands slapped against my ass cheeks. My answer was a muffled howl.

"He says you have bull balls, Hawkins." Once more, his calloused palms slapped against my burning ass. "Did you hear that? Maybe the boy here is just jealous?"

With each sentence he pulled back farther, slapping his hand against my ass with increasing fury. Tears came to my eyes. My skin was burning like a blazing fire.

"Stop," I roared at him.

"Oh no," Stevenson hissed back. "We've just begun. Why don't you just show him your thick balls," he said, turning to Hawkins, who was already ripping his shirt and pants from his body. From below I could see his firm stomach and angular chest. At the sight of his ballsac my eyes grew wide. Calling them "bull balls" had not been an exaggeration. The fat spheres hung down deep and heavy between his legs. Above them, his thick cock dangled like an aggressive snake whose one-eyed head was turned directly towards me.

"Yeah, I can hear you gasping for air," Hawkins mocked. "You're going cross-eyed. But just wait until my friend here comes to life …" With that, he slapped his plank roughly right and left against my cheeks. "… You'll wish you were lying on the bottom of the sea with the mussels."

"I'll report all of this to the captain tomorrow," I tried to intimidate the two of them. The first mate's answer was another slap to my ass.

"Stuff his mouth, Hawkins," Stevenson ordered. "I can't hear this whining anymore."

A second later Hawkins grabbed my nipples tight. As I was opening my mouth to scream out, Hawkins shoved his thick pole deep in my throat.

"Don't dare using your teeth," he threatened. "As I live and breathe I will rip your balls off."

"And I'll help him," the first mate affirmed.

To give weight to his words, he tugged my sack energetically with one hand. Appraisingly, he weighed my balls in his palms.

"Judging by the size of these things I would place this young stallion in the top class. I'm curious to see how wild he gets when we start riding him."

At that moment I wasn't sure if I would survive that day. The two pirates seemed to enjoy watching me suffer. But I wouldn't give up so quickly. Maybe I could distract them, play along with their game for a while and then use the next opportunity to flee. Even though I didn't find it very agreeable to be their plaything, as long as they were having fun with me they would at least not throw me overboard to feed the fish. With his left hand still gripped tight around my sac, Stevenson grabbed my flaccid cock with his right. He rubbed it vigorously, until a thick hard pipe was towering between my legs. I already felt pre-cum dripping from my cock. Stevenson continued his work without hesitating. As I began to fear that a small lake was going to form on my stomach, my asshole suddenly started to twitch involuntarily. The first mate seemed to have been waiting for that. Immediately he let go of my cock, wiped the fluid from my stomach with his hand and pressed his moist fingers against my rosebud. I reared up to resist the invasion but the hand clamped tight on my balls made me think better of it. The hard slaps at my ass seemed to have had the desired effect.

Surprisingly, my narrow hole opened at the first touch, swallowing the eager finger willingly. Hawkins took advantage of the fact that the first mate had let go of my meat. He bent over me eagerly, sinking his cock further down my throat. The fat snake pulsed excitedly in my mouth. I could still manage to tame the beast, but I was afraid it was far from reaching its full size. Hawkins began unrestrainedly sucking my nipples, causing my cock to lurch. Then his rough tongue licked down the fine, hairy midline to my navel to lap up the rest of my pre-cum. But Hawkins' ultimate goal was the tip of my throbbing cock, which was dripping its sticky nectar. His mouth set to work boldly, pressing drop after drop out of the long pipe. He slipped his lips as far as possible over my cream dispenser and tensed them forcefully as his tongue greedily slurped up the wet drops. His own pole quickly reached a size that made it impossible for me to swallow it all the way down. I tilted my head back to keep from suffocating on his giant meat and his thick balls lying on my face. As I began to gag more desperately, Hawkins understood. He stretched his massive legs and gave me some more room to breathe.

"That's good. Give him a bit of time to get used to your giant," said Stevenson. "The young stallion must not have much experience with such big carrots. We'll see how he manages."

The whole time, the first mate had been working over my pleasure gate with his fingers. Two or three of his shameless grips had sunk within me, exploring the narrow canal and stretching it further. Now he pulled them out completely. His moist hands stroked along the inside of my legs, which were still spread wide with their straps attached to the ceiling. Shivers ran through my body as Stevenson clasped my thigh, directed his mushroom head to my rosebud, and forcefully shoved his pole in my ass. For a brief moment, none of us moved. All I felt were three pulsing cocks: my own in Hawkins' mouth, his deep in my throat, and Stevenson's enormous hammer filling up my ass. The hard shaft slid slowly out of my narrow canal, only to push back roughly. Then Stevenson shoved my manhood back into his comrade's mouth, allowing me a second to catch my breath on the other end.

"We'll see how far we get today. What do you think, Hawkins?" asked the first mate.

Immediately Hawkins let my cock slip from his mouth, then stood up and grunted: "As far as I'm concerned we can get going. I've got everything in hand here."

His hands had clasped onto my firm nipples again, tweaking them sharply. Shortly afterwards I felt his thick mast entering my mouth. The two men started to shove me between their hard cocks—first slowly, then accelerating to a feisty tempo. Stevenson's firm balls smacked against my ass as he sunk his shaft within me, while Hawkins' fat rod plowed my throat. The pungent manly odor between his legs became an intoxicating drug for me. My cock slapped against my abs in time with their thrusts, my pulsing mushroom head burned as if on fire, but neither of them paid it any attention. If I could have gotten my hands free, I could have relieved myself immediately. Instead, I could only flail my arms and shoulders back and forth, which pulled the sailors' knots at my wrists even tighter.

"Watch out, Hawkins. I thought we had a lame Dartmoor pony on our hands, but this unruly beast is actually starting to buck. And his stallion cock seems about to burst. Keep going. You'd probably like to pump out your horse cock, right? But first we want to see how long you can last in the first round. When I was young, I rode more than one stubborn horse on our estates. I liked the obstinate stallions best. By the end I could make them all walk like obedient dogs on a leash. The stall boys were impressed by my riding skills. Even my father was proud of me. So you see you're in the best of hands here."

His stiff mast pushed wildly, uninhibitedly between my spread ass cheeks. Now and then he would pull out and smack his thick cock head against my sensitive balls. Then he would ram his manhood back deep into my warm cavern.

"Don't you think it's time to use the harness?" asked Hawkins suddenly. As he made this bizarre suggestion his cock twitched expectantly in my throat. Then as he started to smack my firm chest with the palm of his hand, I feared the worst. I'm sure my tortured skin was brick red. I could feel my chest quaking, burning and glowing hot.

"Yes, you're right. It's time to tighten the reins a bit," the first mate agreed. "But let him watch. He should learn what it means to be tamed by an experienced horseman."

Hawkins freed me from his pole and lifted my head lightly. I watched as Stevenson placed a metal ring around my balls. Several plaited leather straps were secured to the ring. He squeezed the device down to the base of my cock, then tightened the straps around my sac to separate my balls down the middle. Then the first mate shoved his firm torpedo back in my ass, fixing the loose ends of the straps to his cock and fat sac.

"All right, let's try out the harness," he roared and began thrusting his pole in and out of my ass. When he pulled back, the straps tightened and would only let his cock go far enough out that his thick head pressed against my tight rosebud from within. At the same time my cock was pulled inevitably upwards. Bucking like a wild horse, it twitched and rolled while my firmly secured balls struggled against these unusual chains. I moaned in pleasure.

"Ohh … no … that's too much. I can't take it anymore. You barbarian, you're going to rip off my cock."

"Don't worry, boy, I already said I have experience with riding young stallions. Come on, let your horse cock dance for us."

Now that Stevenson's hands were free, he bent forward between my spread legs, grabbed my nipples and rubbed his flat hands roughly over my chest. All the while I tore at the straps on my hands, pressed my back against the hammock and flailed my legs against my foot chains. I moaned out loud as Stevenson's meat rammed back into me. One thing was clear to me: I was not going to escape this brutal lug or his giant appendage.

"Resisting again?" Stevenson purred to me. His voice had taken on a threatening tone. "As you like! Come on, Hawkins, sit on his mouth and give your cock to me." His comrade actually stood spread-legged over me, pushed his throbbing cock into the bent-over first mate's waiting mouth and positioned his asshole directly over my mouth. Restlessly, he shoved his sweaty ass between my nose and chin while his rod sunk deep in his friend's throat.

"Come on, lick my goddamn ass, boy, otherwise you'll have to deal with me," Hawkins spurred me on. His hands were spreading his ass cheeks wide. Carefully and uncertainly, my tongue circled around his rosebud.

"Yeah, stick it in deep. Oh … that's so good. More. Deeper, man."

As if under a spell, my tongue teased his moist cave more aggressively. Suddenly, Hawkins' movements grew more rapid. His twitching rosebud tightened. He lay his hands on the back of the first mate's head and pushed him relentlessly onto his cock. Meanwhile, Stevenson thrust his cock deep into my canal. He clamped his paws on Hawkins' hips, sucking loudly on his friend's pole until his whole body began to shake. Warm streams of sperm shot down the first mate's throat. At the same time, Stevenson's torpedo swelled also. My tight hole stretched visibly under his throbbing weight. In one last wild thrust the pirate's balls boiled over, flooding hot fluid into my ass like a bursting dam. Moaning, the first mate lay on top of me gasping for breath as his meat kept pumping within me. Finally Hawkins spilled from my face. Then he slapped his thick moist cock against my cheeks, laughing.

"Not bad at all for a landlubber. What do you think, first mate?"

He untied the leather straps from my sac and pulled his cock out of my ass. Sensually, he massaged his manhood and slapped the thick mushroom head against my tight balls.

"We should come back later and then decide what we're going to do with this boy. But first I need a proper swig of rum."

With the back of his hand, he wiped off the last of his comrade's sperm. With a pleading look I looked up at my firm, twitching plank. The iron ring wedged around its base squeezed the swollen shaft, and the head had grown dark red. All the veins in my pulsing erection stood out dangerously and my wedged balls seemed to be twice as large as normal.

"And what about me? You can't just leave me lying here. My cock is about to burst and my ass is burning," I cursed.

"You're right about that," the first mate grinned in amusement. "I'll leave my substitute here, that way I don't have to start from the beginning next time to loosen up your ass."

Uncomprehending, I looked at him. He swung a wooden belaying pin in front of my face. These forearm-length pegs were positioned all around the ship in pegboards to secure ropes. As soon as I realized what the rascal was planning, my eyes went wide in horror. Stevenson ran his long tongue over the polished grip of the peg, smacking his lips. Grinning, his face contorted to a derisive mask. Then he shoved the round end of the peg into my moist hole without further warning. My scream was muffled by a thick rag Hawkins stuffed cleverly into my mouth, then tied around my neck. I tried to push the wooden pin back out, but Stevenson had already rapped the loose leather straps around the end of the peg and tied them tight. Panic rose within me. I tore at my chains wildly. The hammock rocked wildly back and forth.

"I can see," Stevenson said, "that as soon as we've gotten back our strength, we'll have lots more to teach this stallion."

Laughing loud, he clapped his comrade on the shoulder. Then the two of them slipped their pants on rapidly, snatched up the oil lantern, and slammed the door shut. It had grown dark around me again. The two of them hadn't even bothered to lock the door, that's how sure they were that I wouldn't be able to escape. But I had to try nonetheless. Cautiously I turned my right hand back and forth in the tight chain, then did the same with my left. If I just twisted my wrists long enough, the knot would hopefully loosen at some point. On one side I had already half managed it. Sweat ran over my entire body. I thought nostalgically of Noah and his revitalizing washing skills.

My cock answered by twitching lightly. Unfortunately my asshole twitched as well, causing the thick wood rod to sink deeper inside me. A hot wave rose up from my legs. My skin burned and prickled indescribably. A muffled moan escaped my throat.

"What you whining now?"

Suddenly Noah was standing in the doorframe holding up a lamp. Wide-eyed, he tried to comprehend the scene before his eyes. Then he freed my mouth from the stinking rag.

"Who did this?"

"Stevenson and Hawkins, those two scoundrels," I managed to croak out before being overcome by a coughing fit. Noah had already freed my arms. But when he saw the long peg jutting out from my ass between my hanging legs, he hesitated.

"Devil take them!" he hissed through his flawless teeth.

"Pull it out carefully and grab my cock tight. I can't get the damn iron ring off in this condition anyway. My cock is going to burst if you don't start right away," I coughed numbly. Noah yielded to my desperate need. First he swiftly loosened the tight leather straps, then grabbed the wooden peg with one hand and my cock with the other. As he pulled on the peg he massaged my tortured meat.

"More … faster … please!"

I moaned and cried out at the same time. When the fat wooden peg slipped from my sphincter all at once, my balls pulled up tight, the head of my cock spread like a sail in a storm and my hot load shot like a cannon ball from my shaft onto the wall behind me. Faster than any cannoneer ever could have reloaded, more white clumps slapped against my face and stomach. Freed from the pressure, I sighed with relief.

"Thank you, Noah. You rescued me."

Grinning happily, my rescuer loosened the straps around my legs and lifted me up.

"I bring you on deck. Then better hide you from first mate. He be very angry when you not here." Noah picked me up in his strong arms, naked as I was, and carried me up the ladderway. My head rested gently on his shoulder. As if through fog I perceived him laying me on deck in a dark corner, slipping a large shirt over me and covering me carefully with a blanket.

"I back in a minute. Not move. Make good hiding place ready," Noah said before disappearing.

Deep fatigue overcame me. Contented, I breathed in the fresh night air. Bright stars shone above me. The white sails gleamed palely in the moonlight. For the first time after my long imprisonment I felt free again. Then my eyes fell shut.

I have no idea how long I laid there. If I moved in the slightest, all my bones ached; my arms and legs still felt numb and I had difficulty keeping my head from falling on my chest. A thousand needles seemed to be stuck in my back. Not to mention my ass, which was burning like hell, setting off wild flashes to ignite my loins. I crawled over to a large barrel and leaned my back against it.

I looked up yearningly at the glimmering dots in the night sky, whose light I had missed for so long. Uncle Walter always used to say that we only recognize the value of everyday things when they're no longer there. Most of the time I had shrugged off this wisdom. But now I realized how much truth there was to it. The sight of the broad canvas of stars stretching over the ocean reminded me painfully how precious freedom was.

I wished I was back in the little cabin in the woods near Plymouth. Where on those clear nights nothing but the stars watched over Brian and me. Suddenly I missed my lover again. His gentle voice, his warm skin, our boundless intimacy. I hadn't thought of him for ages. Where was he now? I'm sure he no longer believed he would see me again in this lifetime. Was he grieving for me? Or had he already found a new lover? Did I myself believe I would ever hold him in my arms again? For a brief eternity, my heart seemed to stop. Time stretched infinitely. But as soon as the moment was over there was nothing left but deep emptiness. Resigned, my gaze turned back to the rolling sea.

In the east, the sun was sending out its first heralds. The first shimmer of dawn flickered on the horizon, bathing the ship in a ghostly light. Dark shadows crept over the empty deck. In a few moments day would once again conquer the world. I had often longed for this moment on the *Margarita*, just before the sun broke above the surface of the water sending its warm rays over the world. Again I was reminded of the loss of my freedom. True, I could move freely now, but where was I supposed to flee? Should I just jump overboard and hope a ship would come soon and pick me up? There was still time for that. Or should I seek out a secure refuge for the time being and wait until we sailed past an island to slip overboard?

Where had Noah gone? He had said he would be back right away. An uneasy feeling spread in my stomach. Then I heard a muffled cry all of a sudden. Something heavy fell off the portside into the water with a loud splash. Hasty steps rushed away along the deck. Alarmed, I jumped up, but in the next instant my legs collapsed beneath me and I fell to my side on the planks. I cursed out loud. A thin cry for help rang up to me from the water. Amid indescribable pain and further curses against my tormentors, I raised myself up and clasped the railing. Down in the water a dark figure was paddling his arms helplessly. Without thinking I tied a rope around my hips, secured the end to the nearest pegboard and jumped overboard. Icy cold surrounded me as I entered the foamy sea. High waves crested above me. I couldn't breathe. I sank underwater. Stillness. A brief moment of peace surrounded me. If I would just ... then, coughing, I resurfaced from the flood. Had I honestly believed, just a few minutes ago, that I could escape by swimming away? I questioned my sanity. Panting, I looked over where I had seen waving hands just a moment ago. They had disappeared. Or not … I saw them again a bit farther off among the waves. With a few desperate strokes I reached the spot. Just in time to keep the man from sinking beneath the waves again. I grabbed him energetically, pulling his powerless body to me. The weight made me sink beneath the surface of the water again. Desperately, I paddled upward. No, my journey was not going to come to an end here. My lungs filled with air again, but I could also feel my legs going numb, and my fingers were cramping in the freezing water. I could barely hold the heavy man. Then my security rope tightened and we were pulled back in the direction of a ship. Loud voices above me bellowed out orders. The next thing I knew, strong arms were grasping me and pulling me on board with the unconscious man.

"Bring them under deck right away and wrap them up warmly," a voice droned from the aft deck. "Come on, grab under his arms. Man, he's heavy!"

Two sturdy men grabbed hold of me. I sank weakly into their arms. They carried me down the steps under deck, tore my wet things off my body and rubbed my icy body roughly until it was glowing. Calloused hands pressed and kneaded every imaginable muscle and spread an oily mass over my moist skin. Their clumsy fingers wandered everywhere, even between my legs and ass cheeks. I was too weak to defend myself.

"Whale oil is the best way to keep the body warm. Our hero will probably survive. A thick blanket should take care of the rest. And later a hot swig of rum. That will bring him back on his feet." I didn't recognize the deep, manly voice. I fell limply into a bunk and fell immediately into a deep sleep. I only woke once, briefly, when the door to my cabin was opened. I heard two sea robbers speaking softly above me.

"Everything seems to be all right. He's still sleeping. Let's give the rescuer a bit more peace and quiet. The captain is already waiting to talk to him."

"And? Any news about who did this?" asked the other man.

"The captain is trying to squeeze it out of every crew member individually. Up until now, he's let them all go. But one thing is for sure: if he finds the cowardly rogues who were trying to get his son out of the way, they won't live long enough to regret what they've done," was his whispered answer.

Later I woke to the sound of soft whimpering nearby. Dim streaks of pale light broke the darkness. Until now I thought I was alone in the cabin.

"No … no … I don't want to … let go," the man babbled in his dream. "I'm cold, so cold."

His teeth chattered together. His entire body cramped up. I sat up and looked over at the miserable wretch. Then I realized who was lying next to me. I could hardly believe it. It was the man I had been devouring with my eyes until recently. The man who just a day before had been commanding the aft deck, proud, inaccessible, and self-assured. Now he pressed himself to me desperately.

"Jack. Jack, can you hear me?" I whispered. "Everything is all right. You're safe here."

"I'm so cold, so cold," he kept repeating. Then I saw that his blanket had fallen off, and he was lying uncovered and shivering in the cold cabin. I quickly sprang up and threw the protective blanket over him. Then I slipped under it myself and scooted up tight against his back to warm him. The poor guy was like an ice block. Only his head was glowing warm.

"What happened?" he asked uncertainly.

"You were thrown overboard. I jumped after you and fished you out of the waves," was my simple answer. "You were unconscious, you've been sleeping here a while. Just like me. My name is Tom, by the way. I'm …"

"Yes, I know," he interrupted me. His whole body was still shivering. "We captured you along with that little catch. I've been observing you for a while as you've been scrubbing the planks on deck. You were quite a worthwhile plunder to save from the sharks."

Then Jack shivered again in the cold. I began to rub first his back, then his arms and legs. First forcefully kneading, then slowly, attentively stroking. My activity began to warm me up as well, and Jack began to relax. His shivering grew softer. By the time I was fondling his stomach gently, it had stopped altogether.

"I'm starting to feel better," he observed gratefully.

My own spirits had fully returned. My cock was already pressed gently against Jack's firm ass. And as my hand stroked further down his stomach I brushed against his hard pole.

"It's still quite chilly," I gasped. "My hands aren't going to be enough to get rid of the cold." I cautiously turned Jack on his back. Then I slipped down and took his hard-on between my lips.

"It's really warm in your throat. That's just what I needed right now," he encouraged me. My tongue surrounded his swollen shaft. My mouth ran along its entire length. Then I let his fat plank out of my throat and set to work on his freezing balls. One after another his nuts disappeared in my mouth. I licked them on all sides, then rubbed them warm with my tongue.

"You must not be completely warm yet either," Jack interrupted me. Then he rolled me on his back. On his hands and knees he rolled on top of me and dunked his head in between my legs. His hot tongue kissed the tip of my cock, then his stiff torpedo disappeared in my throat. His mouth slid down deeper, and his tender lips grasped my thick cock even firmer.

"You can keep going," he murmured, waving his cock encouragingly in front of my face. Then he spread his legs and shoved his hard-on between my lips. I put my hands on his cool ass cheeks. From there I worked intensely, rubbing towards his asshole. Jack moaned softly as my fingers reached his tight ring. Every time he sucked my cock in deep, I pushed my fingers against his tight hole. His twitching rod in my throat showed me how aroused he was.

"It's still cold deep within me. Couldn't you warm up there too?" Jack asked pleadingly, rubbing himself against my finger.

"I'll light a warm fire inside you. You won't be cold after that," I promise him. "Just lie on your back. Leave the rest to me." I sank my whole weight onto my back. My lips warmly touched his. Our tongues met, our bodies quivered together. I pressed my hard cock firmly against his.

"My hot sword will warm you through and through," I whispered in his ear. Then I leaned back carefully and lifted his legs onto his shoulders. When I bent gently forward my moist cock found its soft target. I bent Jack's legs further and increased the pressure at his rosebud. Then our lips touched again, his narrow gate opened invitingly, and my thick meat slipped all the way inside him.

"Oh yeah, I feel your fiery sword," he moaned. "You're so warm."

I rammed my pole in his ass to drive the rest of the cold from his body. I drove into him until the first drops of sweat formed on his forehead.

"Getting warm at all?" I asked.

"Oh yeah, you're heating me up well," he panted.

"Would you like me to stop?" I suggested devilishly. I pulled my cock out.

Immediately Jack slipped his legs from my shoulders and clasped them around my hips. Determined, he pressed his heels against my ass, pulling my plank back into his hole. He didn't release the pressure until he felt my balls against my ass.

"No, quite the opposite," he whispered. "I'd like to get a bit hotter."

To emphasize his words he wrapped his arms around my back and pulled me closer. His warm hands stroked my skin lovingly. His hard cock twitched upright when I lay on his stomach.

"All right," I panted. "If that's the way you want it."

In circular strokes I began driving my cock into his moist canal, my tense stomach muscles rubbing against his firm manhood.

Jack's hands wandered forward to my nipples, tweaking them sensually. This tender treatment spread directly to my cock, causing my mushroom head to swell and sending small flashes of pleasure through my balls, which pulled together from the arousal.

"Does that mean I can put a few more coals on?" I gasped, breathing heavily.

In response, Jack pushed harder with his heels. Each time I slapped firmly against his ass, making Jack's whole body rock along with my powerful thrusts. Moaning, he demanded more—and I gave it to him. Our bodies grappled together like two flints crashing against one another to ignite the wick of a cannon. It was clear to me that even the smallest spark could cause an explosion.

It was Jack who brought out the spark. Lustily he punished my nipples with his teeth, sucking the hard nodes and tonguing their sensitive tips. Then he carefully bit them, causing bright flashes of light to explode behind my closed eyes. With a howl, I threw my head back. With raw power I drove my sword into his ass and flooded him with my hot juice, shooting my enormous load in countless thrusts deep into his ass.

Our heated rubbing brought Jack's hammer to the edge of self-combustion. My heaving stomach touched his brick-red cock head again, and … his thick cock let out a shower of hot sperm. Jack fired his cream across his chest up to his throat. In the dim light his nectar gleamed like little fiery stars. My lips traced up to his throat, healed the burns of ecstasy with my tongue, and finally let him taste his own warm fireworks.

"Thank you for saving me," Jack said after a while.

"To be honest, I didn't even know who was out there in the ocean calling for help," I answered. "But I'm unbelievably glad it was you."

I gave his soft cock a tender squeeze , and it swelled.

"You really seem to be doing better," I said. "The ice-cold water hasn't left behind any lasting injuries."

"Thank you for that as well. Without your caring, warming treatment I wouldn't have survived this mishap. I will never forget you for that. I owe you deeply."

Jack's face grew very serious with those words. But then he smiled again and pulled me close.

"We'd better cover each other well, otherwise we'll start freezing again."

We both grabbed the blanket, moved closer to one another, and cuddled tightly together. Jack pressed his back against my stomach.

"If you get cold again, I'd be glad to warm you again," I whispered.

"I can hardly wait to feel your hot rod inside me again," was his soft answer. "But at the moment I'm simply enjoying being near you."

Shortly afterwards, I heard Jack's peaceful even breath. I pressed myself carefully to him, covered us with the blanket and sank into a long, dreamless sleep.

The next morning I was awakened by the first rays of sun falling onto my face through the half-open hatch. Blinking, I opened my eyes. Jack was still lying next to me. He had hardly moved all night. Every now and then his arms had jerked, his breathing had become uneasy and he murmured incomprehensible words in his sleep. But as soon as I stroked his back gently, he would roll over without ever fully waking, and soon his breathing was even again.

He opened his eyes and turned towards me. His eyes gleamed, large and blue as lakes in a clear white sea of clouds. Astounded, he looked at me.

"I thought ... I didn't know ..." he stuttered. "You were here all night?"

"Yes, of course," I answered. "I drove your bad dreams away and took care of you."

His face relaxed. A broad smile revealed his even teeth, making the jaunty lines of his red lips appear even more seductive. My lips searched his sensual mouth. His soft tongue met mine like a long lost friend. Then after a long, intimate embrace we released one another hesitantly, but also relieved.

"My rescuer," whispered Jack, holding my glowing cheeks with both hands. "You saved me from drowning. I will be grateful to you forever, Tom. When I fell into the cold water I saw my brief life flash before my eyes. That was when I realized how lonely I have been until now. No one would have truly missed me if I disappeared off the face of this earth. You didn't just grab me from the water, you've awakened a whole new life within me tonight."

Embarrassed, I avoided his eyes.

"When I jumped into the water, I didn't care if I survived," I admitted. "I ... I wanted to swim away or die, as long as I never had to go back to that dark hole below deck."

My head sank powerlessly onto his chest. A tear rolled down my face. At that moment I realized how close I had been to dying.

"I'm glad you thought better of it," Jack said encouragingly. He laid a hand on my head. "Your beautiful hair. What happened?"

"I was shaved."

Carefully he took my chin in his hand, lifted my head, and looked at me for a long time without speaking.

"It will grow again and be even more beautiful. I'm sure of it." He stroked my head lovingly. "You saved my life. Now I'm going to save yours. You'll never have to go below deck again, unless it's to warm my bed for me when I get cold. You're really good at warming me up. Otherwise I might not have survived last night."

"I'd be happy to do that for you," I answered gratefully.

Jack jumped from the bed.

"But now we need to see what's going on back on deck. Come on, get dressed. And don't be afraid. I will explain everything to my father. He's not the monster everyone thinks he us. It just amuses him to see people quake before him if he makes a grim face."

While Jack got dressed I simply sat there and watched his muscles playing. Then the door flew open. The magnificent silhouette standing in the doorframe against the light left no shadow of a doubt: this hulk could only be the captain.

"Jack, are you all right?" He pulled his son close and embraced him. "I thought you were done for. All night long, I grilled the crew to find out who was trying to kill you. It wasn't until I broke out the cat o' nine tails that Stevenson and Hawkins admitted to the whole thing. The cords are already rigged. Come on, you should watch these two rogues receive their just punishment."

He pulled Jack towards the entrance. During his flurry of speech I had tried to make myself as invisible as possible. Cowering close to the wall in the darkest corner of the bunk, I scarcely dared to breathe.

"Wait a minute," Jack stopped his father. "What about Tom? He saved me."

Enraged, the pirate captain walked back and bent down to me. His eyes were sparkling with fury.

"You stay here and don't move an inch," he growled at me. Then he shoved Jack in front of him and slammed the door behind him. I heard the lock fall into place from outside. Again I was sitting in a cage. The hulk hadn't even let his son get a word in edgewise. Discouraged, I cowered in bed to await my fate. Then I fell asleep again.

Loud cries of pain awoke me. I shivered to hear the hissing of a whip flying through the air and the strap cracking on naked skin. Sweat formed on my forehead, and I flinched with each crack. After countless beatings, silence finally returned. Then I heard a dinghy being lowered into the water. With a splash, it set down on the surface of the sea. The captain's unrestrained voice shook the entire ship.

"If you somehow survive and I catch sight of you again, I will strangle you with one hand. Any one of the crew members is allowed to do the same with no punishment."

I spied cautiously through the half-open hatch. Two men were lying in a small boat, motionless. Like a tiny nutshell, the rowboat danced on the waves. It quickly moved away from the pirate ship, growing smaller until it finally became nothing but a tiny point on the endless horizon. It was clear to me that Stevenson and Hawkins were the men in the boat. And it was also clear that the two of them had scarcely any chance of survival. It was a tough but common punishment among seafarers to set mutineers out on the open sea. With a bit of water, provisions, and a pistol with only one bullet. Whatever happened with it lay solely in the hands of the condemned men. I shivered to think of my tormentors. So they had been spared the "hempen jig." Maybe it was better that way. Nonetheless, my gloomy memories of those two rogues clouded my senses like dark thunderclouds. Then I was suddenly grabbed by the arm and shaken. I shot bolt upright as if waking from a nightmare.

"Tom, Tom, what's wrong?" Jack was standing in front me giving me a worried look. "You screamed out loud when I came in."

"I don't know what it was," I lied. "But now it's over."

Maybe I would tell Jack the story at some point. But it would have to be later, not today.

"What is going to happen to me?" I asked with concern.

"My father would like to receive you. He can hardly wait to finally meet you. I told him all about you. Come on, get dressed. I'll bring you to him."

Jack put me on my feet and held me in his arms.

"You're still shaking. Here, I have new things for you. You don't want to go in to see Captain Brandon in your birthday suit."

"What should I tell him?" I asked Jack as I hesitantly put on my shirt and pants.

"It's best to tell the truth. My father is a clever man. He will notice right away if something's not right. Just don't tell him all the details about last night," he added with a chuckle, giving me a fleeting kiss on the mouth. "That can stay our secret for now."

When I entered the captain's cabin, my stomach dropped like a ball of lead. Captain Brandon reigned behind a giant table like the lord of the seas himself. His imposing figure inspired instant respect. What I already knew about him was enough to terrify me. Only an experienced seaman could command the heaps of scoundrels and villains on this ship with an iron hand. Only an extremely cunning mind could track down the routes of wealthy trade ships. And last but not least it was thanks to the captain's long seafaring experience that he was always able to escape pursuers at the last minute. Myths and legends about his life abounded among seamen around the world. No one story was like the others. Only one thing was accepted without a doubt: despite his severity, Brandon had impeccable manners. Some said he came from an old line of nobles who had grown poor through intrigues and endless lawsuits; since then, they have had to flee English law enforcers. Others said that his family castle near London was still rotting away, populated by evil spirits.

But this knowledge was no help to me at the moment. I felt impossibly small next to Captain Brian. Helplessly, my eyes wandered over his enormous figure, from his broad shoulders and stately chest down to his powerful arms and hands. He looked at me with calm, attentive eyes. Next to him stood Noah and Jack.

Now it will all come out, I thought. I felt dizzy. I had to grab for the nearest armrest to keep from losing my balance. Jack's father's voice sounded almost considerate when he addressed me this time.

"You must not have your full strength back, Tom. Why don't you sit down." He pointed to the chair I was grasping desperately. Relieved, I sank into it.

"First I would like to thank you for your bravery. Not every man would have been so courageous as to put his life in danger to save my son. Noah confessed to me that he brought you on deck. Apparently he freed you from a dangerous situation. He didn't want to tell me more, but since I know I can trust Noah, I believe him.

All right ... well, it seems those two rogues caused a whole lot more trouble than I originally thought. But they've been punished for that. And now to you: from now on, you are free to move about the ship."

Silent, astounded, I took in his last words. Captain Brandon stood about and walked around the table to me.

"I give you a pirate's word of honor," he grinned and held out his hand.

Still completely surprised at the unexpected change of fate, I grabbed his paw and shook it firmly.

"Yes, yes, all right. Not so forceful, young man. I'm going to need this hand later."

With that, he pulled his hand away, took a step closer and embraced me jovially.

"Thank you for saving my son. If Jack agrees, I will quarter you in his cabin from now on."

He looked over to Jack for confirmation.

"Yes, of course, father, we'll get along well."

The excitement in Jack's eyes was impossible for me to miss, but the captain and Noah didn't seem to notice anything.

"So, that's settled," the captain said gladly, smacking his belly with a laugh. "Tell me, do you have as large a hole in your stomach as I do? We should definitely do something about this. You're my guests to celebrate today. Noah, order the cook to prepare a special feast for us. And an extra portion of rum for the crew."

Several hours later when I entered the aft cabin, a magnificently spread table awaited me. Silver plates gleamed next to polished candelabras. Festive light refracted through fine crystal glasses, sending dancing shards of light onto the ceiling beams. Enormous bowls, serving boards and heavy carafes rested inside the batten. The aroma of crisp baked fish and fresh bread wafted to my nose. My mouth began to water.

It was a very pleasant evening. The strong wine gradually loosened the tongues of all present. I told many stories of my life in Plymouth and my nurturing uncle. And finally I learned more about Jack and the conditions that led to he and his father becoming pirates. It was a long story, full of adventures, and it was clearly not the first time the captain had told it. Finally I was able to confirm at least some of the rumors I had heard about the pirate king. Jack and I exchanged many yearning glances throughout the evening. I hadn't felt so well in a long time. Later, as we lay in our shared bunk, we were able to exchange more than just glances. I warmed Jack again the way I had promised him, and he warmed me—and my eagerly pounding heart.

*T*he next days and weeks passed like a strange dream. I got used to the pirate life surprisingly quickly. My initial insecurity abated with every hour I spent with the rest of the crew in the shrouds in any wind or weather. I enjoyed measuring myself up against these experienced sea dogs. Soon I was no longer in last place when it came to clambering up the topmast quickest; sometimes I even came in first.

More and more unusual clouds were popping up on the horizon. They were shaped like white sails, and—as the lookout determined—clearly belonged to English war ships. We were being followed. For a few unthinking moments I still hoped to be saved by my countrymen. But I rejected this hope quickly. I had become much too accustomed to the free, uninhibited pirate life to want to leave the *Bone*, as this ship was called. I had to admit that sea travel had really drawn me in. But could I really give up on Brian forever? I just couldn't find any answer to that painful question. Since Captain Brandon, thanks to his well-practiced crew and swift ship, always managed to escape our pursuers, these thoughts quickly became unnecessary. After five days of uninterrupted pursuit, the captain suddenly called all men on deck.

"As you see, this damn war fleet has been chomping at our tail for days. I think it's time to say good-bye to our old motherland."

He made a significant pause, making everyone wonder what devilry he would roar out next. Curiously, I looked over to Jack, who was standing next to his father. But he, too, seemed to have no idea what was going on, merely shrugging his shoulders at me.

"I have decided to set sail and conquer the New World on the other side of the known seas. Where the land and people are free, where the sea receives us with open arms, we will be safe from our pursuers. Anyway ..." He emphasized his next words slowly and clearly. "Anyway, the Spaniards unload their gold freight there. We're sure of ample booty. Will you follow me to the New World?"

Speechless silence reigned for a second, then the ship quaked under a salvo of gleeful cries, the likes of which I had never heard before. Every man was beside himself. Excited hoots and yells echoed across the deck. We were all certain that infinite freedom and indescribable riches awaited us in the distance.

"We will make like the wind," Brandon's powerful voice droned over the celebratory cries. "Then we'll make a last stop on the coast of Africa with some friends of ours to take on provisions. Then our new destination is: America!"

The joyful hubbub took a long time to die down, eventually giving way to widespread relief. This cat and mouse game with the English marina and everyone else who was hunting us would finally be over. The crew was visibly glad. Only a handful of men didn't dare come along on this adventure. They spoke with Captain Brandon the next day. He promised to pay them off and set them on land in the next harbor. Soon we were racing towards the West African coast. The crew was 115 men in all, from all sorts of different countries. Only the highest posts on board were manned by English people, the rest of the crew came from Spain, France, or Portugal. Even some men from deep Africa had made it on board. All of the crew members on board the *Bone* were experienced seamen, but they had various reasons for being rejected by their countries and countrymen. Probably not always unjustly. But for me, the crew seemed to be a hoard of athletic, well-built men, good sailors, glad and jovial characters who weren't afraid of hard work. On board, they formed a small community that followed its own rules. Noah was the only one who didn't quite seem to belong. He was a real lone wolf. But for me, since the first time we met, Noah was a good friend.

Our starting point for our dangerous journey to the New World was to be a small bay south of Agadir. The African crew members in particular were feverishly awaiting our arrival. Several years ago, Captain Brandon had saved many of them from a sinking slave ship in the very same bay. Out of gratitude, they had sworn him eternal allegiance. Since then they had never complained about their rescuer, even when he drove them on to hard labor every day like the rest of the crew.

On the tenth day, after the captain had set a new course, the long-awaited strip of land finally appeared to starboard. In a few hours we were docking at the small, inconspicuous harbor. Our stay was supposed to last no longer than five days, just enough time for us to make a few little repairs to the ship and swap some of the sails before the stormy crossing. The African crew members whose families lived nearby were allowed two days off to say good-bye to them.

I was standing on deck trying to make out the approaching coastline more exactly when Jack appeared at the back ladderway.

"Tom, come here!" he waved me closer excitedly.

"My father wants to talk to us. We're supposed to go to him in the captain's cabin."

"Do you know what he wants from us?" I asked uneasily. Jack's father rarely called crew members in to him. It must be something unusually important. But Jack gave me a reassuring look.

"Don't worry. I don't know. But I'm sure he just wants to teach us a few small things about coming into harbor."

I kept quiet, but I was still amazed that the captain wanted to see me. Without knocking, Jack opened the cabin door. Captain Brandon sat behind his giant table, waving us in.

"My men," he began formally after we had taken our places in front of him. "A few days from now when we lift anchor and set off for the New World, we may be leaving the old continent behind forever. I'll make this quick." He coughed significantly. "On a small island close to here, there is buried treasure."

Jack and I looked at one another, speechless.

"I would like you to set out today to dig up this booty and bring it onboard without causing too much commotion. For years, I've hidden my share of treasure here every time I passed by. There should be several chests of gold and jewels at the spot. I trust you, my son. And your friend seems to be the right companion for this crucial expedition. I will send Noah by your side as well. He will be your bodyguard. You just need to more strong, dependable seamen who can help you dig up the heavy chests."

Brandon had stood up and was wandering back and forth, deep in thought.

"I know who we can trust," I interrupted. "Paul Morgan and Henry Torbett are honest and discreet. I'm sure we can depend on them."

Paul Morgan was the provision master. He was responsible for making sure that there were enough rations in the storerooms for the entire journey. An important post. If the provision master was careless with the food stores, the crew would go hungry at the end, which could lead to illness and plague. But if he held back provisions for too long, it could lead to discontent or even mutiny. Paul managed this difficult balancing act perfectly. He directed the storerooms with a strong hand; it was strictly forbidden for normal crew members to enter the rooms. It was an order everyone followed, not least because no one wanted to have to reckon with Paul. He was large as a tree, with powerful arms and broad shoulders. He didn't play around and he was rarely seen on deck. Among crew members he was considered a sullen, quick-tempered tiger.

But that wasn't the reason I had suggested he should help us dig up the treasure. A few days ago, I had had an unusual encounter with the provision master—with him and Henry Torbett. The captain had sent me to Paul to replenish the supply of his favorite Spanish wine. I set off to the storerooms at the front of the ship, where I knew the provision master could usually be found. Over the weeks I had explored every possible nook and cranny of the ship, but I hadn't made it here yet. Loads of chests and heavy sacks towered to the ceiling of the dim storeroom. But I couldn't find the provision master anywhere. I was about to turn around when I heard voices from a room further forward. As I came closer, I could clearly hear Paul Morgan's droning voice.

"Come on, don't get so upset. Put the sacks on top of each other properly, then it will all be fine. Here, I'll help you. See, it works fine that way."

"Be careful or I'm going to break all my bones," another man thundered in response. "The captain will not be pleased if I slip here and end up in the sick bay tomorrow. Damn it, just stay put."

Hearing the men cursing about their heavy loads, I made sure to be careful. I didn't want to surprise them and cause an accident. And I certainly didn't want to get involved in a heated confrontation between the two squabblers. On tiptoes, I bent around the nearest corner. What I saw there nearly knocked me off my feet. I could scarcely believe my eyes. The provision master was standing there, pants hanging at his knees in front of a pile of overflowing sacks, sinking his thick meat into the ass of a man lying in front of him. He was completely naked, stretched out on his back, holding tight with both hands to the provision sacks to keep from losing his balance while Paul held him by the calves and spread his legs wide apart.

"Oh yeah, that's good, Paul. Shove it in deep. Let me feel your stiff plank in my ass. I've waited so long for this moment. Just look how my cock is throbbing," moaned the naked man, who I had recognized as Henry Torbett, first mate onboard the *Bone*. He was nearly as magnificent a man as Paul Morgan. I had observed him as he lifted the heavy anchor chain with the others, driving his comrades on with loud, smutty sailor ditties. But I liked what I was seeing now even better. His thick pole towered in the air almost vertically, bobbing expectantly up and down while Paul's plank boarded his firm ass.

"Believe me, Henry," the provision master roared. "Soon you'll be begging me to release you from my wild torpedo. But it won't do you any good. Once I've fathomed your depths I'll sink into you so hard that last night's hurricane will seem like a mild breeze."

With those words, Paul shoved his long member forward. In seconds, he had found the proper balance for his command. His breath grew faster, he licked his lips again and again. He threw his head back passionately. I could literally feel his mouth watering from the first mate's eager devotion. The veins on Henry's arms protruded clearly as he clasped tightly to the coarse linen sacks. Under Paul's relentless thrusts, the whole pile wobbled dangerously. But the provision master's fury only seemed to make the first mate's hot ass want more, as evidenced by his raging hard-on. My cock was also trying to escape my own tight pants. Intently watching the show in front of me, I leaned up against the doorframe and loosened the ropes on my pants. My firm cock throbbed in my hands. I could barely control my pulsing meat; Henry seemed to be in the same situation. He was moaning so loudly I was afraid he would attract the whole crew. His head rolled back and forth. His sweaty chest rose and sank, quaking. Clear fluid dripped from the tip of his bulging cock onto his tense stomach.

Suddenly, Henry stopped in the middle of his wild thrusts. He tilted his head and looked at me wide-eyed. He held his breath. Paul noticed that his companion had suddenly paused and followed the first mate's glance. For a brief moment there was silence on the rolling sea. Paul's chest heaved up and down as his fixed gaze examined me from top to bottom. His eyes came to rest on my unmistakable sign of arousal. Slowly, the corners of his mouth broadened into a knowing grin.

"You've come just in time, Tom. Henry can barely control himself on these stormy seas. You're a strong boy. Come on, give him a bit of help."

Deliberately, Paul continued thrusting. The muscles on his ass worked furiously while Henry relaxed, carefully released one hand from the sacks, and waved me over.

"Well, come on over. You can help me hold tight when the next storm breaks over me. I think ... ah ... the first ... breakers ... are rolling in."

His last words came panting out of his mouth, since Paul was riding him full force again.

Cautiously, I approached their wild horseplay. In two steps I freed myself from my pants and slipped my shirt off my shoulders. By the time I reached them I was naked. Henry immediately grabbed my ass and pulled me close.

"This is much sturdier," he panted. "Grab my rudder and guide me through this damn storm. Take my ..."

Whatever he had been meaning to say was swallowed in a load moan. Paul must have found a particularly sensitive spot that drove poor Henry crazy. The first mate desperately grabbed my head and pushed it down on his stiff cock. His moist mushroom head was so swollen it barely fit in my mouth. But his powerful right hand at the back of my head allowed no resistance. His juicy meat slipped deep into my throat while Henry's left hand dug in between my ass cheeks. After he had stuck two fingers deep in my cave, Henry seemed to feel a bit more secure. Panting, he waited for the next wave. And he didn't have long to wait. Paul groaned contentedly as Henry's cock disappeared in my mouth. Now he sank his pole back into Henry's hot pleasure gate. With each oncoming wave Henry thrust his cock in my mouth. At the same time, I clasped Henry 's dangling balls, my cock rubbing roughly against his ass and his sac.

"That's the way," Paul grunted. "Hold tight, boy. The next breakers are on their own way."

I had never experienced such a wildly raging storm flood. Henry couldn't last long under the onslaught of Paul's furious battering ram. His long moans gradually became rapid pants. His ass wriggled, trying to escape the powerful surf, but it was easy for Paul to quash the first mate's attempts at escape. He set the sailor's ankles on his broad shoulders, grabbed his victim's hips, and rammed his hard meat viciously into his ass. I stood spread-legged, leaning with all my force against the wobbling sacks. I could tell that this unstable pile was going to fall apart any minute now.

Paul's body began to shake. His chest rose and fell as he panted. His ass throbbed wildly and he pulled his thick cock out of Henry's ass. With a loud cry he unloaded his sperm. Hot spurts shot over my cheek. Surprised by the force of the warm spray, I pulled back as Henry's hard shaft transformed into a bursting cannon in front of my eyes. The last attack had been too much for him. Fire spewed from his dangerous weapon. His steaming load flooded my shocked face.

"Wow, what a sight," Paul joked as I wiped the thick cream from my face, still taken by surprise.

"It's a fit punishment for interrupting two busy sailors at work," Henry added with a laugh.

"The two of you would be buried under a pile of sacks right now if I hadn't showed up," I countered defiantly.

"And if you had done your work responsibly, maybe you would have come when we did," Paul grinned deviously.

"But since you helped us we can help you as well now, right Henry?" The first mate nodded and grabbed me from behind without warning.

"You should always be able to depend on your comrades. Believe me, you can depend on us, Tom," he said, throwing me onto the pile of sacks. Moaning, I came to rest on my back. Immediately, Paul grabbed between my legs and pulled my balls downward. I felt his lips slip over the tip of my cock. His rough tongue wandered along the shaft, exploring every inch. Then Henry's tongue joined in. From both sides the two hulking men pressed my throbbing manhood. Their lips wandered tirelessly over my tool.

"I can't take it much longer," I moaned, breathing heavily.

"Well, it's not like we have all day," was the provision master's laughing answer. Each of them kneaded my nipples with one hand. Their remaining hands searched my ass for its hidden entrance. Two fingers shoved belligerently through my rosebud. At the same time my cock sank between the first sea dog's lips while the second slipped my balls into his warm mouth.

"Ahhh ... uhhh ... you're driving me crazy," I cried, uninhibited.

My sperm boiled up. Bucking wildly, I lifted up as the two men explored my ass with their fingers. I could feel the warm fluid shooting up out of my shaft. When Henry suddenly pulled his head back, my semen sprayed wildly onto my stomach. The second spurt went all the way up to my throat, and the third shot hit me right in the face.

"Well, how do you like the taste of your own cream after tasting ours?" Paul wanted to know.

I licked my moist lips sensually.

"I think I like the taste of my own the best. But I'm not entirely certain."

With effort, I sat up and beamed contentedly at the two men.

"Maybe I could get another taste later?"

I looked between Paul and Henry's legs pleadingly.

"That could be arranged," grinned Henry. "What do you think, Paul?"

"First we've got to tie these provision sacks together properly. If the whole load slips during the next storm I don't want the captain coming down here," Paul pointed out.

At the word "captain," pearls of sweat suddenly formed on my forehead.

"Oh, that's right … I'm supposed to grab wine … for the captain," I stuttered awkwardly.

"Damn, you've got to hurry, Tom. If his food is already standing on the table without his beloved wine sparkling in the glass, the whole crew will have nothing to smile about tomorrow. Come on, I'll grab you a bottle quick," the provision master cursed and disappeared into the next room.

A sailor was just bringing the food platter down the narrow corridor to the captain's cabin as I entered with the bottle.

"The captain's wine," I called urgently after him. He looked at me in confusion as I set the bottle down on the platter without commenting and hastened away. Shrugging his shoulders, he opened the door:

"Ah, finally my food," I heard Captain Brandon roar. "And the wine's there, too. Fantastic!"

So, the Captain had received his noble drink on time. But Paul and Henry still owed me another taste of their special liquid. I hoped that there would be an opportunity while digging up the treasure to settle their debt. And since Captain Brandon didn't have anything against the first mate and provision master accompanying us on our excursion, nothing else stood in our way.

"Paul Morgan and Henry Torbett? If you don't have any problem with them, my son, then you've got a full team."

This little troop wasn't just full, in my eyes it was almost perfect. My cock twitched just thinking of the days I would spend in the company of those four magnificent men.

"When should we set out, and where is this fabled treasure, father?" Jack wanted to know.

"I like the way you talk, boys. You don't beat around the bush, you get right to it. All right, here's the map of the little island. But Jack, I will only tell you its location. Pack provisions for three days. Tonight you will take the large pinnace and sail away."

Brandon embraced his son tightly. Then he came over to me.

"Take good care of him, Tom. And come back in one piece! Make your preparations as inconspicuously as possible. The rest of the crew shouldn't know anything about it."

In front of the door, Jack clasped me by the shoulder: "Are you ready for our little adventure?"

"With you? Anytime, Jack. You tell Noah. I'll let Paul and Henry in on our plans. In two hours we'll meet up for a first discussion of our location in your cabin."

"First we need to make clear who's running this expedition," Jack challenged me.

"Aye, aye, captain. No question who has the command here," I responded with a grin, saluting him dutifully.

"I'd like to show you how well I can command right now."

Eagerly, he grabbed his crotch, then reluctantly straightened his thick cock under the tight fabric. The spot where his thick mushroom head was rubbing the coarse linen was already stained darker. I cuddled up to my captain. My expectant shaft pressed hard against his erection.

"I will carry out all of your orders without resistance," I whispered into Jack's ear. As confirmation I licked his throat tenderly. But before my tongue could find its way down to his chest, Jack took my head in his hands.

"Not now," he sighed. His large, blue eyes looked at me, visibly glum. "We have an order to carry out. But I will test your obedience plenty later, you can depend on it. By the way, what made you suggest Morgan and Torbett?"

"You can trust them, believe me! But it's a long story. Maybe our expedition will give us an opportunity to get to know the two of them better. Then you'll understand why." Jack looked at me inquisitively. Then we parted ways.

Later, when the five of us met in Jack's little cabin, the tension in the air was palpable. First Jack explained the details of the treasure's location and how we could bring it onboard quietly. Paul and Henry went wide-eyed and swore absolute secrecy. Noah sat still and showed no sign of excitement. His face was expressionless, as opaque as ever. Nevertheless I knew I would trust this man with my life before anyone else.

After dark, we met up on deck as agreed. Captain Brandon had ordered the pinnace to be brought down to water level on a false pretense. The next morning, our disappearance with the dinghy would arouse attention, but Brandon had already prepared an explanation: he would say I was ungrateful for being rescued, and had fled. The other four had chased after me immediately. After a few days they would bring me back on board as a prisoner. A fake arrest below deck would be unavoidable, but the captain promised to personally take care that no one harmed a hair on my head.

But first we had to get off the boat without anyone noticing us.

We waited until the first round of night watchmen had finished their circuit, then rappelled carefully down the outside wall of the ship from a cabin in the aftercastle. The weather was ideal: the light, offshore wind would help us to reach our destination quickly. Softly and cautiously we paddled out of the small bay. Our oars, which we had wrapped in thick rags as a precaution, dipped almost noiselessly into the black water. The only accompaniment to our secret escape was the barking of a seal stretched out at the entrance to the harbor. We sailed directly out onto the open ocean. It had been too late for the *Bone* to dock securely in the harbor the night before, so the boat would not be moored at the bulkhead until the next morning. This gave us an extra head start.

When we rowed past the cliffs at the mouth of the harbor we unfurled the small lateen sail. The boat glided out into the dark night. Jack had received exact instructions from his father. Thanks to a precisely detailed route and exact information about star constellations, we reached the small offshore island after a short trip. The pinnace landed on the flat sand beach of the crescent bay with a crunch. In no time, Noah had conjured up a small fire with a few dry branches. After a scarce evening meal we huddled together and waited for sunrise. I slipped very close to Jack. He embraced me and ran his hands softly over my head.

"Short hair looks good on you." He smiled at me.

"I can't wait for my hair to be long enough to tie up."

"By then we'll be in the New World already. But first we need to take care of this important mission."

"I still can't believe it," I whispered. "The two of us on a real search for buried treasure."

"I don't think it'll take long," answered Jack. "The only problem could be if the map is wrong or if we somehow overlooked one of the instructions. But then we'd never find it in a million years. If that's the case we could count on a whole lot more unpleasantness than one of my father's temper tantrums."

I pulled Jack into my arms and kissed him passionately.

"Don't worry. We'll manage. Anyway, your father instructed me to take good care of you."

Jack's answer was no less passionate.

"You're a true friend, Tom," he said, pressing his gyrating hips against my hard cock. I smiled at him gratefully. We spoke no more that night. Our lips found other ways to express our affection.

The next morning, Jack led us to the place where the treasure was supposed to be hidden according to the map. For a long time we followed the path, which was delineated with nondescript markers.

It led us through a thick forest, along a small stream, up to a high, narrow crevice in the rocks. Jack stood still.

"This should be it. According to my father's directions, it's only a few steps from here. The chests we're supposed to pick up should be in the cave over there."

Carefully we squeezed through the narrow crack, one by one. Jack lit a torch. Flat, slippery steps led into the inside of the rock. We climbed down and down until we finally reached a large cavern. The flame brightly illuminated the massive room. A small ship's mizzen mast could have fit comfortably beneath the high stone ceiling. Astounded, we looked around us.

"The three chests should be at the other end of the cavern," said Jack, walking determinedly through the cave. If he hadn't been holding the torch, he probably would have stumbled over the three dusty chests. Instead he stood solemnly before them, pulled a key from his pocket and opened the heavy locks. As he lifted up the lid of the largest chest, dead silence reigned. We all stared at the contents of this shrine as if bewitched. And what a sight they were! Silver coins, gold cups, finely decorated plates, and loads of gems and jewelry glittered up at us. The payload from the two smaller chests was no less magnificent. All together, this treasure must have been worth an entire dukedom.

"Most of these treasures have been our family's property for centuries," Jack said gloomily. "By the time were forced to leave England, there was nothing left."

Silent and thoughtful, he touched a few of the particular beautiful pieces in the large chest.

"The rest," he said, pointing to the two other chests, "is booty from the past few years. But now come and give a hand! Paul and Henry, grab the one up front there. Tom and I will take this one here. Noah, you carry the smallest."

None of the chests were gigantic, but since they were all filled to the brim, it took us some effort to get them to the mouth of the cave. On the way back to the boat we had to pause several times to regain our strength. Once we reached the beach, the sun was already sinking below the horizon. With our last force we heaved our burdens into the pinnace. When everything was safely stowed away, Jack finally looked content.

"The first part of our mission is done," he said with relief. "Thank you for your help. We have reason to celebrate. My father gave me something special to take with us."

Under our watchful glances Jack pulled two large bottles of rum from the provision chest.

Henry disappeared quickly into the forest to gather new wood. Paul kindled the fireplace from the previous night and Noah caught a few fish with a spear, setting them over the fire to sizzle aromatically. We sat in a comfortable circle around the crackling light. Jack and Noah were to my right, Henry and Paul sat on my left. Exuberant, Jack kissed me on the mouth when I handed him the bottle of rum.

"Oh ho, is that the reward for outstanding service? Then we want our share too," Henry demanded with a grin. "Paul and I carried the second biggest chest after all, and I gathered the firewood myself."

"Here, take the flask, Paul. The provision master is personally responsible for extra rations," said Jack, briefly interrupting the kiss. Paul interpreted his invitation in his own way.

"Come here, Henry," he boomed, stretching out sensually in the sand and kneading his thick cock. "With the captain's permission, you've got an extra big portion tonight."

With a greedy look, Henry took another powerful swig from the flask. Then he handed it hastily to Noah and jumped onto his friend's hard schlong. Then he sank to his knees and his head disappeared between Paul's legs.

Out of the corner of my eye I observed Noah slipping carefully beneath Henry. Since the first mate had already pulled his pants off, Noah enjoy the sight of the sailor's round ass gleaming seductively in the fire's glow. Carefully he let a stream of rum fall from the flask down Henry's ass crack. Then he licked the spicy drops up with his tongue. Henry moaned out load as Noah shoved his tongue through his narrow gate.

"Yeah, show him, Noah," Paul spurred the man on.

"Oh no, not him. I'll show you instead," he droned back.

Before Paul could respond, Noah was shoving his fat pole in his mouth. On all fours, Noah knelt over the provision master, thrusting his black snake into Paul's wide open mouth. After Paul had recovered from his initial shock, he eagerly grabbed the hulk's firm ass cheeks and shoved his mouth down greedily on its unexpected invader.

Jack looked at me wide-eyed. I had taken my cock in my hands and was grinning cheekily at him: "I did tell you Paul and Henry were the right ones to take on this adventure. And even Noah finally seems to be part of the group."

The three of them did seem to be getting along famously. Paul's massive paws grasped Noah's black ass like two giant tongs. The black pole slid in and out of his greedy throat in powerful thrusts, while Henry's mouth worked on Paul's cock as if enchanted, his head bobbing up and down rapidly over the provision master's thick meat. Wild shadows danced over the sweaty bodies of this well-practiced team.

Jack observed this unusual ritual for a while. Then he turned to me again, smiled and engulfed my cock. His tongue danced seductively along my pulsating shaft. I sank into the warm sand, overwhelmed with pleasure. I looked up at the clear sky. A sea of stars glimmered in the wide dark vault. I felt Jack's warm hands stroking my quivering body. His tender tongue was trying to bring the heavens down to me. I closed my eyes and abandoned myself to this uplifting movement, until small colored dots began to dance around my eyes, exploding into new glowing heavenly bodies, creating still more stars in magnificent fireworks. This inner spectacle grew brighter and brighter until I looked up one moment and the magnificent show was wiped away by an even more beautiful sight. The most beautiful cock I could imagine was hovering in front of my eyes.

"Remember the night you saved me, how you promised to warm me up whenever I got cold," Jack said with a chuckle. "I think this is one of those times. Our campfire has almost burned down and my friend here is already quite cool."

Jack gently lowered his cock to my face. I gladly took his throbbing manhood into my mouth, anchoring my hands on his cold ass and pressing his sausage harder to my lips. Moaning, Jack bent over to reach my cock.

We had been engulfed in our sensual pleasure for quite some time when we suddenly noticed it had become oddly still around us. Where had the others gone? Alarmed, I let Jack's cock slip from my mouth and looked around me.

"We didn't want to bother you," Paul's voice rang out all of a sudden. The provision master had appeared directly above us. He licked his lips mischievously. "You guys got us pretty heated up. But I think we might have something to add."

Visibly aroused, he rubbed his throbbing meat. Noah and Henry, standing to his left and right, were just as eagerly rubbing their own erections. Jack and I looked at one another. After a quick nod I gulped down Paul's fat rod. On my knees, I took care of his veiny giant while Jack fell upon Noah's thick snake. His black meat was just too tempting.

Henry came up next to Paul so I could suck off my two friends in turn. This direct comparison showed me their clear differences in shape and taste, but they were each irresistible in their own way. Both hulking men moaned with pleasure. And soon both their cocks were pushing into my mouth at the same time.

"I can't take anymore." Paul fell to the ground. Breathing heavily, he lay on the soft sand. "If I didn't know any better I would say your tongue is the tool of the devil."

Henry didn't pass up on this opportunity. Quick as lightning, he bent over and fished for Paul's throbbing hard-on, hungrily attacking his fat prey. As he bent over, his ass hovered lustily above Paul's face. Moments ago, the two of them had found me and Jack in exactly the same position. Now I finally understood how intoxicating the sight must have been. Feeling incredibly horny, I shoved my pulsing rod between Henry's legs and pushed my hot thighs cautiously but unrelentingly against his cool ass cheeks. My cock slipped beneath him, past his balls onto Paul's sweaty forehead.

"Here, mate, now you can have a go at fishing with two rods at once."

The powerful man seemed to have no problem at all swallowing two cocks. My mast disappeared easily next to Henry's manhood in Paul's huge mouth. Shivers ran through my body as I felt the first mate's shaft and Paul's rough tongue rubbing my meat. Spit flowed from the provision master's mouth as he eagerly sucked our cocks. Now I concentrated on what had been my actual goal all along: Henry's firm ass. Finally, I was kneeling directly in front of his magnificent mounds, and I served myself shamelessly. Paul stared at me from below as I pulled my moist mushroom head from his mouth and pointed it towards Henry's seductive entrance. With a thick cock in his mouth he couldn't speak, but his mischievous facial expression spoke volumes. Slowly, I led my moist rod to his magically pulsating point. Immediately, Paul's hands were on the spot helping me to open the first mate's gate. Then the tight grotto allowed me in. Panting, Henry threw his head back while his buddy's hands clamped onto his quivering hips and pulled them towards my torpedo.

"Ahhh … your giant mast will tear my ass in two."

"I can't imagine that," I managed to sputter with clenched teeth. Then I thrust my pole into his ass, slapping my balls rapidly against his muscular cheeks. His broad back gleamed with sweat. I fol-

254

lowed my hands with my eye as they wandered up his spine. I could feel his muscles tensing beneath my fingers as my manhood burrowed deep within him. Then a hand suddenly grabbed my balls from behind and I let out a sigh of pleasure. Paul's greedy fingers shot around my sensitive nuts like a tight iron ring, kneading them painfully. I cried out loud.

"No one can hear you here." I could feel Jack's hot breath on my ear. His powerful arms surrounded me from behind, pulling me avidly toward his chest. "I've got you, you ungrateful landlubber. So, you wanted to flee after we took you among us and tried to help. Well, it's about time we showed you what pirates do with disloyal liars. But as I can see, our provision master has a firm hold on you. Men, I commend you. You've managed to capture the deserter and hold him down. All that's left is for me to cut off the traitor's last escape route from behind."

With those words, Jack shoved his hard shaft against my back entrance like a drawn sword.

"Give in, you miserable louse. It's the only way to save your worthless life."

Jack chuckled as he whispered to me in a commanding tone. "Now you should whimper and beg for mercy."

Now it was my turn to laugh out loud. "I've never seen such miserable acting," I howled.

"Noah," Jack ordered. "Stuff the traitor's filthy mouth."

Suddenly the black giant was standing in front of me. Legs spread above Henry's back, he lay his pipe on my lips. I was about to make another snarky comment, but my answer was muffled by his thrusting meat. His giant mushroom head rammed full force into my throat, filling it entirely. Noah's crotch still smelled of Jack's saliva, which had been smeared all over his magnificent cock. I offered my mouth as well as I could to the invader. After all, I didn't want to give the others any reason to think I had failed at my mission.

"That's good, Noah," Jack moaned behind me, rubbing his cock impatiently against my ass.

"It's about time to take you up in our crew, to make sure you never even dream of fleeing again. Once you've experienced how invigorating a pirate's thrust can be, you'll be begging for more and swearing eternal loyalty."

Jack increased the pressure at my pleasure fortress. His swollen cock head twitched excitedly at my most sensitive spot. Then he grabbed my hips firmly and pulled me onto his hard spear. My protest was suffocated again by Noah's black shaft. The silent black man lay his paws on the back of my head and pushed my cock down further onto his manhood. In one sudden thrust, Jack had shoved his saber halfway into my ass.

"Well, how do you like that, you English redneck?" he joked. Amused, the pirate prince endured my flailing attempts to escape his punishment. Particularly since they caused his manhood to slip deeper between my ass cheeks. But that was fine with me. I turned and twisted until I felt the hairs on his ballsac against my ass. Then I finally admitted defeat. My will shattered, I let Jack thrust his cock into me mercilessly. I had no choice but to allow my own manhood to be thrown deeper into Henry's ass at each thrust. And I didn't defend myself when I found myself immobile, clamped between the two pirates. For a while, none of us moved.

"Well, now the prisoner is secured on all sides," Jack declared triumphantly. The self-satisfaction is his voice was impossible to miss. "Still going to try to slip away, you rogue?"

He slapped both hands loudly against my spit-roasted ass. I was starting to get used to feeling his hard rod in my canal; the gentle vibrations caused by the slaps only turned me on even more. And the giant in my mouth was not a problem any more. Paul's firm grip on my balls swelled my cock inside Henry's ass, making him pant exhaustedly. I don't know who was the first of us to move, or if we all starting moving as if following some secret signal. But suddenly Noah was pulling his cock back out of my mouth, nearly causing my cock to slip from Henry's magnificent canal. Since Paul was still clamping my nuts, our hot connection was undisturbed. Then Jack's thighs slapped against my ass with fiery passion, my own cock sank rapidly into Henry's depths, Noah's pole tickled the farthest reaches of my throat, and Paul's willing mouth swallowed Henry's fat mast.

Noah's dark stomach hovered in front of my face. Bright stars danced over his black skin. My tongue circled wildly around his black tower, causing his balls to erupt. With the uninhibited cry of an African bushman, Noah sprayed hot lava from his thick-headed snake. I only managed to swallow the first spurt, the rest landed on my chest. From there, his semen ran down my stomach in narrow streams.

Jack grabbed my nipples from behind, tweaking them so firmly that I broke out in a sweat. My eyes were still hypnotized by the head of the dripping black snake in front of me. Then I felt Henry's canal jerk tightly around my pole. An uninhibited gurgling noise told me that the first mate was spraying his cum directly into Paul's mouth as Paul held his own hose in his fist and flooded his face with hot fountains.

"Tell us, do you want to live with us as a pirate forever? Are you ready for that, Tom Moore?" Jack intoned behind me.

His hard cock hit the deepest part of my ass. I could feel him quivering as I cried, "Yes, I'm ready!"

"Then I take you here and now, once and for all, irrevocably into our band," Jack roared like a madman. Then his semen flooded my hole in rapid streams at exactly the same time as my first spray of sperm flowed into Henry's ass. When Jack noticed that I was overflowing as well, he pulled me back hastily by the hips, causing the rest of my salvos to fall on the men lying in front of me.

A little while later I lay exhausted but happy in Jack's arms.

"It feels good to finally be a lawless pirate," I beamed at him.

"It feels good to have finally found a true friend among friends," came his whispered answer. A long, intimate kiss made any further explanation unnecessary.

The others had fallen asleep long ago. Just the two of us were lying awake, watching the stars in the night sky. In the east, the first stars of the Pleiades were rising up above the smooth horizon. A little to the left the pinnace rocked gently, splashing back and forth. Small waves of spray rolled sideways onto the sand. As the seven stars rose entirely above the horizon, our eyes met. We each sank into other's gaze, and our souls melted together.

Early the next morning we set out on our way. The fine sand crunched beneath the flat bottom of the boat as Noah pushed the pinnace back in the gentle water, setting his shoulder against the high bow until the boat was freed. With a nimbleness you would not expect from such a heavy man, he jumped onboard.

The sun sent its first rays over the horizon to greet the new morning. Sitting gloomily on the bow deck I looked back at the little island one last time. It could be a long time before I would see a white beach and green trees again. The memory of the past two days, and last night's hot encounter, made the still beach seem even more full of promise. But the wind drove us irrevocably out towards the open sea. Jack came up behind me.

"Well, Tom? Don't tell me you're having doubts, are you?" He pulled me into his arms lovingly. Filled with passion, my mouth met his warm lips. "You should take a careful look at the horizon. That's where we're traveling to."

I turned around softly. My back snuggled against his chest, our hands met on my stomach. I followed his outstretched hand, letting my eyes streak over the broad sea and radiant blue sky.

"Yes, you're right," I sighed. "I'm glad we'll get to experience this adventure together."

"Come on, you two," interrupted Paul. "When you're done exchanging whispered nothings, we'd like to hear from the captain where to go next."

With a grin, Jack released me and went over to the others.

Around midday, we caught up with the *Bone*. We had hid the heavy chests beneath thick tarps, where they would stay until nightfall. Then Paul and Henry would bring them secretly into safety. By that time, I would be stewing away below deck. When we arrived they had chained me up and brought me onboard. In front of the eyes of the entire crew I was banished to a low dark cell for several days. Once more, we were acting out a play. But this time we had to stay serious. In order to make Jack's deep resentment of my escape more convincing, he was not allowed to visit me in my cell even once. That was the only catch of Captain Brandon's otherwise brilliant plan. I missed Jack. I longed to feel his warm hands on my skin, his soft lips on my mouth, to hear his enchanting laugh that made my heart beat in my throat.

To my consolation, Noah at least found some time to visit me in the uncomfortable cell. He did his best to cheer me up in his own special way. Nevertheless those few days seemed to me like never ending years of imprisonment.

After a thorough discussion, the captain and his nearest mates came to the following decision: since I had not been a full-fledged member of the *Bone* at the time of my 'flight,' my escape was not deemed mutiny. Instead, it was written off as the unfortunate misstep of a prisoner. Otherwise I would have ended up hanging from the highest mast with a rope around my neck. But none of the seamen wanted to see me hang. Many of them had already taken a shine to me. So there was only one way out. In front of the entire crew, I had to take the pirate's oath. That way I would become one of them, with all their rights and duties.

"Are you prepared to join us, Thomas Moore?" Captain Brandon asked during the ceremony on deck. "Are you ready to become a pirate, body and soul? Then swear!"

I put my hand on my heart. "I hereby swear to be a pirate from now on … for as long as I live."

"Grab him," called a sea robber from behind me suddenly. Immediately, three strong men rushed up to grab my arms and legs. A fourth grabbed my head from behind.

A stabbing pain shot through my ear, then I was freed again. I stumbled and would have fallen down if Captain Brandon hadn't caught me.

"Now you are indivisibly one of us, Thomas Moore. You now wear the pirate's mark for all to see."

My hand groped inquisitively at the throbbing spot on my ear. A small metal ring pierced my bleeding earlobe. Jack came up to me, smiling.

"Welcome on board, pirate."

He embraced me firmly. Then the rest of the crew broke out in wild hurrahs. From all sides, men clapped me on the shoulder, congratulated me and embraced me.

As a security measure, I would continue sleeping in Jack's cabin so he could keep an eye on me.

"And I promise you, Tom, I will show no mercy if you break your word," Jack announced loud enough for all to hear. The surrounding sailors murmured agreement.

"In the future, the slightest trip-up will leave clear marks on your back."

Jack knew perfectly well he had no reason to worry about my loyalty. I had truly dedicated myself to the pirate life, body and soul. And I was glad of my decision. His threat served another purpose besides ensuring my loyalty. If the night watchmen came by our cabin in the coming weeks and heard wild screams or loud moaning, no one would be concerned. It would be clear to everyone that the Captain's son was punishing the young pirate with his whip. The fact that I accepted Jack's special punishments eagerly and submissively was our own secret. Not only did he cover my back again and again with hot kisses, he found countless spots on my body to torment. But it wasn't any whip that made me howl out in pain, it was the sharp tip of his tongue engulfing me in pleasure.

One night he said to me, "I would like to give you a gift." In the candlelight, he pulled two small rings from a case. They were a gleaming silver, open at one end. "You already have the pirate's mark in your ear."

I nodded gladly. I had quickly become accustomed to my new jewelry and it was an honor for me to be allowed to wear it. Besides, it was a roguish pleasure when Jack teased my earring with his hot tongue or pulled on it with his teeth.

"I noticed you always wear a ring on your finger that you never take off. I'm sure it has a very special meaning. I'd love to hear the story some time."

He held my hands tenderly and stroked them.

"It would make me proud if you would wear one of these rings for me. I'll wear the other."

Not comprehending, I looked at him. "But they're much too small for our hands. Is it for my other ear?"

"No," he said softly. "It goes here."

Jack solemnly laid the ring against my left nipple. I inhaled in shock, but I knew him well enough to know he was being serious …

That night was one of the most special nights in my life. Pain and pleasure have connected Jack and me since then in a way that cannot be described in words. From then on, whenever his sensual lips closed around my mouth, it became even stiller in our shared cabin. We had no more need for words to confess our love.

After a few weeks, I had found my place among the pirates. My skilled ability dealing with sails and ropes made it easy to gain access to their sworn band. And since the others knew they could rely on me, my former enemies soon became my new friends. They accepted me because I felt like one of them, because I had become a real pirate. A pirate among pirates.

Epilogue

All sails were set. Wind from the northeast filled the white fabric. The *Bone* shot across the water light as an arrow. Over the past several weeks I had climbed the masts countless times, loosened the binds countless times, and pulled in the cords. That's what I was doing now. Halfway down, I stopped. A powerful gust tugged at the ropes. The pulling of the taut ropes and the rig swaying in my hands filled me with indescribable happiness. From up here, I could observe Jack. Self-conscious, legs spread, he stood on the aft deck. As always, his white shirt was half open, his wild hair was bound in a ponytail. His eagle eyes checked the trimming of the sails. His gaze examined every single rope. When he caught sight of me high up in the bulwarks, he interrupted his careful inspection for a minute. He nodded to me almost imperceptibly, then continued with his tasks, looking far out over the bowsprit into the open sea. I knew he had noticed my broad smile. On deck during the day, we didn't make our deep connection known. But the intimacy we enjoyed on our shared nights was something no one could take away from us.

I love standing up here in shrouds, the salt wind and invigorating sun on my naked skin. I follow Jack's gaze out over the water.

The sun is slowly sinking towards the horizon. Its bright gleaming white is gradually turning a mild red. The waves glitter like water dipped in gold. Jewels in every color of the rainbow sparkle up within them, showing us the way: they lead towards the west. Always onward towards the setting sun. To the New World and new adventures.

To be continued ...

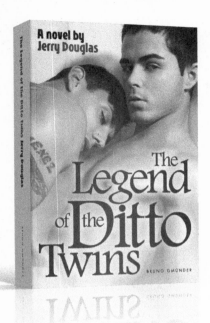

Jerry Douglas
THE LEGEND OF
THE DITTO TWINS
400 pages, softcover
13 x 19 cm, 5¼ x7½ "
978-3-86787-257-7
US$ 17.99 / £ 9.99
€ 16,95 / CHF 25.90

Since they have touched each other for the first time, Eric and
Derrick know they are different. Know they are special. Know
they will be bound together as long as they live. Most of all, the
twin brothers know that no one else must ever discover the secrᵉ
games they play in bed each night—until puberty hits and Eriᶜ
and Derrick begin to understand that they are destined to bᵉ
legendary.

Follow two young men on their journey from a modest
in America's heartland to the glamorous world of Berliⁿ
models, from the wonderland of Prague's adult film inⁱ
fast lane of New York's glittering club life … and ultimⁱ
way to the Supreme Court of the United States.

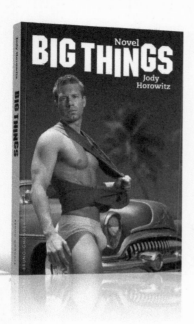

Jody Horowitz
BIG THINGS
216 pages, softcover
13 x 19 cm, 5¼ x 7½ "
978-3-86787-442-7
US$ 17.99 / £ 10.99
€ 16,95 / CHF 25,90
AUS$ 27.99

When David lands in L.A. with no money and little prospect of publishing his first novel, he takes a succession of dead-end jobs. Soon he realizes that he has to do something totally different if he wants to get ahead. So he decides to think big—and cashes in on his largest and most personal asset.

Big Things is a cleverly written story. It's racy, juicy, funny and sometimes sad.

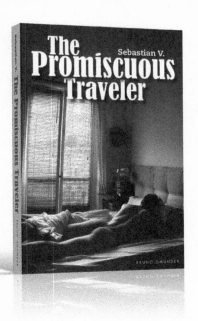

Sebastian V.
THE PROMISCUOUS
TRAVELER
176 pages, softcover
13 x 19 cm, 5¼ x 7½ "
978-3-86787-443-4
US$ 17.99 / £ 10.99
€ 16,95 / CHF 25,90
AUS$ 27.99

It's every gay man's fantasy—to travel the globe in search of sex. One lucky travel writer has done just that, and here he chronicles his diverse encounters while on the road, from a man in wet Speedos on a Puerto Rican beach, to a uniformed Russian train conductor, to a lonely boy in a Senegalese village, to a naked and smiling Aboriginal in an Australian frontier town.

What he finds are the raw universal physical needs of men ' the bounds of race or identity, and the fleeting and intang nature of sex itself. Like any transitory journey, the tales dreams, where in another country the body and the spi one.

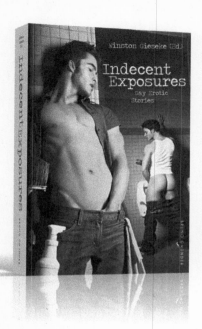

Winston Gieseke (Editor)
INDECENT EXPOSURES
Gay Erotic Stories
208 pages, softcover,
13 x 19 cm, 5¼ x 7½"
978-3-86787-520-2
US$ 17.99 / £ 11.99 /
€ 16,95

The thrill of getting caught is a major turn-on. Which is why getting frisky in a forbidden place — outside of one's comfort zone and away from the comforter — can be some of the hottest sex of all. Compiled by former *Men* magazine editor Winston Gieseke, *Indecent Exposures* is a tantalizing anthology of erotic tales in which sexually charged couples, casual hookups, and nameless strangers get their rocks off by taking a walk on the wild side.